Simon

01516

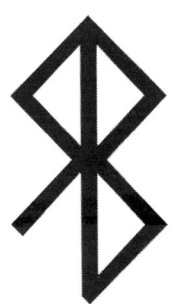

Fireflies from Hell
The Summons

Rob Burgess

The characters and events in this boo are fictitious. Any similarities to real persons, living or dead, are coincidental and not intended by the author.

All rights reserved. No part of this publication may be reproduced, stored in a retrieval system or transmitted in any form by any means electronic, mechanical, photocopying, recording or otherwise, except brief extracts for the purpose of reviews, without the permission of the author and copyright owner.

Cover Art by Lauren Brittany Hanchin

Bandit Press

Copyright © 2013 Rob Burgess
March 2013
All rights reserved.

ISBN 10: 1481288717
ISBN-13: 978-1481288712

DEDICATION

For all my fellow wanderers.
May your world always be full of wonders.

"If I couldn't walk fast and far, I should explode and perish."
~ CHARLES DICKENS

"Not all who wander are lost"
~ J.R.R. Tolkien

CONTENTS

	Acknowledgments	ix
1	Good morning sunshine	1
2	We're off to see the wizard	p. 4
3	Down the rabbit hole	p. 6
4	Once more into the woods...	p. 7
5	How bad could it be	p. 10
6	I had a dream	p. 14
7	You gotta expect rain in the Smokies	p. 16
8	Heigh ho Heigh ho...	p. 18
9	Honey we're home	p. 20
10	Voices of the wind	p. 23
11	Fireflies don't sting	p. 25
12	Lock and load	p. 28
13	Reality has left the building	p. 29
14	Now the rest of the story	p. 35
15	To a mouse	p. 38
16	Gift horse or Trojan horse	p. 40
17	Stromboli...yum, Bad apple yuck	p. 43
18	Just a ride in the park	p. 46
19	Out of the fry pan…	p. 49
20	Now we are brothers	p. 51
21	A history lesson	p. 58
22	A taste of things to come	p. 62
23	Beam me up	p. 65
24	I'll huff and I'll puff…	p. 69
25	Going viral	p. 74
26	Don't give me 'Once upon a Time'	p. 79
27	Son-of-a-bitch that's sharp	p. 83
28	What's a nice werewolf like you…	p. 89
29	Nothing like a burger	p. 94

30	Blood sucking blue butterflies? What's next!	*p.* 98
31	Shoo fly don't bother me	*p.* 101
32	Batter up	*p.* 104
33	Dancing with the lights	*p.* 109
34	Listen bitch, you took my son	*p.* 111
35	Me a flirt?	*p.* 120
36	I don't swing that way	*p.* 126
37	The force is strong with this one	*p.* 130
38	It's not that simple	*p.* 138
39	It just looked me in the eye	*p.* 142
40	Lady, you are a piece of work	*p.* 145
41	There's no place like home	*p.* 150
42	I got some S'plaining to do	*p.* 155
43	Holy flaming fairies	*p.* 160
44	Roger you fool	*p.* 164
45	Bacon, sausage and eggs oh my	*p.* 169
46	Okay, Important safety tip	*p.* 173
47	Fairies in the kitchen, now what	*p.* 178
48	OMG	*p.* 181
49	You are one evil temptress	*p.* 187
50	You'd only anger him anyway	*p.* 196
51	L'Chaim	*p.* 201
52	An STN…Stick Teleportation Network	*p.* 209
53	Magic is fun	*p.* 214
54	A smile would steal the corners of their	*p.* 219
55	It was fairy made	*p.* 225
56	One way or another this all will be a	*p.* 230
57	Your reputation precedes you, Wizard	*p.* 235
58	Burning at the stake was too gentle	*p.* 240
59	Bugger! Bugger! Bugger!	*p.* 244
60	Goldie and Smokie	*p.* 252
61	No one messes with my family	*p.* 257
	About the Author	*p.* 264

ACKNOWLEDGMENTS

My first thanks goes to my family and friends. Your wonderful depth of personalities breathed life into every one of my characters.

Gary and Todd, I would not have started this journey without that campfire in Georgia.

Gooey Rocks!!
You are a mentor and a friend who makes me a better writer.

Annie, Kelly, and Keith, thanks for wading through the typos and grammar errors and…I can't thank you enough.

Last and certainly not least Deb and Tab for well, you know

Chapter 1

GOOD MORNING SUNSHINE

My world was a quiet and restful one until fiddles broke into Miller's Reel. I begrudgingly opened my eyes and slid my finger across the phone's screen to silence my alarm. Passing my hand across my bald pate, I sat swinging my legs over the side of the bed.

I was tempted to lay my head back down but knew I had to get on the road soon. Being late for this was completely unacceptable. I pushed myself up and hobbled toward the bathroom door. My knees were screaming at me, but all they were saying was, "It's morning." I switched on the light and gazed at the haggard old guy looking back at me. I picked up the floss and proceeded with my morning routine.

The shower was hot and the pressure was strong. I could feel the night wash down the drain as the morning settled on me. There is nothing like a hot shower in the morning. Stepping out of the shower I grabbed my razor. I used the corner of the towel to wipe the steam from the mirror. I was scrapping a few days' growth from my face. I rinsed my blade to work on the other cheek and staring back at me in the mirror was the face from my dream.

"Do not forget you duty, Chosen!" He said.

I jumped nicking myself with the blade. "God damn it," I shouted and dropped the blade. "I haven't forgotten," I said as I picked up my razor and found I was talking to myself. As reached toward my face with the blade and found I couldn't keep my hands from shaking. I put the razor down and splashed off the soap.

"Good enough," I said aloud and began to plan the day's route.

The trouble with shaking off the night is the day's events queue up waiting in the wing to ambush you.

Do you know how people say it's all about the journey, not the destination? Dear Lord I wish that were true for this little sojourn. I had a five to six day drive ahead of me and was not looking forward to being there. I could blow it off but others, many others, would pay the price for my reluctance, nay cowardice. I'd never be able to look at the bald guy in the mirror again. I was going.

Enough with the fretting, I left the bathroom pulled on a pair of shorts and a tank top running shirt. Comfortable clothing was what I needed to start this day. I pulled the hair on the back of my head into a ponytail and put on deodorant, plenty of deodorant.

I was almost ready to leave. I found myself sneaking out of the bathroom purely out of force of habit. How many years have I had to tip toe around my sleeping wife? Today there was no snoring lump in the bed and I was both angry and ashamed. The goddamned camping trip set this whole course of events in motion. Screwing with fairies has consequences. The only thing she heard was I was unfaithful and tried to blame fairies, as if they were real. Past is past and cannot be relived.

The coffee gurgled into the waiting cup as I beat the eggs in a bowl. I planned on cooking one last meal before I hit the road. This morning called for an omelet with plenty of butter, cheese, mushrooms, caramelized onions, tomatoes, spinach, and whatever else I could find in the fridge. Cholesterol be damned …this was going to be a great omelet. When it came to turning the bloated omelet I invoked my inner Julia Child, shook the pan and flipped it in the air. When the golden treat landed intact, I found myself speaking in a falsetto voice, "Thank you, thank you, you are too kind," as if I were Julie speaking to an appreciative audience. You might think this would be embarrassing to admit, but this was one of my ism(s), for lack of a better word, when I cooked. And I love to cook.

The omelet was plated, coffee brewed, English muffins were golden and buttered, and all the pans and cook area were clean. Time to eat. Sadly the time to eat a meal was inversely proportional to the time required to create the meal, but it was delicious, if I do say so myself. I found I was sitting there sipping my remaining coffee and looking at the clock.

"Well," I said aloud to no one, "I guess it's time to go." I cleared my plate, washed the few remaining dishes and set them to dry. I double-checked to make sure the stove was off and the windows were locked. God only knew when someone would be living here again. I didn't know when or if I'd ever make it back. I certainly hoped I would.

Chapter 2

WE'RE OFF TO SEE THE WIZARD

The house was buttoned up. The truck was packed, though I wish I could take the bike.

"No," I chastised myself, "let's not start this again. I have too far to go and too much crap I want to bring. Nevermind the unpredictability of the weather from here to there. Crap, am I talking to myself again? Yes, and apparently answering myself as well."

Shaking this craziness off I locked the front door, climbed in the truck, checked the map and turned the key. I plugged my phone into the stereo and selected a book. My choice for today was "Bandits on the Rim" by G. Kent. The narrator began the story as my truck's engine turned over and my trip began.

I turned out of my driveway and headed to I - 75 where I'd spend the day. This trip will take me from Central Florida to the Pacific Northwest but I only had to make Tennessee by this evening. So far, this Friday morning's traffic was light and Chattanooga was about five hundred miles away.

I relaxed into the drive and let the narrator's voice tell me about the visions and dreams of Garrett Kay. This was written by my friend George and he based it on an accident that almost took his life about forty years ago. He never ceases to amaze me.

As expected, the drive was long and boring. On the plus

side, the road was familiar. I passed through Gainesville and it brought back many good memories from days gone by. Luckily the traffic was light and I was moving quickly along this road. As long as I didn't get stalled in the Atlanta traffic for too long I should be able to check into a motel and have plenty of time to catch dinner before my rendezvous with Naomi.

My instructions were to report to Point Park after dark and follow my escort. These instructions came to me in a dream. Don't judge me quite yet because it gets a bit more insane. I was summoned to Washington State, also by a dream. As I tossed this thought around I felt my grasp on reality shift. If not for my experiences on a backpacking trip the year before, I would have checked myself into the loony bin.

Chapter 3

DOWN THE RABBIT HOLE

I was lying on a large flat rock with my head resting on my backpack. The morning sky was beginning to mature as a few white puffs drifted lazily against the blue backdrop. I was tired and last night, oh God, could last night have really happened?

"We better get going. I want to be at least a hundred miles from here before the night falls again." Ted said as he shouldered his pack.

"And we're going to stay in a motel, in a city, agreed?" I said as I checked the bandage around my neck absently.

"Agreed!" Ted said quickly.

"Hell yeah," added George.

We hoisted our packs and hit the trail.

Chapter 4

"ONCE MORE INTO THE WOODS..."

The events that follow will haunt me till my heart's last beat. I need you to understand I'm not a nutcase. I am a regular guy with a regular job and I'm not given to flights of fantasy.

George Koff, Ted Clark and I are three friends who teach at the same high school in Florida. We enjoy each other's company as we commune with nature, be it a hike, partying by the lake or the occasional camping trip. We are what society calls middle-aged men. Our ages range between fifty and sixty but we refuse to believe our ages puts limitations on us. We simply have to go a little slower and take more breaks. George Koff is the heart of the group. He's the guy who is always comes up with the plans for the hike or the canoe trip and even the plan for this backpacking trip. He is the finest History teacher at the school and some would say in the county. He loves to travel and spends most of his summers on one adventure or another. When the time comes to plan he usually knows or has heard, or has been to the site or on the trail we're thinking of tackling. Ted and George have been best friends for the past 25 years. I'm a relative new comer, but more on this later. Ted is by far the soul of this group, simply by the way he approaches life. He is a teacher of English and some would say philosophy. I am not saying he teaches a philosophy course but he challenges his students to become their own philosopher, while looking through the eyes of the greats to see if they agree or if they have their own thought. To say he is a man who thinks things through would be a bit of an understatement. If asked what he teaches he will be quick to say English, but all you have to do is to listen to him discuss literature and you will hear the philosopher who resides in his soul. He treats his life with the same thoughtful introspection. Where do I fit in? As I said, I'm a relative new comer. I only began my teaching career a few years ago. I moved here with five of my six kids a few years back. Currently, only two live at home. Before the move, I flew planes for Uncle Sam and after twenty-five years decided it was time to do something new. The question I have been asked most often is, "Why didn't you go fly for the airlines?" It's not what I wanted to do with my life. I love mathematics and I love teaching, so this is what I do. I got to know George and Ted by a simple twist of fate. I was assigned the room next to George and the rest as they say is history. Get it? George is a history teacher; This isn't a comedy.

About three weeks before the end of the school year, amidst all the paperwork of finals and posting grades and lesson plans for the fall, Ted suggested to George a backpacking trip right after school let out. George and I were onboard at the get go, and our destination was the Smoky Mountains. George suggested a trail he'd taken with his wife fifteen years ago and it sounded great to Ted and me. Forgive me if I don't tell you the specific trail we were on, because honestly I hope they close the campground and people stay the hell away from the place. It will probably take a few more years for my fear and loathing of that place to abate even a little.

For the last three weeks we have been gathering equipment and creating menus. We were mentally and physically preparing for this wonderful retreat. The plan was to camp along the way, pack in, stay a couple of nights, pack out, and camp on the trip home. All the campgrounds were picked and reserved. So plans were set, bags were packed and repacked, water bottles filled, and the cooler was loaded and iced. We were ready to go.

Now I need to point out, this wasn't the first backpacking trip for any of us. Between us, we can account for dozens of trips including camping, backpacking, and hiking. Ted and I have never been up this trail before, though we'd been up many like it. The fateful Sunday morning arrived and I drove to pick up Ted. We stowed his gear in the bed of my truck, he said his goodbye to his wife, and we drove to get George. We secured all the gear in the truck, I programmed the GPS, and off we went, not unlike Don Quixote's quest to slay a dragon.

Chapter 5

HOW BAD COULD IT BE

The drive was long but the mood was light as always. There was plenty of conversation and laughter. The miles slipped by quickly and before we knew it we were unpacking equipment and setting up camp. The original plan for dinner was to head to town for a quick burger. We ate a late lunch and none of us wanted another large meal, so we nibbled on gorp and jerky instead.

Another side of these trips is the beverage side. Being adults we chose to enjoy adult beverages, which is to say we like to drink on these trips. So with camp set I unscrewed the cap of my flask and proceeded to converse with my buddy Jim Beam. George was a wine drinker and Ted loved his beer. His love of the barley pop was a bit of a challenge for him this trip. Beer is way too heavy to carry on a four-mile hike with a fully loaded pack, and he only likes hard liquor if it's mixed with soda over lots and lots of ice, usually a gin and tonic. So he had to find a new drink of choice to enjoy in the backcountry. He was introduced to ice tea-flavored vodka and his problem was solved. But tonight we had our cooler in camp and ice cold beer was on hand.

After we had a few drinks George suggested we have a look at the canyon this park was formed around. I tossed him the keys and off we went. It only took about five minutes to get to the other side of the park. Ted and I carried a drink with us,. Mine was diet coke and his was iced tea, both of the leaded variety. George left his wine in camp.

The canyon was beautiful. The suggestion to come here was excellent. We wandered the paved trail taking pictures and acting like a bunch of tourists named Griswold. We walked the length of the paved trail and discovered a set of steps constructed from large stones, leading to dirt trail.

As I descended the stairs a young man bumped into me as we passed.

"Excuse me," I said and he turn giving me a look of malice.

"What the hell was that about," George asked seeing the look I received.

"Beats the hell out of me," I said and proceeded along to a stone outcropping that provided a view which was breath taking. When we arrived, someone was there.

A pleasant looking young woman stood there. When I say pleasant looking I mean she possessed the girl next-door look. She was quite attractive but seemed unaware of her beauty. She appeared to be nineteen or maybe twenty years old. She had with her a portable drawing box with a slanted top. The top was hinged, covering a compartment for ink, paper, or whatever she chose to carry. The unique part of this box was the carving around the outside. The combination of designs resembled a written language of some sort and fairies. Yes fairies like the Tinker Bell variety except they looked ferocious. They all had swords in their hands and scowls on their faces all ready for a battle.

This box sparked my curiosity, so I proceeded to talk with this young lady.

"Are you an artist?" I asked gesturing to the box.

"No," she answered meekly. "I do calligraphy."

"Really, that sounds unique. Is this a professional pursuit or a hobby?"

"More of a hobby, I've sold a few pieces but mostly I like doing calligraphy."

"By the way, my name is Roger," I introduced myself.

She pointed to herself, "Naomi."

Her accent told me she wasn't from around this part of Georgia. Her accent placed her in Eastern Europe.

"I can tell you're not originally from around here. Where was home?"

"Originally Romania but we moved here some time ago. I now call Tennessee home."

"Hey we're headed up to Tennessee to do some camping."

Her eyebrow rose and she seemed to take an actual interest in what this old guy was saying.

"We are backpacking in the Smoky Mountains around Gatlinburg."

"I'm from a small town a bit north of there called Cosby." As she was speaking to me, she took a step closer and placed her hand on my forearm as a friendly gesture. I wasn't really sure what to make of this. Hey, I was a bit flattered to be sure. Heck, an old guy like me and a young lady such as she, but the feeling faded quickly and it soon became uncomfortable. I know this sounds weird and she only had her hand on my forearm, but I felt violated. It was as if she were taking something from me. She stood there with her hand on my arm smiling and nodding her head. It was more than a bit creepy.

"Well, we have to get back to camp," I was looking for any excuse to break this contact.

She smiled and looked straight into my eyes, "I hope we get a chance to meet again." Her eyes held something ancient. No, she didn't look old, but within her eyes there was a sort of worldly understanding a twenty something girl simply could not possess.

"It was nice to meet you, Naomi. Who's to say if our paths will cross again. Goodbye now."

As soon as we were out of earshot I turned to George, "Did that seem odd to you?"

"Hey the only thing odd is you shamelessly flirting with a twenty year old girl," he said grinning.

"No, I'm serious. When she put her hand on me I got this weird feeling. I don't know how to describe it."

"Sounds like she hit back and threw you off balance. You're not used to getting a response from all your flirting."

I could see this was going to get me nowhere except the butt of their jokes. Honestly, looking back from their point of view I probably would give them the same sort of crap. So I sat and took the good natured ribbing. How bad could it be? The fire was lit, the drinks were cold, and went down easily.

Chapter 6

I HAD A DREAM

As I sat sipping my bourbon and diet coke with ice, I saw the evening light up with a chorus of fireflies. They were everywhere and circling outside of the campfire's light. I have never seen so many before and the way they danced on the breeze was beautiful. We sat back and watched the fire crackle, swapped stories, and drank, letting the evening wash over us. This was why we went camping.

Soon it was the time of night when the conversation seemed to taper off and the fire began to fade and our glasses were near empty. We each headed to our tents for the night. Before crawling in I headed into the woods to brush my teeth and water a tree.

With the necessities complete, I crawled into my sleeping bag and quickly fell into a deep slumber. The dream came flooding into my subconscious. In it I met Naomi again, but we were in a forest glen surrounded by massive trees. Naomi was older now, actually I would put her age close to mine, but these things happen in dreams. Even though she looked older, she was still beautiful; she was far more beautiful than her younger self I met earlier. Her eyes came level to mine. Her tunic was white with embroidered delicate flowers all over it. It was like a robe and was fastened in the front by a bit of flimsy lace. The tunic did not leave much to the imagination. Her breasts presented themselves like those in a pushup bra commercial for Victoria's Secret and her legs were long and perfect.

"Come untied, come untied," I chanted in my mind trying to will the lace to untie. This was nice, I haven't had one of these type of dreams since I was a teenager. Naomi glided towards me from across the glen with a grace, which was part ballerina and part feral cat. As she came closer I noticed a laurel leaf crown upon her head.

"Hello Roger, I've been waiting for you," she said.

In my dreaming mind I thought, "nice," but I found the rational part of my mind answered her.

"You have? Why would you be waiting for me?"

"Today you and I renewed a connection and you have something I need."

I was beginning to feel a bit self-conscious, "What could I possibly have that you would need?"

"You'll see," she laughed and I found myself laughing with her for no apparent reason, but that is how dreams work sometimes.

"When will I see?"

"Soon, but for now sleep, and she put the heal of her hand on my forehead and pushed. I fell backward into another unrelated dream.

Morning light woke me from my slumber and as I woke, the dream flooded into me with a feeling it was no dream. As I climbed out of my bag I found a twig and some leaves. There is no way this detritus could be here. I am always careful, almost anal about brushing off my feet before climbing in my tent. I also noticed my tent's fly was unzipped. There is no way I would have miss this. It seemed my dream was feeling way too real now.

God, I need to coffee up. I only hoped it would make the willies go away. I busied myself with packing up my equipment and striking my tent. Soon we were all up and packing the truck to head out on the next segment of our journey. Maybe I needed to put some miles between this place and me. Maybe then the weirdness of last night would fade.

Chapter 7

YOU GOTTA EXPECT RAIN IN THE SMOKIES

The drive to the trailhead was mostly unremarkable. We stopped and had our big breakfast at about two hours into the trip. These stops allowed us ample time to drink our coffee and allow the coffee to do what coffee does best. This is why we try to eat at places with clean bathrooms. Eating a late breakfast also staves the hunger so we don't need to eat again until suppertime.

After breakfast we headed up through the gauntlet of Pigeon Forge. What used to be a nice country town has turned into a joke, complete with neon and some of the tackiest displays I'd ever seen. To make things worse, there seemed to be a stop light every ten feet and we had to stop at every damnable one of them with nothing to look at except the land of tacky. We finally limped through and pressed on to Gatlinburg looking for signs leading to the trailhead. The GPS said we had about a mile to go to the final turn when I spotted a road sign for Cosby, Tennessee bringing Naomi back to mind. Do you know the feeling that goes up and down your spine? It's sort of a warning that something bad is about to happen. Well I was having the feeling right then.

"Rog, are you ok? The turn is right there." George was pointing at a small road off to the right.

"Sorry, zoned out for a second. How far to the trailhead?"

"From here about four miles. Then all we have to do is hike another four and we'll be home for the evening." George added with a wistful smile.

"Don't tell me, four miles of flat, easy, and downhill both ways trail," Ted quipped.

"You know it." George replied.

We all had been looking forward to this trip after a long year of teaching pubescent teens. This was a great way to kick off summer vacation. We drove up the road passing many day visitors, but the closer we came to the trailhead the fewer cars we passed. When we reached the parking lot we got out to stretch our legs and unpack, then hit the trail. After we unpacked and opened our ceremonial beer, the sky opened up. I'm not talking a light shower. It was one of those showers where you ask who's got the keys to the ark. We quickly covered our pack and dove into the truck. The storm passed almost as quickly as it arrived and soon we were on our way, slightly damp but spirits high. After all, you gotta expect rain in the Smokies.

Chapter 8

HEIGH HO HEIGH HO...

George led the way, he was the one who picked the trail and had been here before. The hike was tough. George neglected to remember the four-mile hike was uphill all the way. I spent six hours in a car and now was hiking uphill with a pack filled with way too much crap, ouch! At least the hike out will be easier.

I thought I was in better shape than this but the hike took quite a while, especially with all the breaks I forced upon them. About the half-way point was this bridge; well it functioned like a bridge and got us across the river. It was a huge log that looked like it escaped from a lumberyard after its first pass by the saw. Along the top someone had glued a gravel texture for better traction as you walked across. Below the bridge were raging rapids and the sights and sounds of this place were breathtaking. About now I was hoping there were campsites so we could be finished with the packs for the day, but we were only halfway.

We did take a break and I headed back to the bridge, sans pack, to get a few pictures. I snapped a few shots and found myself looking over my shoulder. I felt as if I were being watched. We hadn't seen a soul since we left the parking lot so who the hell would be watching us? Naomi flashed in my mind and I shook it off.

Damn, the dream was still freaking me out. This is weird,

I've hiked trails all over the world and never have I been affected like this, by a stupid dream. The woods were a sacred place to me, a safe place, not one to make me feel like this. Well I should probably leave the bourbon alone. I'd only had a nip or two but it had to be the booze that was making me paranoid.

When we were rested we shouldered our packs and marched on. The trail was rocky and strewn with roots trying to twist our ankles or throw us off the trail to tumble a few hundred feet down to lay prostrate before the river gods.

We carefully placed our feet and trudged forward. We came around the final bend and our campsite opened before us. The welcome was wonderful and we simply rejoiced in the fact that we had made it. We dropped our packs and took a look around trying to figure out which piece of earth would be ours for the duration. Once it was decided, we pitched our tents and settled in. We all wanted to explore our surroundings and head to the river to freshen up from a long day's hike.

Chapter 9

HONEY WE'RE HOME

It took about fifteen minutes to erect the tents, stow our gear and hang the hammocks. Hammocks are always essential camping equipment. I grabbed clean clothes and my camp soap, which is very eco-friendly, then changed out of my boots. It felt wonderful pulling them off. I slipped on my river shoes and headed for the river. George rediscovered the trail at the back of the camp, which led to the river. We walked through the over grown bushes and had to carefully traverse a steep muddy trail down to the bank. This was the tricky part of the trail. It was steep and quite slippery. One misplaced foot would result in a nasty tumble.

The river was beautiful and frigid, but I welcomed the cold. I quickly disrobed. There is no false modesty amongst us and into the water I went. The water washed across my skin, shedding the dried sweat I earned from today's march and carried my day's effort quickly downstream. I emerged refreshed from my mountain baptism as the sins of my journey were cleansed from my soul. My body and spirit were renewed.

We spent a bit of time traipsing up and down the river. We explored with a curiosity which is usually reserved for the very young. Being miles away from all civilization on a trip with my brothers did wondrous things for my soul. I became a child of my surroundings, with no cares except for my primal needs. All those worries of the world about my family, work, bills, etc. were left at the trailhead. We had no wallets or phones. Modern technology consisted of flashlights and butane lighters. All we had was our clothing and camping gear. We protected ourselves with our wits and our knives. Oh and George packed his Smith and Wesson 38. Some of the predators grew large in these parts. Soon, the arduous march was forgotten as muscles and attitudes adjusted to the relaxing sound of the water tripping over the rocks in its race to reach the bottom of the hill. The banter we exchanged seemed to dry up and a quiet ruled us all. It was a quiet of reverence, one you would find in the presence of the divine. We were truly in a holy place and our spirits soared. We sat as the river tumbled by and Apollo's chariot raced across the sky.

Our stomachs soon reminded us that our last meal had been breakfast and was gone by the time we reached the bridge. I gathered my belongings and headed back to camp.

I was cooking a stew for dinner. Cooking in the backcountry has its challenges and I don't buy backpacker meals from Walmart. I use fresh ingredients and spices from my own cupboard. The beef was braised and dehydrated in my kitchen. The spices were vacuum sealed in bags with the dried beef. The vegetables were fresh. We packed in whole potatoes and fresh baby carrots. You have to love the durability of root veggies. They were tough enough to handle this trip. I got the stove cranking and put on a pot of river water to boil. I dumped in the beef and spices. Then sliced up the veggies, covered the stew and let it simmer. This complete, I raised my flask to the heavens in thanks and let the brown liquid warm the cockles of my heart.

George and Ted soon took up residence in the hammocks with drinks in hand.

"When do we get to eat? It smells great," Ted asked.

"Do you want us to get our bowls?" George added.

"No, we have a little time. We can't rush good food," and the steam filled the air of the camp. It did smell good and my stomach rumbled with anticipation.

We drank and soon the stew was finished. There is something about the illusion that camp food tastes better. It could be the distance from home or because you are truly hungry, but this beef stew was ambrosia. We ate like starved beasts and the pot was scraped clean in a matter of moments.

We all sat back with stupid, sated grins on our faces. George and Ted toasted the cook and I joined them. Any excuse to raise our glasses was fine with me.

I cleaned up the camp kitchen, after all, we wouldn't want to attract bears in these parts, and I stowed my cook gear. Ted built the fire in the pit and poured a little Girl Scout juice on the damp mess. He wanted to kick-start the wet wood. We has bellies full of stew and bourbon and weren't in the mood to fiddle with breathing a fire to life. With a flick of the lighter, it kicked the flames into high gear, and soon the wood was blazing.

Chapter 10

VOICES OF THE WIND

George is the one who assigns all the nicknames and titles. Ted was given the name, "gatherer of wood." This proved to be an apt title. Ted could find enough wood for a bonfire in the middle of an arid desert. So here in the wooded mountains the pile of wood was enough to heat a small village for a week during the middle of winter. My title after creating the stew became "cooker of food," and George's is, of course, "namer of things." Ted awarded him that title.

We had a good fire as the sun fell below the western peaks and the gloom of night fell around us.

Here, as in Georgia, the fireflies came out in droves. Again I'd never seen so many in one place. I found myself feeling a bit drunk and quite happy. We all were enjoying this perfect end to a good day, a hard day but a good one. Our bodies were tired and our bellies were full, so our eyelids grew heavy.

I looked out beyond the fire's reach and watched the fireflies flit from here to there. The sense of being watched came over me again, but this time I felt as if I were on stage being watched by many. I shook my head and put the cap back on the flask.

"That's enough for me, boys," I announced. "I think I'm going to hit it."

"Sound's good to me," agreed George.

"I think I'll have one more. Good night boys," said Ted.

George and I ambled off to our tents. I grabbed my water bottle and toothbrush and headed off to prepare for my sleeping bag. I was brushing my teeth about twenty paces in the bramble. I rinsed and spit. As I walked with my toothbrush in my teeth I found a spot to take a leak.

"Tonight," I heard as a whisper on the breeze.

"Very funny, George," I called out.

"What's funny?" George called from the opposite direction.

"Uh, nothing. I thought I heard you say something," I'm not ashamed to admit, I was more than a little spooked. I headed back to camp and met George as he was climbing in his tent.

Chuckling he asked. "What did I say?"

"You whispered, tonight."

"What in the hell is that supposed to mean?"

"Shit man, how the hell would I know? You are the one who said it." And we both laughed at how ludicrous this conversation sounded.

"I guess I'm hearing things. I must be over tired. Goodnight George."

"Goodnight Rogo." Yeah, Rogo was a nickname he was working on for me. I stripped down and climbed in my sleeping bag and boy did it feel good. The evening was cooling off nicely and the warmth of the sleeping bag felt divine. I was ready for sleep and fell off to the land of slumber.

Chapter 11

FIREFLIES DON'T STING

At first, my sleep was deep and free from dreams. The dream started suddenly and came to me live and in high definition 3-D. I was back in the same forest glen with the older Naomi.

"You will come to me tonight, my love."

"My love? Now I'm my love? Lady, I don't even know you."

"But I've known you from your earliest days," and her eyes locked with mine. The details get a bit fuzzy here. I can only say, I got lost in her gaze. I fell off a cliff and literally, fell into a pool that was she. I don't understand this myself. One second I'm freaked out by the weirdness, and the next, all stress and anxiety melted away, making everything okay. A surreal sense of well-being washed over me in a wave.

Do you remember when you were a child and skinned your knee? Mom would scoop you up into her lap and make everything better. Her love would ease your pain and sooth your soul. Your hurt would begin healing from the inside out. You were still bleeding but you didn't care. You were safe and loved in your mother's arms.

Naomi's gaze did that for me. All you fans of Freud need to put your analyses away. A weird, foreign, sensual being was stalking me and invading my dreams. It all seemed okay as if everything was going to be fine. She was threatening my very existence, but I felt loved so there is no need to worry. I am a proverbial sixties flower child tripping on acid, but she was so damn beautiful nothing else mattered.

"My queen, when shall I come to you?" Son of a bitch, what did I say? Did those words come from my mouth? What in the holy hell was happening?

"You will be called. Come then and you will know my love." With those words a thrill of expectation shot through me.

I snapped awake and sat up in my tent. I took a deep breath and blew it out slowly, trying to control the pounding of my heart.

"Son of a bitch, this was one freaky dream, what the…?" It was then I noticed I had an erection. Somehow this fairy bitch turned me into her lap dog and I was excited. I let out another breath and checked the time. It was half past midnight. I rolled over and fluffed my tiny pillow and tried to fall back to sleep.

I must have nodded off quickly, because I woke again, this time needing to pee. I got up and threw on a shirt. Underwear was good enough for a 4 AM pee. I unzipped my tent as quietly as possible, and then slipped my river shoes. The full moon lit up the camp like a streetlight. I could clearly see both George and Ted's tents standing tall in the gloom. I decided to forego the flashlight and headed into the brush to relieve myself.

The fireflies were still out. They were everywhere. A swarm was buzzing around my head. One came close to my face. I swatted it away and it stung me.

"Ouch," I said aloud before I realized the words were out of my mouth. I instinctively put my wounded hand to my mouth. I discovered a thorn, or a stinger or a splinter, or an I don't know what was sticking in my hand. I'd never been stung by a firefly before. I pulled the hard stinger out with my teeth and spat it to the side. I then sucked on the bleeding wound. I stopped at the next tree and relieved myself.

This night was weird. I turned to go back to camp and

the swarm of biting fireflies were headed for me. I began swatting and they began stinging.

"Son of a bitch," I said aloud. I turned to retreat from this mass. Stumbling, I fell down the bank toward the river.

Chapter 12

LOCK AND LOAD

George was sleeping soundly when he heard the zipper on my tent. As an avid camper, the sound of a tent zipper, always seemed to catch his attention. It was a way to watch out for each other. He heard me traipsing into the woods and knew why. Actually, he was trying to decide if he needed to do the same. As he was deciding, he heard me yell, "Ouch," as the first firefly stung me. This seemed to wake up a little more. He pulled himself free from his bag, for he decided to pee and was unzipping his tent when I shouted, "Son of a bitch," and took my tumble. He scanned the area where I fell looking for my flashlight beam to pinpoint my location, but of course, couldn't find it. He knew I wouldn't accidentally stumble down an edge and noted I'd been acting a bit distracted all day. Something wasn't right so he reached into his pack and drew his .38. He then went to roust Ted.

Chapter 13

REALITY HAS LEFT THE BUILDING

At the bottom of the ravine, where I gracefully descended, I checked to see if I had broken any bone or if I cut myself. I found, aside from a few bruises and minor scrapes, I was okay. I rolled on my belly to push myself up. On a rock, inches from my nose were three to four of the fireflies except, they weren't fireflies. They were tiny men with insectile wings and swords.

Dear God, they were the fairy carvings on Naomi's box, come to life. They stood there with all the confidence and attitude of Roman Centurions standing over a conquered foe. They motioned with their swords to go in a certain direction. My brain was having trouble processing all was happening. At least I wasn't crazy. There are no biting fireflies, but now I was seeing fairies. Did I bang my head on the fall? No, fireflies are fireflies and I'm seeing fairies. Yep I was insane.

I turned to look where they motioned and the path was lit up like an airport runway at night. I saw literally, thousands of these little guys and gals. They lined the path and all had swords. So I decided it was in my best interest to play nice and see where this led, as if I didn't know.

The walk was intriguing. As I passed a section, the fairies, they would, sort of, flit to the front in a leapfrog fashion. It was quite a light show. I walked for about fifteen minutes. Imagine my surprise when I was led into the same glen from my dreams,. As I entered, my escort flew up into the trees around the glen. They lit the area creating a Christmas wonderland. I wandered to the center with the moving lights disoriented me.

I realized then, I had no earthly idea how to get back to camp.

My mind raced and was trying to figure out a way back to camp. I could yell to the guys and see if they could hear, or I could follow the river upstream. As I worked through this dilemma, a bright light, brighter than any of the other fireflies, descended to alight on the ground in front of me. From the light appeared the older version of Naomi.

"Welcome, Roger," she said in a heady, sultry voice.

"Would you please explain, what in the hell is going on here? I mean, are you real?" I took a step and raised my hand to touch her, to be sure I wasn't dreaming. Out of nowhere one of those goddamned fireflies from hell zipped down and slashed the back of my hand. The pain and the blood were very real. I quickly retreated a step.

"Roger, please sit, and relax. All will be explained." She motioned to a table and chair being formed from the roots of the surrounding trees. Roots rose from the ground and morphed into a table and chair. Yep, I was seriously freaked.

I sat and she offered me a cup filled with a clear liquid, but I declined. God only knows what was in there. She sensed my hesitation and took a sip from the cup and then offered it again. This time I accepted and took a sip. It was unlike anything I'd ever tasted. It was water flavored with the fragrance of flowers and sweetened with honey, and there were fruit flavors. I don't know all I tasted but it was sweet and it was good, real good. I quickly drank the whole cup and thought about asking for more when I remembered where I was and how I got here.

She sat next to me and took my hand. Her touch was inviting and sensual, and she only held my hand. I was glad I was sitting at a table because I found myself getting aroused by her touch. She was well aware of the power she had over me and she smiled a wistful smile.

"Let me begin. My name is Naomi and I am the queen of all the mystical beings of these woods."

"These woods, you mean this local area?"

"The area you call the Great Smoky Mountains National Park."

"Shit, you are the Queen of the Mountains?"

"Some have called me such."

"Wait a second. What were you doing in Georgia? Does your kingdom stretch that far?"

"No, that area is ruled by a loathsome creature named Uke. He rules his kingdom through power and intimidation. All who serve him fear his wrath."

"So he's a fairy king? And you were there with this foul being, why?"

"He called a council meeting of all the ruling parties of the southeast. He is attempting to annex several domains to increase his power base."

"And he's more powerful than all the other rulers? Including you?"

She looked bothered by my question. "It has not always been so, but my powers are waning. To protect my realm from Uke I need you, the Chosen, to complete the ceremony before this full moon passes." Her words caused much unrest in the trees. The fairy folk seemed worried about this, Fairy King Uke. He must be some piece of work.

"So how do I fit into all your plans? Don't you mystical types prey on virgins for this sort of Bacchus ritual? Hell, I've been married for thirty years and lady, I am no virgin."

"Virginity is nice," she purred, "but sexual purity isn't the only source of power. The Chosen's power comes from pureness of heart."

"I say again, me? Chosen? No way, don't get me wrong...getting laid in the woods by a gorgeous fairy queen does sound enticing. Hell, if I weren't married, I'd be your man."

This comment drew a sinister laugh from our audience, for lack of a better word. Even Naomi's smile didn't make it to her eyes.

"Did I say something funny?"

"This ceremony is more than a sexual coupling. For my strength to be renewed I need the purity of your heart, the heart of the Chosen."

This was beginning to take a wrong turn. "So you're going to eat my heart? And what is this Chosen crap?"

"No," she snapped with disgust, "I shall not eat your heart and you were Chosen from before birth. Do you truly not remember the cleansing when you were a lad of eight years?"

"No, I don't. So what is this ceremony then?"

"You'll see," she said.

"If I refuse?" With this she leaned in to me and placed her hands on either side of my head. She kissed my on my mouth and breathed. I inhaled her breath and she owned me, body and soul. I could offer no resistance and frankly, I didn't want to. She took my hand and led me to the center of the circle.

"Circles focus power and the center is the heart," she explained as we walked. This was when I noticed the glen formed a perfect circle. We stopped at the very center and she began to undress me. I stood there as in a drugged haze and lusted after her. She pulled the shirt over my head and I looked up to see all the fairies flying counterclockwise within the circle.

I pointed up and asked, "Naomi, what are they doing?"

"They are focusing the power to me."

I stood in front of her, naked as the day I was born, and She pulled the lace holding her tunic together. It fell open exposing her glorious body. She shrugged the garment off her shoulders and let it drop to the ground.

She stood before me and she was perfect. I can think of no better word. Her skin was soft and smooth and the color of alabaster, pure and clean. Her scent was a mixture of flowers and that fresh smell the air has, right after it rains. I found myself breathing deep. I tried to make her part of me by inhaling her scent. Her curves were soft and voluptuous. Her face was ageless and more beautiful than Helen of Troy, more desirable than Aphrodite. Finally her breasts, oh god they were perfect and either the air was chilly or...

She came to me and I wrapped her in my arms pulling her body up against mine. Her thighs were against mine, her breast against my chest and our lips locked in a deep kiss. Her breath possessed me like a drug and now her kissed washed through me from head to toe with a wave of pleasure, exploding every nerve in my body. I struggled to keep from bursting right then.

Somehow during this kiss I ended up on my back looking up at the swirling lights and the beautiful Naomi straddling my hips. My heart was pounding so hard I thought it would leap from my throat. She raised her hips above mine and guided me as I entered her. I met her moist welcome with a powerful thrust. She let out a small scream of pleasure as I moaned trying to restrain myself. She rocked back and forth and I met her motion with my hips. It wasn't long before I was ready to release and she leaned down to my neck and licked me. I saw a flash of blue light and felt a sting where she licked, I should have been more concerned but I was in the throes of passion and found something erotic about the pain.

I was moments from my final pleasure as she sat up with my blood upon her face. It was then I came with violent thrusts and she moaned and met each thrust with her hips as she licked her lips. I took a deep breath and settled back on the ground in exhausted pleasure and saw her raise a knife above me with both hands. She began chanting something with her head raised to the sky and my blood dripped off her chin.

The hold she had on me was broken. And I reached for the knife.

Right then there was a flash of light with an explosion and something slammed into her shoulder knocking her to the ground. I rolled on top of her and grabbed for the knife, when a set of hands pulled me up and pushed me to the outer circle. Ted had pulled me off her and was directing my escape.

George was calling for him outside the circle to lead us back to camp. Ted and George had sticks in their hand and both were taking batting practice on the 'friendly fireflies'. As we ran, I began to laugh but it was more of a hysterical laughter. This was a bizarre night. Complete with the fireflies from hell, a fairy queen screwing me to within an inch of my life, literally, and now I am running naked through the woods. You tell me, laugh or scream. I chose to laugh.

The run seemed to last forever and we arrived in camp as the sun made her appearance above the mountain. From what I've read, most of the mystical stuff happens when the sun was down. With the sun up, humans are safe. My first stop in camp was to get some shorts on. I was feeling a little self-conscious.

My blood was all down my chest. My neck still bled slowly but was beginning to clot. We had run for about half an hour, so the blood and sweat made a big mess of things. I grabbed a sock out of my boot and my first aid kit.

"Don't worry about being fancy. Just cover it up and let's get the hell out of here."

"Are you going to explain what that was all about?" Ted asked.

"Later, let's get on the trail." So I wiped my neck with the sock and Ted covered it with a bandage. We struck camp in record time and hit the trail.

Chapter 14

NOW THE REST OF THE STORY

After our first break, I could put their curiosity off no more.

"Roger, what the hell happened back there?" George asked.

"Okay, what did you see?"

"Not much. I heard you fall down the ravine and I got Ted and we came after you. By the time we got to where you fell, you were gone, but down the river there was this light."

"Yeah," Ted added, "we figured you were there. As we got to the clearing, the fireflies were swirling and we saw you with the girl in the center. It looked like you guys were having a good time but it was obscured by this curtain of light around you."

"By then we didn't care anyway. It was like we were stoned. We stood there and watched the pretty lights," George said.

"Yeah, just looking up at the swirling lights," Ted said laughing as he remembered.

"All of a sudden, our heads cleared and she was there with that knife," George continued.

"George took aim and shot. Boy, did that piss off those fireflies. Did you know fireflies could sting you?" Ted said.

"Fairies," I said, "the fireflies were fairies with swords. I found out the hard way too."

"Anyway, I put the gun away and grabbed a stick and went all Hank Aaron on them. Ted ran in and grabbed your naked ass, you know what I mean, and the rest is history. So how about you fill in the blanks."

For the next hour I filled them in on the dreams and the voices and all the other weird shit I'd experienced on this trip. The miles passed quickly and we soon found ourselves at the trailhead. The packs were thrown unceremoniously in the back of the truck and we drove with reckless abandon to get the hell out of Dodge. We drove all day and by nightfall were approaching Atlanta. We found a nice roadside motel and rented a couple of rooms for the night. There were no wooded areas around this motel at all. I felt safer after I locked and bolted the door. I let the sun set without me. I showered and changed the bandage on my neck. We ate delivered pizza and drank the plentiful beer in the cooler. When I crushed my first beer can, I turned to Ted and George, "I want to thank you guys. I'd be dead if you didn't show up when you did."

"Hell, we had to. We didn't want to tell your wife you were screwed to death by a fairy bitch," George said and we began to laugh.

"I still have a hard time believing this really happened."

"But it did," Ted added, "and the question is what do we do about it?"

We all agreed this was my tale to tell and no one would share this till I was ready.

As I slept, my dreams were once again hijacked. There I was in the glen again, but this time I got to keep my clothes on.

"Hello, Roger."

"Naomi."

"I wanted you to know you saved my kingdom. The ceremony was completed with your blood on the knife and my prayer. Thank you."

"Then why were you attempting to plunge the thing in my chest."

"No, I realize it may have looked that way but no, your life would not have been forfeited."

"Then I'm sorry you were shot. My friend thought I was in mortal danger and acted."

"The iron passed through me and I healed quickly. Know you and your warrior friends are always welcome in my domain."

"But they must have really pissed off the little fairies."

"No, your friends acted nobly in the face of battle. My warriors respect nobility and have already created ballads of their bravery. To be truthful, I believe they enjoyed themselves. It has been a long time since they engaged an enemy."

"Good to know."

"So please return to my kingdom and come without fear."

"Thanks, but it will be a while before we plan a trip your way."

"This is understandable."

"Goodbye, Naomi."

"Farewell, Roger.

And the dream faded leaving me with dream free sleep for the rest of the night.

Chapter 15

TO A MOUSE

Atlanta was finally in my rear view mirror and traffic was as bad as I feared. It was bumper to bumper all the way through. I can't imagine having to do this day to day. This was a reason I found a quiet little town in Florida to settle with my family. Well, that was the plan. In the words of Robert Burns,

> *The best laid schemes of Mice and Men oft go awry,*
> *And leave nothing but grief and pain*
> *For promised joy!*

Even with the Atlanta delay, it seems my early start paid off. I would get to the hotel with plenty of time to get a nice dinner and maybe a beverage or two to help steel my nerves.

The truck's air conditioner was blasting icy cold air but still, sweat dripped down my back. It seems the backpacking trip was the beginning of all this craziness.

The GPS showed I had eighty miles till I get to stop for today. I was ready to stop now. On this side of the city, traffic was light and actually after the gauntlet of Atlanta, was a pleasant change. The sun had passed its peak and trees blurred by casting stunted shadows on the roadside. The odometer ticked the miles as they counted down to this day's destination.

As the state line approached, the traffic increased, though not to the insane levels I experienced earlier. I had to pay closer attention to where I was going. For the first time today I was off I - 75. Exit 1-A loomed ahead and my turn signal was on.

Chapter 16

GIFT HORSE OR TROJAN HORSE

I pulled in front of the office at the Days Inn. I headed in to claim my room. I had a reservation, so I wasn't expecting any surprises. My needs were simple. A clean room, a comfortable bed, and a cup of Joe in the AM. The clerk handed me my plastic key card and I headed to my room.

There was something about how he said, "I hope you have a pleasant stay," that rubbed me the wrong way. He accented the word pleasant, a bit too much and wore a saccharine smile as he said it.

When I walked to my room, those little hairs on the back of my neck began to rise. That familiar feeling of being watched or impending doom was on me. This made absolutely no sense. I had nothing to worry about. I was given safe passage till the meeting.

"Get in the room," I mumbled to myself. I slid the key in the lock, the green lights beeped and I opened the door. The smell assaulted my nose. Roses, fragrant long stemmed roses were on the table. There must have been two-dozen and a bottle of Jim Beam Black with a ribbon.

I took a step backward and pulled the door shut.

"Damn it, you'd think they could give me the right room. There are only four other cars in this parking lot." I was a bit pissed as I stormed back to the front office.

"Mr. Burr, is there a problem with your room?" the wiseass clerk offered.

"Yeah, I think you gave me the wrong key."

"Room 112?"

"That's what you gave me but I think there was some mistake."

"How so, sir?"

"There were roses and such."

"They were delivered for you this afternoon."

"For me, Roger Burr? Are you sure? Because nobody knows I'm here."

"Yes sir. I received them myself. I remember because it was a bit unusual."

"Wait a second, what is your name?"

"Justin."

"Okay Justin, what do you mean unusual?" I was a bit freaked out right now and I think I was spooking the kid.

"Well it wasn't the normal delivery guy. It was this lady and she insisted on taking them to your room herself. I don't think she trusted me."

"So you gave her my key?"

"No!" he insisted. "I took her there and watched her place the flowers and the bottle. Oh yeah and the card. She acted like you were, uuhh, friends."

"Uuuhh friends?"

He looked from side to side to be sure we were alone, "Actually I was going to say lovers. I didn't want to presume. I mean, red roses, bourbon...the good stuff, and when she kissed the card, I have to say it was kind of hot."

"What did this mysterious lady look like?" I asked but I think I knew who it was.

"That's the funny thing, I don't remember details about her. I only have an impression," he said with a confused look. "She was very sexy, not coed sexy, but movie star sexy."

"Naomi," I said quietly to myself, nodding to his response.

"Justin, you got a girlfriend?"

"Yes sir I do, why do you ask?"

"Come by the room in about ten minutes and take the flowers. Chicks love this stuff and yours might be very grateful." I said giving him a little wink.

"Thanks, Mr. Burr."

"No problem kid," and I headed back to the room.

I took one flower out of the vase. I put it in a plastic cup with water, and grabbed the card. Right there on the cream colored envelope was the proffered kiss in bright red lipstick. I tossed it on my bed and grabbed the ice bucket. I hiked back down the hall to the ice machine and filled the bucket.

I walked back to the room and Justin met me at the door. I handed him the vase.

"Are you sure, Mr. Burr?"

"Absolutely kid, absolutely. I hope they work for you."

He smiled and headed to his car. I closed the door and grabbed a glass by the sink. I filled it with ice and covered the ice with bourbon.

"Thank you, Naomi," I said as I raised my glass. As the rim of the glass touched my lip I heard a whisper on a breeze. "You are welcome."

I finished the drink in one pull as a shiver went down my spine. With as much weirdness happening to me this year, you'd think I'd be used to it...I wasn't.

Chapter 17

STROMBOLI...YUM. BAD APPLE YUCK

I'd heard about a small bistro across the river called, appropriately enough, the River Street Deli. I was told to order the Stromboli. The entrance was from riverside and it had the atmosphere of a New York delicatessen. The smells from the kitchen made my mouth water and my stomach rumble. I was hungry. I ordered the Stromboli, and I got to see several on the plates of satisfied patrons as I headed to the counter. I ordered mine to go and grabbed a bag of chips and a diet coke.

I knew I had nothing to fear tonight but this felt like a last meal. I settled myself in the grass of Coolidge Park and laid out my meal. There were still a few folks enjoying this beautiful evening. I ate my Stromboli and watched the world of Chattanooga walk by.

The shadows began a race to the river as the evening announced herself. The day's heat began to recede and mothers were herding children to their cars. The business elite in their fancy suits crossed by at a determined pace as it was time to be home. I sat there with a full belly, sipping my soda. My rendezvous wasn't till much later. You see, fairies prefer the dark. So right now my time was my own.

"Hey you," I heard as someone tapped my foot. "Wake up. You aren't allowed to sleep here."

"What?" I asked as I looked up to see a policeman roust me from my slumber. "Oh, sorry officer, I must have dozed off." Shadows from both directions met on the river as darkness crept into the park. I checked the time on my phone and saw I had been asleep for over an hour. The cop stood there watching me impatiently, willing me to hurry and get up. "Sorry officer, does the park close after dark? " I asked a bit sarcastically as I rose.

"No, but you need to move along."

"Did I break some law?" I was feeling a bit put off by this guy's attitude.

He refused to answer and simply pointed toward the street.

"So is it only me or are you the designated representative of the tourist bureau. Listen, I fell asleep after eating a meal in a park. I'm not a squatter so back off."

"Tell me something I don't hear every day."

"But do they have hotel keys?" and I flashed my key card. I was getting more pissed by the second, but decided this jerk wasn't worth it. I walked away, stopped and turned. "You know I use to think this was a nice friendly place till some self-righteous asshole had to flex the six ounces of authority he had. I hope you have a wonderful evening asshole." and I climbed the stairs to the bridge crossing the river. I took a few deep breaths and forced myself not to let this one bad apple, well you know what I mean.

I walked back to my room, feeling refreshed from my nap. The evening was cool and the sky was darkening from blue through black. I stopped and bought a couple bottles of cold soda for my room. I went in my room, filled a glass with ice, added some bourbon and topped it with coke. I took a sip as I undressed to take a shower.

The hot water felt good as I washed the day away. This cleansing ritual was an excellent way to prepare myself for the evening ahead. I wrapped the towel around me and headed over to the table. I sat in the chair and picked up the card, which earlier, was nestled in flowers. On the front was a perfect impression of her lips in a deep red, almost a strawberry color. On the back it was sealed in wax with a rune design. It sort of looked like the letters, TFAMI. It was pressed into the red glob of wax. I broke the seal and removed the card. This was no hallmark. The paper was heavy and fine. I'm no expert but this was fancy stationary.

On the front of the envelope was simply my name, Roger. It was done in beautiful flowing script. It seems Naomi really did do calligraphy. The front of the card had a rune embossed. I have no idea what it means but I suspect it was Naomi's signet. In flowing script that matched the envelope with a one-line message.

My Chosen,

I welcome you to my realm and await your audience with a light heart.

Your Queen
Naomi

So her realm extends to here now and she's my queen. My stomach clenched. She was welcoming me in earnest but the wording of this felt wrong. I had no fealty to any monarch. Was I in for another tussle in the glen? I had no back up this time. All this anxiety and I still had another hour till I had to leave.

Chapter 18

JUST A RIDE IN THE PARK

The appointed hour arrived and I headed to Point Park. It was a short drive from the hotel, but seemed to take an eternity. The sun was down and the parking lot was deserted. I was a few minutes early so I sat there and took a few deep breaths.

"Shit," I said aloud. I turned the rearview mirror and talked to my reflection. "I thought you were done with fairies," I said. "Me too," I replied. I found myself chuckling as I realized I was having a conversation with myself. "Well buck up old man, it's time."

I got out of the truck slowly and scanned the area. So far there were no fireflies. Was this a good thing or a bad thing? I headed toward the gate. Leaning against the gate was a park ranger, complete with uniform and a name-tag sporting the name, Steve.

"Evening sir," he said as I approached.

"Evening," I replied, wondering how I was going to get around this guy.

"Park's closed."

"Oh?" I replied stupidly. I wasn't sure if I was relieved or not. I mean, I did try, but couldn't get in to the park. And there was no one to guide me.

While I was having this diatribe with myself, ranger Steve stood there watching me.

"You're Roger Burr aren't you?" This caught me by surprise. You would have thought by now I'd be used to expecting the unexpected, but alas I wasn't.

With style and elegance I replied, "Uuhh, yes I am, and you are?"

"I'm another fly in Naomi's web." He extended his arm forward with his palm up exposing a tattoo on his wrist. It looked like the rune pressed into the wax on Naomi's note.

"What's this?"

"Wow, you are new. This is her mark. My guess it's some sort of rune language. Anyway, it's Naomi's mark."

"So you are my guide?"

"Yep, the name's Steve, Steve Coy. Pleased to meet ya."

"So what's the deal, Steve."

"Are you carrying any metal?"

"I'm not packing, if that's what you mean."

"No, I mean, are you carrying any metal, specifically iron."

"Well aside from my keys, a few coins, and my zipper, no. Why, do you want to search me?" I offered sarcastically.

"Actually Rog, I was counting on it."

"What the...?" I started as he pulled up his shirt and pointed to an ugly scar running down his side.

"I got this little reminder because I missed a pen knife. It was in the guy's boot."

I put my arms out and said, "Go ahead man. I haven't got anything to hide." He reached into his golf cart and pulled out a wand. It was like the one the TSA folks at the airport use. He waved it up and down and around me. It beeped when it crossed my zipper and the pocket with my change and keys. All else was clear of metal.

"So Steve, who gave you the little trophy?" I asked gesturing to his scar.

"Naomi told one of the little fuckers to do it, but he seemed to enjoy himself way too much."

"A pen knife?"

"Yep and he couldn't have gotten to it if he wanted to. It was in his boot," he repeated shaking his head.

"Your boss is one tough bitch."

"Tell me about it," Steve said as his eyes rolled.

"How did you get tangled up with the fairies?"

"Like most good stories, this one starts with, I was drinking moonshine with my buddies and was headed home through the woods. I literally stumbled and fell into them. I thought it was a moonshine-induced dream. Anyway, they convinced me to play their game with them. Fairies never play for fun and it was their game, and here I am. It's not so bad. I have to escort a few folks like you every now and again. But I don't have choices. They call, I come."

"Do you ever want out of your contract?"

"No, not really, but the pay is pretty good and it puts money in my bank every month. It doesn't suck."

"Okay, so what's next?"

"Hop on," he said as he pointed to the golf cart.

We climbed in and he headed into the darkness of the park.

"This gets a little weird, so hang on," Steve warned.

No sooner did he finish speaking, than a light flickered to life. It was only a pinprick off in the distance and was headed straight toward us. It was growing larger as it came closer. I looked to Steve and he had a wild look in his eyes, but was smiling from ear to ear. I thought a train was coming and I was tied to the track. The cart started shaking when the light hit us. I hung on to the seat with white knuckles wondering what in the hell was going on. As quickly as it came, the light vanished and all movement stopped. There we were outside that goddamned glen. What had I just stepped in?

Chapter 19

OUT OF THE FRY PAN...

Steve sat there and pointed for me to follow the bouncing light.

"Oh boy," I feigned excitement, "fireflies." I reached out my hand to Steve and he took it.

"Roger, you be careful in there. They can be tricky bastards."

"I know, good luck to you Steve."

"I'll be waiting here for the return flight."

"Shit, we gotta do that again?"

"I'm afraid so."

"Okay then, I'll see you later."

"Good luck, Roger," he called out as I headed to the trees. I waved thanks and pressed on.

The glen was exactly as I remembered. A circle of ancient trees was lit up like Christmas Eve by those damned fireflies from hell. I was prodded to the center and was as nervous as a cat. In my mind, I was reliving the night from last year, minus the tumble down the hill.

A bright light descended and I instinctively knew it was Naomi. It, or rather, she alighted on the ground a few feet in front of me. From the bright light, Naomi stepped toward me. I instinctually raised my hand and retreated a step or two. This seemed to please her. Her smile widened and it actually hit her eyes.

She raised her hand reassuringly, "You are safe here Roger,' she said. Her voice was so sultry and inviting.

"No!" I mentally chastised myself.

"I have brought you here, so we can talk. You need to understand the perils awaiting you along your journey."

"Perils? There are perils? I thought I had a long boring road trip. I'm only supposed to have a nice chat with this King Aelfric, dude." At the mention of his name all hell broke loose. The fireflies, okay, the fairies were filling the air and screaming their battle cries. There had to be millions of them. Just a thought, but I'd bet they weren't too fond of this Aelfric fellow.

"Quiet," Naomi spoke in a whisper but the sound of her voice filled the glen. Before the final letter t was annunciated, all the fairies fell silent.

"Holy shit," I said under my breath. Naomi smiled but this one did not touch her eyes and it scared the hell out of me.

Chapter 20

NOW WE ARE BROTHERS

Naomi motioned and the ground shook as a pair of comfortable looking chairs grew right beside us from what I assume to be the roots of the trees.

"Please,' I said as I motioned to her chair indicating she sit first. She may be this powerful scary fairy queen but she was a woman. Well she appeared to be.

"Thank you,' she replied graciously as she sat. I took the chair opposite her. She motioned to the side and a tray bearing two mugs and a pitcher floated across the glen. I noticed two of the fireflies were carrying the tray. I took comfort from the fact that it was carried and not self-propelled. Somehow I accepted these bugs into my perception of real.

Naomi watched me with amusement as I followed the tray. She seemed to enjoy the childlike wonder I expressed.

"Roger, before I start I need to clarify something for you. My subjects, nay my friends," and she gestured to the trees, "who assist me are not bugs, nor are they fireflies, as you like to call them. They are proud and fierce warriors. Many are ancient, by human standards. We are of a race of fairies called pixies. We find your derogatory titles both insulting and demeaning. Please, refrain from using this terminology in our presence.

I was embarrassed but didn't remember calling them

anything out loud. This could only mean she could hear my thoughts. Oh this was lovely. "My apologies, I spoke only in ignorance and meant no offense." I offered in reply.

She took the pitcher and poured two cups of the clear liquid. I remembered this drink from the last time we met. I was looking forward to trying it again. She offered me a cup and I took a deep drink.

"Why am I here and why do I have to travel to," I paused not wanting to cause another commotion, "to King, uh you know." I didn't want to say the name and have all the fire…eerr pixies go all nuts again. As I corrected my thought from firefly to pixie, I saw Naomi smile. Did it get cold in here? Because I had a shiver travel all the way down my spine.

"You travel to my brother's realm because you have been summoned. You are Chosen and he is King." She said this rather as a matter of fact.

"Chosen? I am constantly being named as this 'Chosen.' Would you please explain this to me?"

"You were selected before you were born, as was your mother's father and his mother's mother, as was your granddaughter."

"Wait a second, did you say my granddaughter? What the hell have you done to Harmony?" No one messes with my grandbaby.

"Easy Roger, she hasn't been touched and we want no harm to come to her. Actually, we are watching over her much like we did for you in your youth."

"My Mum told me how you took me away for several days. Will that happen to her?"

"Yes, when she is older."

"I want to go with her when she goes. I am Chosen don't I have the right?"

"In fact, this is within your right, but first this journey must be completed."

"I need your promise, Naomi."

"If you survive the trials in front of you and are alive at the time of her cleansing, then you may escort and remain with Harmony."

"Okay," Wait did she say survive? "That's settled. I was picked because of lineage, but what does it mean to be Chosen?"

"Your grandfather descended from an old line of magic keepers from across the ocean. Your mother brought the old magic with her she when she travelled to these shores.

The Chosen is a vessel, a holder of the magic, a container. All humans have magic they have forgotten how to use. There are bloodlines where the old magic runs deep."

"Wait, Wait, Wait," I interrupted. "Are you saying I am magic?"

"No, I am saying you hold the magic."

"Can I access it? You know, use it?"

"Possibly, but mostly humans have forgotten or lost the ability to access their magic, though we are able to use it.

There was a time when humans and Fae lived together in this world. We lived in peace, exchanging magic freely. This is the lore my mother taught me at her knee about five hundred of your years ago. In the time since the break, much magic was lost. Now, not all humans have magic. There are only a few bloodlines left. Even they have bred impurities into the magic. This is why we took you as a youth. We must cleanse or purify the magic when you are young. This allows the magic to grow within you. I did this with you when you were younger and we will do this with Harmony."

"Can any fairy take my magic or do I have a say in who gets access?"

"We cannot take your magic without your consent. Last time we met here you gave yourself to me."

"Hold on, I gave myself? You sent these fi...pixies out to get me and then you took my will."

"No, you misunderstood their intentions. They simply showed you the path and invited you along." She smiled.

"Showed me the path with their swords."

"Though I recall, you considered them harmless fireflies?" she quipped sarcastically.

"Touché, but how about my will?"

"You didn't put up a fight."

"I didn't have a chance to express my will."

"That's not totally true. I could not have taken you without your consent. Some part of you wanted to be taken."

"Okay, I see we can go round and round on this and will never agree with your assessment. Let me ask this. How can I resist being taken, again? I don't want to lose my free will or be a slave to anyone."

"First, you can bear my mark and then no Fae will touch you, for you will be mine."

"Somehow it feels like I'd be branded, and I won't be owned like cattle."

"You could bend a knee and declare fealty to me as your queen," she offered earnestly.

I returned this with a look of disdain. "And so I would bow to your every command. How is this different than being branded?"

"There are differences, but your point is valid," she said and smiled a sly grin.

"Is there an amulet or a sword of power or some sort of magical pendant I could carry?"

Her smile brightened, "Are you wishing to enter a bargain with me?"

"Hold on, haven't I given you enough? Wasn't it my magic providing the power you needed?"

"Needed? Why would I have need?" she snapped back as if the word tasted sour in her mouth.

"I noticed you came and got me freely, from what I remember as Uke's realm," I started saying.

"Uke was a toad," she spat.

"Yes, maybe but I recall a toad beckoned and you went. Yet, now I get zapped from his domain, without so much as a glimmer of permission. I also remember you said your power was, and I quote, 'waning'. You needed my power to fend him off. I'm guessing, my 'old magic' was enough juice to, let's say, depose a King? Tell me fair queen, where are the boundaries of your kingdom now?"

"You saw more than I expected. Yes, my realm has

expanded. I am now Queen of the East."

"East of what?"

"East of the country you call the United States. My boundary connects your cities of New Orleans and Chicago."

"Holy crap, my magic gave you this? If I'm not mistaken only truth can be spoken in the hallowed ground.'

"This is so, only truth can be spoken in this place. Your gift allowed me to pursue the annexation of these weaker realms."

"Now we are back to my original statement. Haven't I given enough?"

"Well spoken. I can offer you a warrior escort on your journey.'

"You are gonna send a pixie with me? I know they are tough but being so small and only one?"

"Are you willing to share some of your power with him?"

"Wait a second, I don't swing that way."

Naomi laughed when she realized what I was saying. "No, No you will not need to couple with Kalen to exchange power," she said while laughing. "Coupling for magic is reserved for when large amounts of magic has to be transferred. There was much more to the ceremony than you were made aware. For you to share power with your escort, Kalen, you need only say the words and share a drop of your blood."

"Again with the blood, are you some sort of vampires? You cut my neck and drank my blood. Now I need to give some to, uh...Kalen? What if he decides he wants more?"

"He is loyal and the words bind him, giving you the ability to control the magic he receives. Your blood is a way to establish a conduit of power. He won't be able to take magic from you. You will have to give it to him. As for me drinking, I didn't drink. I wet my lips in accordance with the ancient ceremony. Your blood acts as a conduit of power, not the power itself.

Here are the words in your tongue. I don't believe your mouth could form the old words.

I offer you the strength of my heart's blood. Please accept my gift.
"How often must we perform this ritual?"

"Only once, unless you sever the bond. Then it will need to be performed again to reconnect."

"So, he can take the magic now and hold on to it until he needs to use it?"

"No, when need presents itself, you will have only to will your strength. If you are unable, you may grant him permission to take power as needed. Again the choice is yours to make."

"Will he remain small?"

"I forget you are still so new to our ways," she said sounding very much like my second grade teacher. "He will walk with you in your world and appear to all who gaze upon him as a human." She turned and said something in what I expect was the old tongue and the only word I caught was Kalen. From high within the trees, a bright blue light dropped down and alighted on Naomi's palm. She closed her eyes and blew on the light. It floated out of her hand on her breath and fell toward the ground. As it fell the light flared to a brilliant sky blue and out stepped a young man. He look to be in his late twenties and had light blonde hair and emerald green eyes. He was not at all what I expected. He had a slight build but moved like a tiger stalking a kill. His eyes were serious, much too serious for a man of his apparent age. He bowed to Naomi.

"Rise, Kalen," she said.

"My Queen, how may I be of service?" Something about this guy seemed familiar. I couldn't put my finger on it but I'd seen him before.

"You will escort the Chosen to and from the realm of King Aelfric." His face twisted into a look of disgust. I wasn't sure if it was because of me or their beloved king. "Do you have a problem with this?" Naomi asked sounding a bit perturbed.

"No, my Queen," but it was obvious he did. "I will do as you command."

Oh what a joy this trip is going to be with Mr. Sourpuss.

The Summons

Now I have to give him my magic.

"Roger, this is Kalen. He is the head of my personal guard and the finest warrior in my army. Kalen, this is Roger, our Chosen, the savior of our realm. Guard him well." I offered my hand in friendship. He grasped my forearm in a firm grip, very firm. I took his and tried to return the favor. As we released grips he grinned at me in a relaxed smile.

"Kalen," Naomi continued, "the Chosen has offered you his strength. Will you receive his gift?"

He now started to walk around me looking me up and down. He was sizing me up.

Curiosity got the better of me. "Naomi would you please explain what is happening?" I pleaded. I thought it was already settled.

"Please remain quiet, Roger," she asked politely. Kalen looked into Naomi's eyes and gave a single nod, albeit a slight one.

"I accept," he said turning to me.

"Roger, would you please prepare your gift." I don't mind telling you I was clueless. Prepare my gift? What the... One of the pixies flew down so fast it was a blur and the damn bug stabbed me in my left index finger. The blood welled up to form a perfectly round drop of blood. I pressed it into my right palm and spoke the words.

"I offer you the strength of my heart's blood. Please accept my gift." I extended my hand to Kalen. He took my hand in his, again in a firm grip. The air seemed to still and become silent. Our hands began to glow and a brilliant light travelled up our arms and down our chests. I felt a sense of peace and strength emanating from Kalen. His eyes were locked on mine and contained an acceptance of sorts. His face was warm and friendly. It even held a tinge of affection. This was a very happy place.

As suddenly as the light wrapped around us, it winked out, but I still felt closer to Kalen.

Kalen looked me in the eye, "Now we are brothers."

"Yes we are," was all I replied.

Chapter 21

A HISTORY LESSON

The ceremony with Kalen was exhilarating and exhausting all at the same time. My heart still raced as I sat again with Naomi. She sent him to prepare for the journey. He bowed and snapped to a little blue ball of light and flew up into the trees.

"Kalen will protect you well."

"Somehow, I know you are right. Please explain to me what happened."

"You have been given the privilege to see each other." I shook my head slightly, saying I didn't quite understand. "Let me say it this way. You two glimpsed each other's essence, your true selves." I still wore a stupid expression. "You were able to see each other's soul?" she offered.

At this I nodded my head, "I think I understand. Magic did this?"

"Your magic, Roger. The old magic is quite potent. This is why we must talk. Aelfric summoned you, because of the magic. He too wishes to use it."

"Like you did?"

"Yes, but I only wished to protect my own. The rest..." she waved her arms to indicate her realm, "came because of Uke's greed and the greed of his allies."

"Go on," I prodded.

"Shortly before our ceremony, Uke led his army to my

borders demanding I bow to him giving him my realm. He convinced the nobility with land upon my borders to rally to his cause. More accurately, he used intimidation and coercion. We were surround by enemies. With a normal strengthening, he knew, I'd be able to withstand his army but not an attack from all sides. He did not know you held old magic."

"So I take it my family carries a powerful bag of mojo."

"Your family descended from powerful mages. Our families have been connected for more generations than I can count. Aelfric and I came to these shores around three centuries ago to establish our own realms. Aelfric picked the northwestern part of this continent and I fell in love with this place." A smile of pure joy was on her face as she was remembering this journey, so long ago. "We each had enough magic to create our realm and hold the area of our choosing. But time erodes magic and the power this land holds pales next to the old magic.

When your mother came across the ocean to this land, she chose to settle closer to me. This made her a ward of mine."

This confused me. "If my mother was your ward, why wasn't she aware of this?"

"You were my ward too. Did you know?"

"No, so by ward what do you mean?"

"There are many things in my world wishing to own your magic. Many would have no regard for your life. Others would only like to keep the magic from us and wait for our magic to erode and remove us."

"Like Uke?"

"Yes, Uke was one who wished me gone."

"I was wondering something. I have four brothers. Why don't they have magic?"

"They do, but in them it is much less. I am sure you could see it in them."

"How do you mean?" She had lost me again.

"By their talents."

"Talents?"

"Yes, we often heard William perform music. He is very good. Anthony-there isn't a piece of wood he can't bend to his will. James, I understand, had much talent in the culinary world. Finally Matthew, he was a unique one. His talent is his passion. He has an ability to love, like none I've ever seen."

"Then how was I chosen?"

"When you were conceived, the moon and stars were in the correct position and the magic flowed into you. It wasn't in the stars for your brothers."

"So the conditions were right or rather perfectly controlled for my conception." She nodded. "I'd be willing to bet the odds on these events coming together at one particular time would be astronomical, if you'll pardon the pun."

Naomi answered without emotion, "Yes, they were."

"Holy shit lady, you arranged my conception?"

"Of course, as we did you mother's, grandfather's, your daughter's, and granddaughter's as well." She said this so calmly we could have been talking about the weather. This felt like some sort of perversion. My whole existence was orchestrated from conception, to birth, and through my childhood.

"This meddling with my family...exactly how long have the Fae been arranging conceptions?"

"Ever since the breaking."

"This breaking...you mentioned this earlier. What was this?"

"This would take more time to explain, than we have here. I can offer a simple explanation."

"Please, explain away, a short version will do."

"In the years prior to the break, the head of the Mages and the King of the Fae had a disagreement. The head wizard Bartholomew, or as he came to be known as Bart the Black, felt the fairies were taking too much magic. He claimed this made the mages too weak to defend themselves. Of course this was far from the truth. He wasn't interested in the truth. He was trying to learn the Fae art of receiving magic. Our king accused him of wanting to take all the magic into himself and become the most powerful.

Bart called together his council but one mage. Charles the Keeper, was away on council business and unable to attend this session. It is believed he was sent away because he was the only one powerful enough to prevent what became the breaking.

Bart was able to bend the council to his will, and declared war on the Fae. The war didn't last long and ended with many unnecessary deaths. Bart and our King killed each other in the final battle.

Upon his return, Charles became the head mage and decided the cost of the war was too great. The whole council and many Fae perished needlessly.

He and Queen Breena decided it was best for all, mankind and Fae alike, if this kind of power was kept from man. Charles being the only surviving member of the council, agreed. Breena used both human and Fae magic to wipe Charles' memory. This enabled him to forget his ability of manipulating his magic. Fae and man would now live separately. From that moment forward we have kept ourselves hidden from mankind, with the exception of you family. You are a direct descendant from Charles and our need of magic has kept our families intertwined in accordance with the bargain Charles and my mother struck."

"Your mother?" This shocked me a little.

"Yes, Breena was Aelfric's and my mother and Charles was my friend."

"Thank you for telling me this."

Chapter 22

TASTE OF THINGS TO COME

"Before we finish here you need to know of the realms you are passing through."

"Before you start, there is one more thing I need to ask. I had a long talk with my mother about you. In the conversation she mentioned something about how you tried to take me when I was an infant?"

"You are talking about the lake incident?"

"Yes."

"It wasn't us," and she waved her hand indicating her subjects.

"But my Mum heard you. She recognized your voice."

"I was there, but we didn't try to take you. I had six of my warriors protecting you from the local wilds. It was considered easy duty, for the wilds generally weren't organized. A somewhat charismatic young fairy discovered your magic. Roger, even as an infant, before your cleansing you had more magic than any before you. This wilder," she spat this word as if it left a bad taste in her mouth, "decided he would take you and raise you as his own. Your magic would then be at his disposal. He organized his tribe and they outnumbered your guard, ten to one. The coward didn't even join the fighting. My friends fought bravely and defeated many of their foe, but alas after the fifth of your guard was vanquished the last survivor came to me. Your mother heard me address the traders telling them to stop and return you to your mother. The young coward who started this mess has paid for his treasonous acts."

"How many warriors did you assign to me after this incident?"

"Fifty, but enough with this history lesson. We need to discuss the trip and talk about the dangers awaiting you."

"But I'll have Kalen and I do come from powerful wizard stock."

She rolled her eyes with disgust. I guess sarcasm isn't a form of humor here. "Kalen will be very helpful but you need to know about the perils between here and my brother's realm. There are three bands of wilders you need to avoid. I don't know for certain if they know of your travels. We need to assume they do."

"How would they know? I'm not completely sure of the route I will be going." I said with frustration. "I should have flown."

She shook her head. I felt like a petulant child right now. I am a highly intelligent man, but these fairies and their magic have turned me into an ignorant child.

"You could not have flown," Naomi said with such authority. "This trip is needed to prepare you for the trials in Aelfric's court. Kalen will show you the way. Please accept his counsel. If one of these bands captures you, they will want what you hold. Our magic is able to extract power from you with a small amount of pain and blood because of the long history of our families. There are those who believe to gain the magic, one needs to consume your fresh marrow."

"Marrow, as in bones?"

"Yes and it must be removed while you live to get maximum benefit."

"Shit." I paused. "Oh cute, marrow is where blood is produced. Once again we are back to the blood factor. Now do all the bands believe this?"

"No, only the most civilized one. The other two are very primitive. They hunt as a roving pack much like wolves."

"These thing are going to be hunting me?"

"Yes, as soon as you leave my realm."

"When I cross the Mississippi it's open season on Roger."

"I do not know what you mean by open season, but the hunt will indeed begin."

"Oh joy," I proclaimed. The blue light descended from the treetops. I knew without a doubt it was Kalen. Must be the bond. Right before he touched the ground the light faded and out stepped my protector. He was dressed for the part as well. He had a sword at his hip and bow and quiver across his back. In his left hand he carried a small satchel that looked like clothes. In his right hand was another sword and bow with quiver. He approached and offered the weapons to me.

"These are yours, my brother," he said.

"Thank you, but I can't," I said.

"Why?" and he was perplexed.

"I'm afraid I don't know how to use them properly. I'd probably stick myself with that sword."

He smiled a sardonic smile containing no warmth. "You will learn. I will teach you." His face had a determination telling me he wasn't going to relent, so I accepted his gift.

"It is time Roger," Naomi interrupted. She was right. I needed to get a little shuteye before we hit the road. I'd been here quite a few hours.

"Okay," I turned to Kalen, "shall we go?" Naomi stood and stepped in front of me. She placed her hands on either side of my head and kissed me on each cheek.

"Roger, be safe and return to my realm."

"I will," was all I could think to say.

She turned to Kalen and did the same except she paused to place her forehead on his and she spoke in what I assume to be a fairy dialect. Before Kalen answered he looked to me, frowned, and replied reluctantly, "I will."

A pleased smile crossed Naomi's lips. We turned and headed out of the glen.

Chapter 23

BEAM ME UP

As we left the glen, Steve was waiting, as promised.

"Hey Steve," I greeted.

"Hi Roger," he looked at his watch. "Finished already?"

"Already? I'm not wearing a watch but I was in there at least five hours."

"Try five minutes," Steve laughed at my disbelief for he knew time passed differently in the fairy world. "Don't worry Roger, this is normal. Time is different in there," he said as he pointed toward the glen.

"Wow, this will take some getting used to. Anyway, allow me to introduce, Kalen." I gestured to my bodyguard. As soon as I said Kalen, Steve bowed his head in respect. "My Lord," he said with a tone of reverence.

"Steve," replied Kalen. This exchange took me by surprise.

"Every time I turn around, there is something I don't know. Steve, Kalen, would one of you care to explain what this is all about?"

"Roger, you really don't know?" Steve asked.

"Obviously not, please explain."

"Kalen is the Lord General of the Fairy Army."

"Yes, he's head of Naomi's warriors." At this Kalen smiled a knowing grin.

"No you ass, HE'S THE LORD GENERAL." And he

annunciated each and every word slowly. I guess he thought I was slow in the head and speaking slowly would make it better. Maybe I was.

"Okay Steve, pretend, just pretend I'm new to this whole, Fairy Thing," I actually used air quotes.

Steve turned to Kalen, "My Lord, may I?"

"You have my permission."

"Thank you, My Lord. Do you know anything about the breaking?"

"Naomi gave me the short version," and I nodded my head toward the glen.

"Did she talk about the war? How they beat the powerful mages?"

"Yeah."

"Lord Kalen led the fairies into battle, beating the mages and their army. If you knew their history, you'd know there was no way the fairies should have won. But they did, and the victory goes to Lord Kalen."

I looked at this young man standing next to me. "So you're a big shot to the Fae?"

"Apparently, yes," Kalen responded. I see he could be a wiseass too.

"You need to know, I don't do bowing and scraping. There'll be no My Lord, this or My Lord, that. Are you okay with this?"

"It will be a refreshing change."

"Okay Steve, take me home. Shotgun!" Yep the front seat was mine. "Did you ever think of putting NCC-1701-A, or G for golf cart, on the side of this puppy?" Steve gave me a blank look and Kalen acted as if I was talking a foreign language. Perhaps I was.

"Am I the only one who every watched an episode of Star Trek? The identification numbers on the side of the Enterprise? We went warp speed to get here? Hello? Captain, I'm giving her all she's got? No? Beam me up Scotty. There's no intelligent life down here. Okay, I give up. You two are a tough crowd."

"Anyway, Roger," Steve said speaking slowly again and

sounding a bit exasperated, "are you ready to go?"

"Yea, Yea, let's go," I said as I showed Kalen to the backward facing seat. These had seatbelts.

"Steve, are the belts necessary?" I asked.

"For the back seats, hell yea." I showed Kalen how to strap in and settled in the front and prepared for the jump to warp speed. They may not appreciate the Star Trek references, but I do.

The light appeared again and Steve headed toward it. The cart shook as it did, apparently, only ten minutes ago.

We landed back at Point Park. If it weren't so dark I'd have been able to see Lookout Mountain. Steve drove us back to the parking lot and all the way to my truck. We got out and Kalen needed help with the seatbelt. After all, he was in my world now. This all seemed new to him, like fairy was new to me.

Before climbing in my truck I showed him how the seatbelts worked. He climbed in and it only took two tries to get buckled. I got in the driver's seat and started the truck. "Kalen, in our world, what are your needs?"

"How do you mean?"

"Like sleeping and eating, you know, the day to day living part."

"My body in this world is essentially human and I'll require what every human requires."

"Good to know. Are you hungry?"

He appeared to consider the question. "Yes, I am."

"I'll hit a drive thru on the way back to the room." We drove in relative quiet. Kalen watched the world go by the window. The light of the city and the passing cars seemed to interest him greatly.

"How long has it been since you were here?"

"I was in the colonies right before the nasty war with your kin from across the ocean."

My kin from across the ocean? What was he saying? He continued, "I believe the year was 1774, yes January of 74. The talk in the taverns was about a tea party, in the city of Boston."

"Holy crap, you were here right before the Revolutionary War?"

"Yes, and none of this," and he waved his hand, "was here. Other Fae have talked about your cities and modern automobiles, but this is incredible."

"It gets a lot more interesting than this," the conversation paused as I pulled in to the Wendy's drive through. He said he ate meat, so I ordered a couple of burgers and fries. I parked next to my room and we carried the weapons and food into the room. We took seats at the table and tucked into the food. He seemed to enjoy his meal.

"Would you like a drink?" I asked as I held up the Jim Beam. He looked at me with an unreadable expression, or as if I should know the answer. But I didn't. "Okay do you want some bourbon, you know, spirits?" I said a bit sarcastically.

"Is it like whiskey? If so, then yes please." I went to the bathroom and retrieved a couple of the glasses sanitized for our use. I poured a generous portion in each glass and pushed one across the table.

"Cheers," I offered.

"To the Queen," he replied. While I enjoyed a leisurely sip, he threw his back and shot the whole thing. He sucked in a breath as the brown liquid burned its way down and then smiled. "This is good," he said appearing half buzzed.

"How about we hit the hay," again he gave me a puzzled look. "Okay, time for bed."

"I agree."

"Are you going to get small, anytime soon?"

"No, while I'm in your world I will remain as you see."

"Okay, you get the bed on the right."

"Are there washing facilities close by?"

"Right through the door," and I pointed to the bathroom. I gave him a quick tour and how to use the indoor plumbing.

"Turn the knob and water comes? It is said you don't have magic here but I see they are mistaken." We prepared ourselves for bed and laid our heads down for a good night's rest.

Chapter 24

I'LL HUFF AND I'LL PUFF

Surprisingly, the morning routine was somewhat normal. Had I not known Kalen was a fairy, I would have thought he was human. After we dressed, we packed the car. We walked to the restaurant and ordered breakfast. Kalen order the daily special. It consisted of two eggs, two toast, two pancakes and coffee. I found it a bit weird, he was eating eggs. With him having wings, I'd never have guessed eggs would be on the menu.

After our second cup of coffee, we talked about our route. Kalen studied the map and pointed to a small town in Kentucky called Wickliffe.

"This is a safe crossing area. It falls between the borders of the Warg and Phengard."

"Warg sounds like some wolf type creature from a Tolkien novel."

"Yes, Tolkien got it right. Did you know your family and Mr. Tolkien had spent time together?

"My Mum sent me a newspaper clipping of Mr. Tolkien summering at the family's hotel. Was my granddad aware of your world?

"Yes, he was also my friend," Kalen said.

"You knew him?" I know he told me but I needed to get my brain around this fact.

"Yes," he replied not the least bit phased by the

redundancy. "I was able to travel there in the late 20's."

"The 1920's?"

He nodded, "I met Eric when he was a teenager. He was a delightful lad. He was quick to smile and always ready to help anyone. He was aware of us and knew his role."

"His role? You mean as Chosen?" I asked.

"Yes," was his reply.

"This is too weird. In my world you look to be barely more than a teenager. But you are talking about hanging out with my grandfather when he was a teen. My youngest child is the same age as my grandfather was in the 20's. This is so bizarre. Okay, let's get back on task. What roads will we be driving?" He pointed out the roads and the stopping points for the day.

"I'll pick tomorrow's route when we stop for the night. I need to see what this day brings."

"Let me get this straight. Today we are going to skirt along the border of the Warg and the Phen something?" I asked.

"The Phengard," he added.

"Is there anything I need to look for? What exactly does a Warg or a Phengard look like? Do they have any special skills?"

"Warg are as you read. Tolkien must have been told about them to be so accurate. Your family probably swapped stories with him. They are large canine like creatures who travel in packs. They are very organized and intelligent. The Warg typically avoid contact with humans in their wolf form. Phengard are quite different. They appear as a small blue butterflies or moths, but don't be fooled by their innocent exterior. I've seen them strip a deer to bones in a matter of minutes. People who wander into their realm are usually never seen again." Kalen shivered as he said this.

"On one side we will have demonic wolves and on the other flying piranha with fluffy wings. Good to know. How will we keep from attracting their notice?

"Very carefully," Kalen smiled at his own sarcasm.

"Wiseass," I replied.

I programmed my GPS, very carefully, and we headed out. We stayed to the back roads and country highways for most of the trip. I actually preferred this route. We got to see lots of main streets this way and the drive was pleasant. A little past eleven my phone buzzed letting me know I had a text message. I ignored it for now because we were stopping soon for lunch.

We found a quaint diner on the side of the road. There were about ten cars in the parking lot, which is always a good sign. We pulled in and found an empty spot. Kalen headed in to get a booth while I checked my messages. The text I received, was from my oldest daughter, Sam, and it simply said;

'Dad, WHAT THE HELL! Please call.'

"Shit!" I said to no one in particular. Not only did I have to deal with this fairy stuff, now I have to put fires out on the home front. I dialed her number.

"Hello Dad," Sam answered.

"Hello Babe," I replied, hoping a familiar nickname would help diffuse the situation, at least a little...Nope.

"What's going on? First Mom is down with Grandma and Grandpa and you are...where are you?"

"Not sure I can fully explain."

""Daddy, you need to try," Sam sounded exasperated. Samantha was my oldest daughter and mother of two of the most beautiful kids. Harmony was one of these. She lived close by and we were quite involved in each other's lives. So this was a fair request.

"Do you remember the encounter I had last summer?"

"Don't tell me it's about the fairy crap, again."

"Okay, what do you want me to say?"

"How about the truth?"

"Listen little girl, this is the truth and you better wrap your head around it, too." The story she got was a PG version of the truth. Okay, I left out the sex part. No daughter wants to hear about her daddy having sex, least of all with someone who's not Mommy. But she asked for it, so she got the whole story this time. I also gave details of this trip up till now. She stopped me twice asking clarification questions, and then she was silent.

After a prolonged pause, "So, you are saying fairies are real?"

"Yep, got one in the diner saving me a seat."

"Harmony is involved in this?"

"I'm afraid so, but they promised me I can be fully involved. Honey, your mom is pissed at me. She has every right to be. I did cheat with Naomi."

"Did you have control? You said she removed your will."

"But I guess I could have fought it. I didn't know it at the time but I've been told anyone has the ability to resist if they want to bad enough."

"Mom will come around, maybe. Can you let her meet your fairies?"

"I don't know. I haven't really thought about it. I've been dealing with this trip."

"When do you get home?"

"If all goes well, next week."

"If not? she asked.

"I'd rather not think about the *if not*." I really didn't want her to think I could die. Shit, I didn't want to think about it.

"Are you in danger?"

"Nah, I've got to avoid a few fairies. Besides, I got this crazy ninja warrior fairy to protect me." Never fails as soon as you say there is nothing to worry about… Right then I heard a growl, a deep throaty growl. It came from the shadow cast by the diner.

"Babe, I've got to go, I love you," and I hung up and dropped the phone on the front seat of the truck. I reached to the back seat, wrapped my hand around the handle of the sword and slowly extracted the blade. It might have been my imagination or adrenaline but I swear the sword vibrated.

"All right you son-of-a-bitch," I even chuckled at the statement because it was a son of a bitch. Then I saw the two iridescent blue eyes shining from the shadow and I heard the menacing growl.

I looked around for Kalen. I caught him watching me

from the diner and he was smiling. For a fraction of a second, I wondered why he wasn't out here with me. I put Kalen out of my mind. I needed to concentrate on the bag of fur. I did not want to be lunch.

I held the sword awkwardly in front of me with a two handed grip. I gripped it like a baseball bat. This was one of those defining moment in my life and I was scared and pissed all at once. This damn dog was a symbol of the weird, negative crap in my life. My wife was gone and she took my youngest son with her. Fairies have been screwing with me, in my dream, on my camping trips, and this little jaunt across the country. Now this rabid mutt wanted to eat me. And Kalen, my guardian, had a front row seat.

"Hell no, come on you stupid mutt," I screamed. And he did. He moved so fast. All that I saw was a massive blur coming toward me like a freight train. I cocked the blade back. The only thought in my head was keep the elbow up and your chin down and I swung for the fence. My world went dark as the train hit me.

Chapter 25

GOING VIRAL

My next coherent thought came as I felt Kalen's hand on my shoulder, I found I was staring up at the clouds.

"You are all right? Roger are okay?" he kept repeating.

"What the hell?" I snapped, rubbing the back of my head.

"You got him." I sat up as my head throbbed from where I smacked it on the asphalt. On either side of me were the halves of the wolf. It did look like a wolf, a big ass wolf, but nothing demonic about it.

"Kalen, was this a Warg?"

"Yes, a nasty bugger too."

"But it looks like a wolf."

"In daylight and near humans, the Warg revert to this form to protect the secret."

"How many others are there?"

"I believe he was alone. I sense no others close by."

"Cool," I looked down and my shirt was covered with blood. Also folks were pouring out of the diner. They were coming to see the spectacle of a killer wolf cut in half.

"You okay son?" an older gentleman asked.

"Yes sir, I believe I am. This isn't my blood," I gestured to the wolf, "It belonged to him."

"What happened?" another asked.

"Not really sure," I said. "I heard a growl. I grabbed this sword. He charged; and I imitated Babe Ruth and voila."

A man with an apron called out. "Got a hose around the side if you would like to wash off. Oh, and the cops are on their way."

"Thanks," I took off my shirt and cleaned the blade on it before putting it back in its sheath. I tossed the shirt in the bed of the truck.

I turned to Kalen and held up the sword. "Thanks for this." He simply nodded. If I didn't know better, I'd say Kale looked disappointed.

I grabbed a clean shirt from my bag and headed around the side of the diner, this time Kalen was with me, and he was armed.

"Let me get this straight, you can sense other Fae? Did you sense him?" I gestured over my shoulder with my thumb. "Before I almost got eaten?"

"Yes, I felt his presence when I entered the diner. I thought it was someone in the diner and was trying to figure out who it was when I heard your battle cry."

"You mean when I screamed like a little girl."

"Sorry, I heard no girl, only a fierce cry calling me to battle. You should be proud. I have never heard of a human defeating a Warg, without magic."

"I feel lucky," I said. There was no way I'd feel pride from this. "Do we need to leave soon?"

"Yes, but we have time to eat."

"I'll have to talk to the police. Is this going to be the typical stop for us? I mean stop for lunch and slice a dog. Stop for dinner and what? Swat a moth?"

"We do need to be cautious, but I believe this was an unlucky encounter."

My heart was still racing as we sat to eat. The police were here. They cordoned off the perimeter and pushed the gawkers back. My truck was moved around the back to get it out of the way. People still walked around snapped pictures with their cell phones.

I found out later that some kid caught the whole thing on video. He heard me call the Warg an SOB and started filming the crazy guy. It was grainy and a bit far away but you saw my sword split the beast in half. Kalen was right. I didn't sound girly at all, cool. The video went viral. But thankfully, my face was out of focus.

My statement to the police was a simple process. As the cop approached our table, Kalen excused himself. He didn't want to deal with the human authorities. I can't blame him, I didn't either. For the police, this was a simple, though bizarre, animal attack.

"So Mr. Burr, shall I begin?" he checked his pad to be sure he got my name right, "where did you get the sword?"

"I picked it up a dozen or so years ago, overseas." The cop looked at me with a raised eyebrow as if he wanted more information. "I was in the Air Force, flying through Japan."

"Would you please tell me your version of what happened here?"

"I was talking to my daughter on the phone, over there, by my truck. When, I heard a deep, menacing growl. I have to admit, it spooked me a bit. I grabbed the sword from the backseat purely by instinct, for protection. The wolf charged at me from the side of the diner. I swung the sword and here we are." I took a bite of my burger.

"Okay, thank you sir," he closed the notepad, "that should cover it."

"Officer, do you get a lot of wolf attacks around here?"

"Can't say we do. This is the first I've had to deal with. Thank you again, Mr. Burr, for your statement. I have your number if we come up with any more questions." He extended his hand and I shook it as he rose to leave.

When he was gone, Kalen found his way back to the table and tucked into his food.

"I need to ask you something, but I not sure how to phrase this. As I understand, you were sent to provide me protection from the supernatural threats we encounter. Is this a fair assessment?"

Kalen nodded and I continued. "On our first stop, I encounter a threat that could have ended me," another nod. "Where were you?" I held up my hand to keep him from replying. "You, were in the diner. Why didn't you use that precious magic to help?"

"It doesn't work like that," he replied casually.

"Basically, you had a front row seat, to what could have been my death." I finished my rant.

Kalen smiled a cold grin, "But that did not happen, did it?"

"No," I said to Kalen and took another bite. I took a few calming breaths and decided this line of questioning was futile. "Naomi has human servants like Steve. Do the Warg or Phengard have humans on their payroll?"

"I don't really know, but it is possible. Why?"

"These people," and I pointed to the gawkers outside, "are going to post pictures, video, and any other information they find online. This little event is sensational enough to catch on like wildfire and could be seen coast to coast probably within a couple of hours. If they have pet humans, I may have shot up the proverbial flare."

"I see what you mean. Queen Naomi has many contacts with this World Wide Web thing, but I have no idea if the Warg or Phengard have the ability."

"We'd better get on the road. We might want to rethink the route." I finished my meal in silence. When I went to pay the bill, the man in the apron was working the cash register.

"Your money is no good here, boy. This meal is on the house. Anyone slicing a rabid wolf in my parking lot gets a free meal."

"Thank you," I said and turned from the register. A news truck was pulling up. "Kalen, we need to be gone, right now."

I turned back to the man in the apron, "Do you have a back way out of here?"

He took us through the kitchen. My truck was right out the door. I stood by the door and looked out into the woods behind the diner. Something was watching us.

Kalen seemed to notice too. I saw him scanning the surrounding woods with a look of concern.

I know I'm a math teacher, but a stanza of a Robert Frost poem came to mind.

> *The woods are lovely, dark and deep*
> *But I have promises to keep,*
> *And miles to go before I sleep,*
> *And miles to go before I sleep.*

Chapter 26

DON'T GIVE ME 'ONCE UPON A TIME'

We both climbed in the truck with our eyes glued to the surrounding forest.

"Did you see anything?" I asked as I backed out in a hurry.

"Not with my eyes," he replied in his usual cryptic manner.

"How many were there?" I asked.

"Enough," he replied, again with the vague answer. He was beginning to piss me off.

"Wait a second, enough? Enough for what?"

"There were enough to take you and kill me, plus extras of about two hundred," he said this with no emotion. He was simply relaying a mundane fact.

"Looks like we got out at a good time, right before they could come get us."

"No, they chose not to."

"Not to what?"

"Kill me and take you," Kalen replied a bit irate at having to repeat himself.

"I know, we got out in time."

"But we didn't."

"Didn't what? It seems like you are trying to tell me something without saying it. Please stop the cryptic nonsense."

"Roger, they were waiting for us there when we arrived. I couldn't sense them because magic blocked their presence, a very powerful form of magic. They could have easily sent 10, 20 or 100 against you instead of only one. The one they sent was a champion, one of their greatest warriors. You killed him with ease. When we went to the truck, why did you stare into the woods?"

"I felt like someone or rather many were watching me. You know the feeling, I saw you looking too."

"I sensed their life forces and magic. The veil was lowered as we walked to the truck. I saw them with my magic. There were hundreds of beings watching."

"Hundreds of the Warg?"

"Warg and other beings. I am not familiar with these others."

"You're freaking me out, Kalen." I looked at the speedometer and noticed the accelerator was firmly pressed and we were rocketing down this country highway. My GPS was showed me the turns to expect. I knew when I needed to slow to turn a corner. I wasn't slowing down for anything.

"Roger, to be honest I am a bit, what was the phrase?"

"Freaked out?"

"Yes, I'm freaked out myself. I think you were being tested."

"What the hell for?" I paused, "Screw that...did I pass or what?"

"I'm sorry, I don't know." For the next two hours we drove in silence, alone in our thoughts. I was going over and over the events until the silence was broken by Sam's ringtone. We both jumped as the music started and I reached to pressed answer on the GPS. You gotta love this hands free stuff.

"Hi Sam," I started.

"Hi Daddy, so you're in Missouri?"

"Yes," I answered cautiously. I wasn't sure how she came by this information. "Why?" I volleyed back to her.

"I was wondering if you could pick me up a wolf skin rug?" At this comment Kalen's face twisted in revulsion. I quickly hit mute on the phone.

"She doesn't mean it. She was being a wiseass like her mother."

"Like her mother?" he retorted and I unmuted.

"What do you know?"

"You split a wolf in half."

"How do you know it's me?"

"Let's see. I saw you and the truck. You ruined the shirt I gave you on Christmas. What the hell happened Dad?" Her voice was starting to get shaky as her emotions rose.

"Easy, Babe. It came at me. I was only defending myself."

"I know, but where did you get a sword? From some stone on the side of the road? And where did you learn to use it?"

"Honey, it was a gift from Kalen, and I got lucky. That's not important now. Did they identify me in the video?"

"Dad, we went over this. I saw you."

"I know you did, but did the video identify me, you know by name?"

"What does that have to do with anything?"

"Samantha Kay, it's important. I need to know."

"Let me look." I heard the clicking of a keyboard. "No, it says an unidentified man."

"Good. This attack is related to the conversation we had earlier."

"How is a wolf attack related to fairies?" I could almost hear her eyes rolling at me.

"Not a wolf, a Warg. He was like something out of the Lord of the Rings."

"Did you say he was a Warg? Do you take me for an..."

"It was a Warg. Think about it. A lone wolf in a populated area. It was the middle of the day. It came right at me, not from the side. If you saw the video you saw how fast it moved. Warg are real. I was lunch and he was hungry."

"You were attacked by a Warg in Missouri."

"Yes," I replied.

"Daddy, do you know how this sounds?"

"Yes, certifiably insane, but it doesn't make it less true."

"When you said earlier, if you make it through this trip, you weren't talking about coming home early. You meant if you live through this trip?" Her voice trembled with this last statement.

"Yes love," I said gently. "I still have a fairy ninja warrior here with me."

"I didn't see him kill a wolf, I mean Warg."

"True, but I did. And I am alive to tell the tale. I bet my video has gone viral by now." She chuckled through her sob.

"Daddy, that's not funny," though she sounded like she was smiling.

"A little funny," I said as I held up my finger and thumb to indicate a little. "Babe, I need to go. I'm driving down a back road at warp ten," I knew she'd get the reference. "Please Love, keep this to yourself. No need to alarm your brothers and sisters and especially your mom. I love you babe."

"Love you too Daddy, and I will."

"Big squench and kisses to my little darlings."

"Will do, Dad. Please come home as soon as you can."

"I will love, as soon as I can. Bye." As I hung up a tear streamed down my face. I wiped it with the back of my hand and kissed it. I let it evaporate and fly to my baby girl.

Chapter 27

SON-OF-A-BITCH THAT'S SHARP

The drive continued uneventfully. We stopped for gas in the middle of nowhere. I stepped out of the car with my sword in hand. I held it against my side, ready to carve wolf.

"I sense nothing here, Roger," Kalen explained trying to convince me to put away my sword.

"As I recall there was nothing at the last stop. I feel safer with this." I quickly filled the truck with gas and got back on the road. I felt even safer moving. The afternoon and evening passed with Kalen sensing no Fae. It was a boring drive as the miles rolled by. After the morning we had, boring was nice, very nice.

Soon, we were pulling into a motel parking lot. I was exhausted and ready to stop for the night. A weird thing was happening to my memory. Today's events were starting to move to the part of my memory reserved for dreams. I now viewed whole wolf encounter as surreal. It made more sense as a dream than reality. I was beginning to convince myself it hadn't really happened. While I was on the subject, this whole mess with the Fae was like a bad dream. These thoughts were going through my mind when Kalen broke the silence and the reality of the whole mess was restored.

"Yes, and that field looks good," I heard Kalen say. He had been talking, but the last bit was all I caught. He pointed to a vacant. grass covered lot adjacent to the parking lot.

"Good for what?"

"I said it looks like a good place to practice," he repeated.

"Practice? Practice what? All I want to do is choke down a burger and hit the rack." In response he only smiled and helped me carry the luggage into the room. Outside the sun was setting as we put our weapons and bags on the beds.

"You will need to dress in comfortable clothing."

"Kalen, I need to get some food and sleep. Don't you think I had enough practice today?"

"No," was all he said. No explanation, simply no.

"Shit," I muttered. I changed into shorts and running shoes and grabbed my sword.

"Don't forget your bow," he prompted. Kalen began unwrapping what looked to be an energy bar from a large leaf. He broke it and handed me half. He ate the remaining half. I took a bite and it was delicious. It has a sweet, fruity flavor. I didn't recognize any other flavor. It brought to mind the clear liquid I had drunk in the glen.

What happened to me next was somewhat amazing. The exhaustion I'd felt fell away. I actually became more alert. I felt refreshed as if from a long sleep. "Kalen, what is this stuff?"

"Bread," was his reply tinged with a wry smile. He picked up his sword, bow and quiver, and a small stick. The stick was about a foot and a half long and looked like a branch snapped off a tree, which as it turned out, was.

I grabbed my weapons and headed for the door. I noticed the radio alarm clock and saw it was a few minutes after nine. We hiked over to the field. It was a simple grass lot bordered by the motel parking lot and two streets. We crossed the parking lot and Kalen put a hand out to stop me from stepping on the field. He went to his knees and put his palm on the grass. He spoke but his voice was too low and I believe he was speaking a foreign language. He then laid the stick on the ground. A light flashed below the stick as it made contact with the ground.

"Cross here," Kalen said as he rose and stepped over the stick. He vanished.

"Kalen? Damn his fairy magic." I said as I followed. Do you when an elevator in a tall building plummets from the thirtieth floor to the lobby? The way your stomach rose to your throat is what stepping across the stick felt like, until I landed in the forest glen.

"Holy, mother, puss bucket...not here again!" We were back in Naomi's glen.

"No, this isn't quite what you think," Kalen said.

"Are you saying I'm not in Naomi's glen?"

"No, well yes, it is a replica. The branch was from one of the trees and its memory is what you see. This looks like the glen, but it will serve as our practice ground. Prepare yourself to work." His smile was eerie, sort of mean and sadistic. He looked like he was going enjoy this lesson, but me, not so much.

I took a few minutes to stretch these old muscles and prepare mentally for my beating.

We started with the bow. I have to admit it was fun, at first. We were shooting across the glen at a standard archery target and I even hit it once or twice, but Kalen never missed. He wasn't pulling a Robin Hood by splitting his arrows but the center ring of the target looked like a pincushion when he was finished.

His teaching style was meticulous. He made me stand perfectly so and hold the bow with my hand here, not an inch this way. I apparently didn't know how to breathe correctly either. When I emptied my quiver I had to sprint, not jog, and definitely not walk, down range to retrieve the arrows. Let's not forget the return sprint. Granted it wasn't a long distance, only thirty to forty yards, but we did the trip dozens of times. Toward what I thought was the end of the session I began hitting the target more often than not. I wasn't hitting the center, but finding arrows was definitely easier.

My left forearm was red and bleeding in spots from being hit by the bowstring repeatedly. The fingertips on my right hand didn't want to pull the bowstring anymore. They too, were red, swollen and bleeding. I can't describe the mental, happy dance I performed when Kalen announced, "This is the last round."

"Thank goodness the bread kept me going, but now I am ready for bed. How about you?" I said as my last arrow leaped from my bow to find the center ring. "Yes!" I exclaimed doing my imitation of Tiger Woods. "Did you see?" I turned to Kalen in time to see him charging me with murder in his eyes and his sword raised above his head. I got my bow in a two-handed block and was able to deflect the blow. I dropped the bow and drew my sword.

"You must always be ready to defend yourself," Kalen offered.

"Son-of-a-bitch, Kalen. What the hell was that all about?"

"A warm-up, now defend yourself." He came at me again. I parried the first attack but his second landed on my arm above my elbow leaving an inch long gash that began to bleed.

"What the hell? Kalen, I thought I was here to learn not to be chopped up into bite size morsels."

"Okay. Lesson One: Don't let me cut you." He smiled the sadistic grin again and it chilled me to the bone. He attacked, I defended, which is to say I bled a lot. I did get a block in, now and then, but I was fighting a supernatural being who has been doing this since swords were invented. After about five minutes of steady attack, I could barely breathe. I tripped and fell, panting and bleeding to the ground. He stood over me with the tip of his sword grounded in front of him.

"Would you kindly tell me the purpose of this exercise?"

"Gladly, it serves two purposes. One, today's success with the Warg was mostly luck. And secondly, I was seeing what skill, if any, you had with the blade."

"I'll make it easy for you. I suck and was lucky. Message received. Will you please stop cutting me and give me a hand up?" We had been in the glen for about two to three hours and I was drenched in sweat, bleeding and dirty. Kalen looked fresh, not a drop of sweat. His clothes looked laundered, and not a hair on his head was out of place. He reached down and gave me a hand up. I staggered to my feet. He reached in his bag and pulled out what looked to be a jar.

"Put this on your cuts. It will help." Kalen handed me a jar labeled, face cream.

"Face cream? Face cream will help my cuts?"

"No, that's only the jar I used. I make my battle salve myself." The salve was a thick creamy substance with a very pungent odor. I dipped my fingers in and applied it to the first cut.

"Ouch!" I yelled. It hurt worse than the initial cut. "What the hell is this stuff?" I accused Kalen.

"Look," he said with an impatient smile. The cut was healing before my eyes. The skin came together and the line where a scar should be simply vanished.

"What the hell is this stuff?" I asked again with amazement. Despite the smell I put this on all my cuts with the same effect. Even my fingertips healed.

"Now we begin," Kalen said. This time he showed me stances, forms, and the proper ways to use my sword. He had me do every stance, form and drill repeatedly with both hands. Finally, I could barely hold the sword tip off the ground when Kalen called it quits.

"Good work, Roger," Kalen announced. "How about we head back to the room?"

"I finally wore you out?" I replied sarcastically.

"Well," he said pulling his sword from its sheath.

"No, No, kidding. Please, no more," and this put a pleasant smile on Kalen's face. Boy, I was glad the evil smile was gone. We gathered all the weapons and stray arrows and headed out. Actually, I forgot where out was and had to follow Kalen. Stepping through the threshold had my stomach leaping again. We landed back in the parking lot. Kalen turned to kneel before the stick. He spoke the words and again the light flashed with a popping sound as he lifted it. He placed the branch reverently into his quiver.

The walk back to the room was pleasant. Our

conversation was about showering and heading to the diner next door for a bit of repose, as Kalen put it.

I slipped my keycard in the lock and with a beep and a green light it opened. I checked the clock and it read nine twenty-five. The whole workout had lasted about twenty minutes. I am not sure what came over me but I literally broke into song.

"Let's do the time warp again. It's just a jump to the left," I jumped. "And a step to the right," I stepped. "Put your hands on your hips. You bring your knees in tight." Yes I did. "But it's the pelvic thrust that really drives you insane. Let's do the time warp again."

Kalen watched me with a look of concerned amusement. He raised his eyebrow as if to say, huh?

"Sorry man, I'm a little punch drunk. We were only gone for twenty to twenty five minutes. The fairy time warp stuff drives me a bit," and I sang again, "insane," Kalen laughed. "When we are finished with this trip can you teach me the spell and leave the stick with me? I can't imagine the stuff I could get done."

"We will see," was all he said as he headed into the shower.

Chapter 28

WHAT'S A NICE WEREWOLF LIKE YOU...

Within thirty minutes, we were showered, dressed and ready to go. The night air had a chill so I grabbed my jean jacket. Before I put it on, I asked, "Kalen, how can I strap this on my back so it's hidden?" I asked, holding up my sword.

"Like this," he said as he removed his jacket and turned to show me how his sword was strapped.

"Wow, I couldn't even tell you were wearing it."

"That's the point." He helped me and it strapped on comfortably across my back. The handle was down by my right hip and the sword tip was below my left shoulder. I twisted and stretched my arms and it felt good.

"Thanks."

"Try a draw," and he reached back, drawing his blade so quickly it was a blur. He reached back again with his left hand to guide the blade back into the sheath. My first attempt never cleared the sheath, but after a little coaching I got it clear after the third attempt. I was good to go.

We walked to the diner and found a booth in the back. It was an old place and seemed like it had been there a while. It had a counter as you walked in and a few booths along the walls. The wall decorations were mirrors with logos painted on them. A Coke, Pepsi, and some beer brands were a few of a very eclectic collection. Kalen sat facing the door, but the mirrors afforded me a full view of the diner.

Our waitress was a middle aged, heavy-set woman with a friendly smile. "Hi ya'll, my name is Jackie. What can I get you?"

"Jackie, I'd like a burger and fries, please."

"How would you like it cooked?"

"Medium, and a glass of water, thanks."

"And you Hon?" she said to Kalen and her smile brightened. I do believe she was flirting with him.

"Please, pretty lady, I'll have the same." I hadn't noticed till then how British he sounded.

Jackie actually blushed as she walked away. "Kalen, you old dog," I kidded.

"Don't worry, Pup. I'm old enough to be her great, great, and add about six or seven greats grandfather." Every once in a while, I'm reminded, he was really old. Here sat this young looking man. This was weird.

I looked around the diner and saw we weren't alone. There was a young couple at the opposite end of the diner. She was in her mid-twenties and blonde. She had on the short shorts and a spaghetti strap top, complete with the push-up bra, leaving absolutely nothing to my imagination. He, on the other hand, was a little older and had a head of black hair that hadn't seen a comb in weeks. A full beard framed his face and a Harley t-shirt with jeans, complete with a chained wallet, complete his outfit. She was talking constantly and he sat wearing a scowl.

The only other patron was sitting at the counter nursing his coffee.

"Roger, I'm sensing something. Don't move. I need to look outside."

"How many?"

"I only sense faded magic. It seems many hours old, but I didn't feel it on the way in and this is quite curious."

"Sounds like you are being drawn out? Be careful. You sure I can't come watch your back? You know another set of eyes and all?"

"No, you are safer in here and I won't be long. I want to step outside of these metal walls to get a better look at the magic."

I watched Kalen go out the door and walk into the dark with a curious look on his face.

Down the diner I heard biker boy say, "Okay, Okay I'll get it." He rose and the scowl deepened, if that were possible.

As he approached the door Blondie yelled, "Don't forget, the blue one in the green bag, not the red one."

He waved his hand, "Okay."

She rose and walked toward me. She didn't really walk. She sauntered, strutted, sashayed, you pick your adjective, but it was intoxicatingly sexy. I noticed the ladies room was at our end of the diner and assumed it was her destination. The whole way across the diner she was pressing buttons on her phone. So when she passed by me, spun and sat in Kalen's vacated seat, I was more than a little surprised.

"May I help you, Miss?"

She growled at me, a low menacing growl. I found the handle of my sword.

"You won't need the sword," she said and looked toward my right hand.

"What can I do for you? I didn't catch your name," I asked gruffly.

"I am called Chepi Lupa, and today I heard you killed my brother. I am here to find out why you have declared war upon my family."

"I killed your brother because he was about to end me. It's more like he declared war upon me."

"I was told you attacked him. Why are you lying to me?" She was leaning toward me aggressively and her eyes were glowing red. I do believe I saw her teeth grow into fangs.

"You were lied too, but not by me," I too was getting pissed and let it show. "I can prove it."

"How?"

I pointed to her phone. "Do you get the internet on your

phone?"

"Yes," she said more as a question.

"YouTube the attack. I believe it was called Wolf Attack in Missouri." She picked up her phone and began typing. She watched the video and I saw the aggression melt away.

"Damn him," she said to herself.

"Would you explain why your people declared war upon me?"

"I don't think I can. I was sent to bring you to trial for murder before our elders. It was to be a quick trial followed by a quick death."

"As you can plainly see, it wasn't murder."

She looked at me curiously, "Who are you? I mean, my pack has been searching for a travelling wizard. He is supposed to be rich with the old magic. Now this happened at the same time. Are you a wizard?"

"No, but my ancestors were. Let me ask you something. Are you a wolf? I'm sorry, I mean Warg? If so can you guys change back and forth to human form at will?"

"Yes I am, and we can change if we have the magic. Humans have called us werewolves or lycanthropes for centuries, and some of the legends are true."

"Full moon?"

"Don't we all go a little crazy during the full moon?"

"Fair enough." I was so caught up in the conversation I forgot about Kalen and biker boy. "Why did your friend follow Kalen out? Did he plan to try and hurt my friend?"

"Hurt Kalen? No he went to keep him busy. Lead him away so we could talk. Maybe take a little stroll together."

"Sister, I don't plan on going anywhere with you."

"You won't have to now. I will take this back to my pack," she raised her phone, "and see what the elders have to say."

"I'm a bit curious. What does your pack want with a wizard?"

"We want him to fight with us and help unite our packs with other Fae to regain our ancient hunting grounds." She said this with a look of hope and longing in her eye.

"The Pacific Northwest territory? Aelfic's domain?"

She growled again, "Yes," she spat. "How do you know this?"

"Oh," I acted innocently, "A good guess is all. I am involved with all this somehow, but I really know very little about your ways."

The front door on the diner slammed open and Kalen stepped in with his sword drawn. His eyes were locked on Chepi's and he headed straight toward her with his sword at the ready. I stood, putting myself between Kalen and Chepi.

"Hold on, Kalen," I commanded and raised my hands to stop him. To my surprise he stopped. He didn't lower his sword, but he stopped. I was feeling pretty full of myself till I turned and saw Chepi on one knee, her hands clasped behind her back, her head held to one side exposing her neck. I took this to be her white flag. I found out later this was the sign of complete submission for the Warg. Kalen put his sword away and motioned for her to sit next to me, and took his seat.

Chapter 29

NOTHING LIKE A BURGER

"Okay," I said acting as mediator. "I believe an introduction is in order? Kalen meet Chepi. Chepi, this is Kalen."

"What does she want?" Kalen said slow and deliberate, making each word crack like a whip.

"What every woman wants," and I paused., "Me!" I found out quickly humor wasn't going to ease this tension.

"No, that's not quite true," Chepi replied. "I first wished vengeance for the murder of my wolf-brother, but I have been misled by one of my Alpha's advisors. I was told this human murdered him in cold blood. I now know the truth."

"How did you come by this truth?" he demanded.

"YouTube," I chimed in.

Kalen turned his scowl on me, "My tube? What is my tube?"

"No, I said YouTube. It is an internet application showing videos that people post."

"Where your daughter saw the video she spoke about?"

"Yes, I had Chepi watch the video on her phone. She saw the whole incident for herself."

He turned back to Chepi. "You said first was for vengeance. What is second."

"We have heard tell of a wizard passing through our domain and I wish to enlist his help."

"Roger," and he gestured toward me, "is not a wizard, but you knew that."

"Yes, but the magic is there. Can you not smell it?" and she breathed in.

"I know he has magic, but it is not for you to take."

"There are some who say as long as he is in our lands his magic is ours to do with as we choose."

"And what do you say?"

"It has to be given freely," she said, "or else it will be corrupted."

I raised my hand like a schoolboy. "Would someone care to explain what you two are talking about? It sounds like you are talking about me and the 'me' is right here. I believe I should be included in this little discussion."

"You are right," Kalen agreed. Chepi only nodded.

"So let me see if I am following you correctly." I said to Chepi, "you want me to take a little side trip." She nodded again. "Then, I humbly decline. I have a date with destiny and only a couple of days to prepare." Chepi grimaced and I continued. "If I maintain my ability to breathe after the meeting, then perhaps on the return trip we can have a sit down with your pack and say Kalen and a few friends?"

Kalen smiled at this suggestion. He was glad I was leery of her pretty face. I went on, "What do you wish to gain from my support?" I asked Chepi.

"My dream is to unite the two packs and all the," she paused, "as you call them, wild Fae of this region."

"Under whose rule?" Kalen asked.

"The Alpha of the Moon Runners," she said as if it were a matter of fact.

I looked to Kalen but he shrugged. "Okay, I'll bite. Who are the Moon Runners and what can you tell me about this Alpha? Was he the one who sent you to kill me?"

"NO!" she exclaimed vehemently. "My father didn't send me. He is running up north."

"Wait, Wait, Wait a minute," I interrupted. "Your father is the Alpha of the Moon Runners?"

"Yes," she gave me an exasperated look, "May I finish?"

She paused slightly, "I was sent by his closest advisor. The Moon Runner's pack range from this area and south."

"You said your father was up north?" She rolled her eyes at me again. "Sorry," I defended, "the dots weren't connecting."

"This is true, but father has been running with the Alpha of the Shadow Killers. They are trying to find a way to join our packs. They find it difficult to agree on the terms of this merging and thought hunting together would help. Once our packs join, we might be able to approach the other Fae. The next step would be to reclaim our ancestral lands from a foreign usurper." She turned to Kalen, "No offense."

"None taken, but which usurper do you wanting to over throw?"

"Aelfic!" She said without hesitation. "When he came to our land he took his realm through violence. At the time there was a third pack whose hunting ground he now rules. The Silent Death were numbered far greater than both our packs combined, but only a few of their numbers survived by joining our packs. Their blood runs through my veins. This is why I want Aelfic gone. He used his magic to destroy thousands of my ancestors. They had no defense because the magic was too powerful."

"Won't he be able to use his magic to stop you now?" Kalen asked.

"This is why we seek the assistance of a wizard," and she motioned toward me.

"I'm no wizard!" I exclaimed.

"But you have the magic. You need to learn. Our mages could guide you in the use of your power."

"Kalen, is this true? I could learn to use the magic? Naomi said the art was lost. She forgot to mention it could be relearned. So Kalen, no bullshit, could I learn to use my magic?" He remained silent and his expression was unreadable. "Kalen you said you could not lie especially to me while we are bonded. Once again, is Chepi speaking the truth? Could I be a wizard like my forefathers?"

"Yes it is possible," was all he said.

"I assume Naomi knows this?" He lowered his eyes to the floor.

He answered in barely a whisper. "Yes, please no more. I do not wish to betray my queen."

"Fair enough. Chepi who among your people can guarantee my safety? I don't wish to end up wolf kibble. Also I wish safe passage for Kalen," I turned to him, "if you are willing, to be my companion."

"The Alpha's word is law."

"Can I get both Alpha's protection?"

"I don't have the authority to give this to you, but I will take it back to the packs."

"Is there some kind of talisman or spell I can use to contact you?" Yes my stupidity was obvious to all but me. Now in my defense I was all caught up in the magic.

"I could simply give you my phone number," she replied a bit too joyfully.

"Yeah, okay, I guess it could work too." I stammered as I put her digits in my phone.

Chepi stood to leave. She turned to Kalen, "General Kalen, I was raised on the stories of your deeds in the old wars. All our youth strive to be as strong and cunning as you. I want you to know it has been my honor to meet you."

Kalen stood and bowed gracefully, "Princess Chepi Lupa of the Moon Runners, the honor of your acquaintance is mine."

I felt completely out of place with all this scraping and bowing. "Chepi, it was a pleasure meeting you. I look forward to seeing you again." At this last comment she turned and almost giggled. Oh crap what did I just do? Kalen shook his head with a grin. We sat down and our burgers arrived.

Chapter 30

BLOOD SUCKING BLUE BUTTERFLIES? WHAT'S NEXT?

I was glad to be on the road again. I hoped to make up for lost time, now I wasn't worried about the Warg. Today, I was shooting for Colorado, but it was an ambitious goal.

I wanted to take the interstate. I turned, "Kalen how about we jump on the ole interstate and make up a little time."

"We might be seen. It's too risky."

"Might be seen? This is your rationale? We might be seen? During our little visit yesterday and last night we snuck by unseen? Really?"

"Roger, you haven't met the Phengard. I don't wish to be among them again." Kalen seemed physically shaken by his memory and this peaked my curiosity a bit.

"The Phengard seemed to cause you great distress. Tell me about them."

"They look like harmless little blue butterflies…"

And I interrupted, "Like you, pixies are harmless fireflies?"

Kalen's face flashed in anger but he continued, "but," he heavily accented this word. "If they choose to, they can swarm and devour their foe in a matter of seconds. Broken bones are the only remains. They are broken because it's the only way to get to the marrow."

"What triggers this response?"

"Usually, it is a response to a threat, and the threat can be real or perceived from anyone or anything. Now I've heard of them targeting animals but I believe it is as food."

"Can they take human form?"

"They can, but their magic is weak and so it is done only by a few and if there is a great need."

"Do they have much contact with the outside world?" I was wondering if they had internet access.

"A difficult question to answer. No, it isn't often they wander in their human form to connect and learn of the outside world. We use folks like Steve to gain information, but the Phengard somehow are always current on world events. They tend to stay away from populated areas as a rule. One theory is that they have spies or emissaries who live among the humans. The life as a spy is risky for fairies. Humans tend to try to eliminate any insectual presence. For a fairy life to be snuffed out, like an insect, is unthinkable to Fae. We live for hundreds of your years, so to lose life for so trivial a reason as gaining human information, seems wrong.

Another theory is that they gain knowledge through blood. If they bite a human they will know what he knows. If one Phengard knows then his whole swarm knows. It's as if they share one mind."

"Kind of like the Borg. You know 'Resistance is futile.' Oh right, Star Trek allusions are lost on you. Anyway, they were creatures on the show, I told you about. They too share one consciousness." Kalen looked at me blankly waiting for me to shut-up. "Sorry, you were saying?"

"Yes, they bite a human and gain the knowledge, but this too can be a suicide mission. Humans tend to swat anything biting them."

"Maybe they do have their Steve. They bribe him somehow, or threaten, and he gains the knowledge. He goes to them and they bite."

Kalen nodded his head. "This does sound reasonable."

"Is there a certain distance limit to a swarm's telepathy?"

"I do not know."

"Is it likely they saw the wolf attack?"

"Yes."

"And knew it was me? And also I will be crossing their domain?"

"Again I don't know. This is why we stay off the big roads."

"Okay, lead on McDuff," and he did.

We had to go a little slower but at least it took longer...UGH. They say it's the ironies in life that makes it interesting. I want to meet 'they' and kick his ass.

When the route was in the GPS, Kalen went quiet. He wasn't sleeping, but he sat there without moving, talking, or even blinking.

My mind was wandering as the miles ticked off the odometer. I wondered how I was selected for this honor, for lack of a better word. I now knew I was selected before conception, and this triggered my thoughts of my visit with Mum this past summer.

Chapter 31

SHOO FLY DON'T BOTHER ME

I am reluctant to write this next part down. My mother was not very forth coming with this story. Actually I didn't recall any of this prior to our conversation on the night of copious amounts of wine.

My visit was about a month after my little trip into the woods. I hadn't planned on telling Mum anything about my experience. I was home to visit family and friends, like I do most summers.

It was a beautiful summer day. The sky was blue and there was a light breeze. We swam in the pool till dusk. I fired up the grill and cooked a couple chicken breasts while Mum made pasta salad. It must have been the wine we had with dinner that loosened our tongues.

"So Roger, something has been on your mind since you got here. What is troubling you, love?" Mum asked directly.

"Not sure how to say this Mum. It's a bit...weird. Yeah, weird is as good a word as any."

"Start and the words will take care of themselves."

I finished my wine in one swallow, poured myself another, and filled Mum's glass to the brim. At this action she held her tongue but raised a questioning eyebrow, which I answered with an affirmative nod.

"Mum, do you believe in fairies?"

Her eyes widened in shock or awe, I'm not sure which.

"Why do you ask?" she replied abruptly.

"Let's say, I now know they exist."

"Oh God, no," her eyes filled with tears. And she tipped her glass back. "You met Naomi? I'm guessing?"

"Shit, Mum, how do you know her name? And yes, but met is putting it lightly."

"I guess I owe you a story first," Mum admitted, taking a deep breath. She placed her glass down gingerly and folded her arms to steel herself and began...

"It was a bitter cold afternoon, even by October standards, on this Friday. This was the day you were born. My water broke early in the afternoon and I had to call your dad home from the mill so he could take me to the hospital.

Dad drove like a maniac to get me there, but he pretty much drove that way everywhere." I nodded in agreement.

"I remember he skidded to a stop in the gravel lot next to the hospital. He ran around the car to get my door. You were already two weeks late and I was finding it difficult getting around. Snow flurries were falling and a swarm of small flies buzzed around my head.

This was quite odd because it was so bitter cold and the wind was cutting me to the bone. These flies flew all around my head and a couple actually landed on my belly, of all places. It was very unsettling to have these flies and contractions all at the same time. I shooed the flies away as best as I could as I lumbered to the door. I guess I was cussing at them because your father, of all people, told me I needed to watch my language." At this, she smiled wistfully and rolled her eyes at the memory.

"As soon as I crossed the threshold to the emergency room the flies retreated. Your dad was holding the door open with my overnight bag in his hand. I remember looking back to see where they had gone. By the car, I saw small lights blinking as they moved away. I actually saw green, blue and a couple of white and pink lights blinking as they moved to pinpricks. There was one white one that was brighter than the rest. By now the other were out of sight. The white one stayed behind. I swear it was looking at me. It was frozen in the air. Your father was urging me along, but right before I turned away it flashed like as if taking a picture and then was gone.

I wouldn't be saying those fireflies were fairies if this was the only time I'd seen them."

"Not your only time?"

"It's hard to believe you don't remember."

"I don't, Mum."

"I'm not crazy and nor do I wish to appear as such, so please love, let keep these stories to ourselves."

Chapter 32

BATTER UP

"Mum, you are not crazy. They truly exist."

"I know," Mum said with her eyes focused somewhere in the distance. She looked like she was trying to see the memories I was dredging up for her.

"So, what don't I remember?"

"No not yet. I want to tell this in order, but I am a bit surprised you don't remember. Anyway," she said waving her hand as if to wipe the thought away. She lifted her glass, "be a dear?" I got up, took another bottle of Chardonnay off the rack, uncorked and filled both glasses. We clinked the crystal and took a long drink.

"Let me see," she started cautiously, "you were only a babe about a year and a half old. It was a few months after we had moved into this house. Remember all the apartment complexes out back and about half of the houses in town weren't built back then. This area was mostly woods and farms.

The day was a beautiful summer's day. The sky was a bright blue and free from clouds. There was a light warm breeze. It was a perfect day as far as weather was concerned. You boys were up at the crack of dawn, as always, raring to go do something. Your dad left for the mill right after breakfast, and so began the daily ritual of begging and promising. You guys wanted me to take you to the lake.

Well, your brothers were begging. Aunty Shirley and I were planning a trip anyway, but it was always fun to watch Tony and Willy do the dishes or wrestle with the vacuum cleaner. I typically had to redo any chore they attempted, but it was fun to see how much they wanted to go to the lake.

While Tony washed the breakfast dishes and Willy pushed the vacuum around, I went up to get you ready. You were still fast asleep in your crib. I remember it clearly because you were very punctual even as a baby. You woke at 7:30 every morning. You would climb out of your crib and usually on to Tony. He would whine and I would come collect you. You always had a big mischievous smile across your face." Mum paused for a moment. She had an expression on her face and it probably matched her expression on a typical day way back when. "Yes, you would be climbing over your brothers, usually giggling. The more they complained and moaned the more you giggled. Sorry. Right, the story, where was I? We got a late start, so I called Shirley and decided we'd make a whole day of it. So I packed hamburger meat and hotdogs along with the perfunctory peanut butter and jelly and all the usual stuff. I wrote a note to your dad telling him to join us when he got home. We headed over to Aunt Shirley's in the station wagon. Shirley strapped Jane in beside you in the back seat and the rest of the kids scrambled in the back fighting over who got to sit near the back window. About fifteen minutes later we were pulling in the picnic area."

Let me put this trip in perspective. We lived in a small town, actually a tiny town. There are lots of open fields and patches of woods and forest. For little kids growing up in a small town, the center of town was a place of wonder. The town hall was down the street from the elementary school. The gas station was next to the soda shop that served the world's best ice cream sodas and milkshakes. It was right across the street from a family owned drug store. We also had not one, but two grocery stores. Each one no larger than a gas station convenience store you find populating small towns today, but back then it was something. On a trip down Main Street, you were never hindered by stop signs or stoplights. The town didn't even own a stoplight. Our trip to the lake passed right through the center of town. We turned down West Street, drove past the lumberyard, and up past the dump road.

Yes, the road the dump was on. Now we call them recycling centers or landfills and everyone has curbside trash pickup. Back then you loaded the cans in the car, drove to the dump, waved at Bill, Fred, or George, dumped your trash in the appropriate place, and gave them a wave as you left.

Anyway, we drove past the dump road and through a portion of the state forest and popped out at the lake. As we drove through the forest it was always a bit eerie. The road was shaded and the leaves cast a greenish hue on everything. Also, the sunlight would fight through trees, throwing spotlights randomly about.

Mum continued, "Roger, do you remember that when we drove through the forest, you boys would always stop what you were doing and stare out at the trees?. Your brother Willy called it the magic woods. The magic woods gave me goose bumps. I would always speed through there, actually, Aunty Shirley would too. It probably has something to do with those damn fireflies.

After we parked, I took you and Jane to our spot. Shirley and the boys dragged the rest of the stuff down and headed for the lake. You and Jane played on the blanket and chased each other around the field. Shirley and I talked or read while keeping an eye on you guys. It was a normal day, complete with PB-&-Js and warm lemonade, because we needed the ice to keep dinner from spoiling.

As dinnertime approached your father and Uncle Dan showed up carrying the beer cooler. You boys loved the ice-cold soda they would always bring you. Do you remember the bottles? Sorry, where was I? Dad and Dan lit the charcoal and cooked the meat. A little after dinner Shirley and Dan and your cousins left for the night. Your dad wanted to get in one last swim with your brothers. He'd throw them around to laughs and giggles. I left you on the blanket drinking a bottle and walked to the water's edge. I looked back every so often, but you were almost asleep. I turned back once more and you were gone. We were the only ones still at the lake. I couldn't imagine who could take you. In this town, at that time, nobody took children. It wasn't done.

I ran back to the table and stood looking and listening. I heard you laugh and I headed into the woods after the sound. I saw a small trail and ran down it toward you. I saw you, or rather, I saw the blanket flying with a lump in the middle. The edges of the blanket were glowing with multicolored Christmas lights. I screamed at them and the blanket stopped and gently lowered to the ground. The lights then flew between you and me blocking my way. They look like fireflies.

I was tired and quite peeved. These bugs stole my baby. I grabbed a stick and walked forward to swat a few of these fireflies and get my baby. I swung the stick right at a little green bugger and the little bastard caught it. He twisted it up and wrenched it from my grip. The damn thing was no bigger than a speck and it hoisted the stick above my head, as if to clobber me. As the stick came down a loud, clear voice called, 'Stop!' And the stick stopped dead, six inches above my head.

'I said, Stop! Do you dare defy, me?' the voice said. It was a woman's voice, and the tone was very commanding. The stick went flying through the brush. I don't think your father could have thrown it so hard.

The blanket was already on the ground and the flies zipped out of sight, so quickly, if I hadn't seen it I wouldn't believe it was possible. I grabbed you, blanket and all, and ran as fast as I could back to the picnic area. My arms and legs had a few scrapes and cuts from the bushes, but you were completely unscathed. You were happy, laughing and smiling as if we played a game. I held you and rocked you to calm my fear and you fell right to sleep on my shoulder.

I sat rocking you in my arms when your dad and the boys came back and packed us up to go home. I never told anyone because I wasn't sure I believed it myself.

Roger, they tried to take you away and I thought I was losing my mind."

I reached across the table and held Mum's hand. Retelling this story was dredging up all her old fears and I felt powerless to stop it from happening. I needed to know.

"Mum, I don't know what to say," I stumbled.

"I know what you mean. It was real…but not. I wish this was the end of it all, but they kept coming back."

Chapter 33

DANCING WITH THE LIGHTS

"How do you mean?" I asked.

"Every once in a while they would come and visit you. This started the summer after you turned four. It always happened at dusk. The fireflies would come out. You would put your arms out and spin. Laughing and smiling in complete joy. You used to say you were dancing with the lights.

Do you remember the baseball bat I always kept in the closet by the door?"

"Yeah, I do. It had a leather strap on the end. I never knew why you had it, but it was so they couldn't take the bat away, right?"

"Yes. Every night I'd be watching you from the kitchen window. But they never attempted to hurt you or lead you away. You would twirl and laugh with such joy."

"Mum, I do remember, dancing with lights. There was such a feeling of peace and love. God how could I have forgotten?"

"How about when you were ten? Getting lost when we were camping in Maine?"

"Vaguely. I don't remember being lost. I do remember all the rangers. Dad was pissed, yelling at me about taking off and being so inconsiderate. You know a typical rant at me from Dad. What I remember most is you crying and that somehow I was the cause. I never understood why. I mean, I was only gone for an hour or two at the most."

"If I'm going to finish this story, I need to take a break."

"I'll put on a pot of coffee. Do you want a cup?"

"Please dear, I'm also going to need something to pick at. Are you hungry?"

"Yes, I'll get it." I filled the coffee pot with water and coffee and turned it on. I headed to the liquor cabinet debating with myself on the virtues of making the coffee Irish. I decided against it. I needed to remember these stories if I want to figure out how this all fits together. I grabbed the leftover chicken, tomatoes, lettuce and anything else that would taste good on a sandwich.

It felt good doing something normal. I made the sandwiches and brought them back to the table with the coffee.

Chapter 34

LISTEN BITCH, YOU TOOK MY SON

Mum cradled the cup in her hands, as wisps of steam rose from the cup. She watched the steam as she took a sip testing the temperature of the brew.

She began, "It was the summer of sixty-nine. Hell, this sounds like a song lyric."

"It is Mum, which was the name of the song too. So the summer of sixty-nine?" I prompted.

"More precisely it was July of sixty-nine. We were going on holiday, something we didn't do much when you were young. Your dad wanted to head up to Maine and show his boys the real woods, as he would say. Let's see...you were nine, making James seven, Willy eleven, Tony twelve, and Matty wasn't even a thought."

"Is this the trip we stopped for a night in Hampton Beach? We collected shells, and play on the beach." I added.

"Yes, I had to talk your father into spending a couple of days on the beach before we headed into the woods. His plan was to spend the whole time hiking around the Allagash. Your dad's friend let him use his hunting cabin. It was out in the middle of nowhere. There was a hand-pump in the kitchen for water and outhouses. There was no electricity, no running water, no toilets. This was a dream and I was living it," she added sarcastically.

"I shouldn't complain, his original idea was to do the

same except live in tents. At least we could lock the bears out of the cabin."

"I remember the cabin," I said. "It was a real log cabin with a big porch. We slept in the loft on real army cots."

"You boys loved the place almost as much as your father. We had to drive five miles down this rutted dirt trail simply to get to the town road. It took over thirty minutes to get to town.

The day we arrived was fairly uneventful. We got to the cabin at noon and unpacked the car. I had to set up the kitchen, if you could call it that. There was a sink with an old hand pump for water and a table beneath a set of homemade cabinets. The cabinets were old wooden boxes glued together. Once I got the Coleman stove set up, I started with dinner while your dad tested the hammock and you boys explored.

Dusk came, and I remember being extra vigilant searching for fireflies. There wasn't even one that first night.

You boys came back all excited. Tony discovered raccoon, deer, and even bear tracks. Willy found fox and bobcat tracks. You and James brought me flowers, well dandelions, but you two were proud of your discovery and I put them in a beer bottle with water. In that cabin beer bottles were considered fancy vases. As we ate beef stew you guys went on and on about the adventures you were going to have. It sounded like you were planning an African safari. This is a wonderful memory. You were all so animated, feeding off each other's energy. Do you remember how your Dad usually got when you guys got excited? That night he didn't yell at you. He was more relaxed than I'd ever seen him. We were all happy. We didn't have many of these nights, so this made it especially memorable.

You boys were up half the night giggling and talking. I heard Tony tell a story about a ghost with a bloody something or other. He finished with the line, 'Okay big daddy, put a baaaaandage on it.' and you all laughed as if it was the funniest thing you'd ever heard. It's odd what comes to mind.

Needless to say, you were all sound asleep till about nine the next morning. I started cooking the bacon about 8:30 and the smell brought you down, one by one. We had pancakes and bacon and you guys ate almost as fast as I could put it on the table. Once finished you all ran back up to the loft, changed into your play clothes and were ready to go before I could do the dishes. By ten o'clock in the morning, we were out the door. Your dad had a pack with sandwiches and snacks. You boys had your canteens from the Army/Navy Surplus store filled with red Kool-Aid and off we went.

Your father knew all the trails. He had spent many hours talking with his buddy at the bar. We saw all kinds of wildlife. We saw deer and turkeys. We startled a few pheasants and they flew out of the bushes and scared James, making him cry. I think it was Willy who brought me a snake and had to show me." Mum made a disgusted face as if she was looking at it now. "Oh yes, there was a field covered in flowers, and it was right next to a waterfall. It was something right out of a storybook. We stopped there and had lunch. You men went for a swim, after lunch, to cool down in the pond below the falls. We were out all day and got back to the cabin as the sun was starting to set. Your dad piled us in the car and we headed to town for dinner. I had mentioned to your Dad, I wasn't cooking after the hike, so we were off to town for burgers."

"And ice cream," I added.

"Yes, and ice cream at a real, old fashioned soda fountain. With a whole day of hiking and a full belly, you boys fell asleep in the car and we shuffled you off to bed as soon as we got back. I took a lantern to the front porch to read my book in the hammock for a bit, when I saw it." She paused to take a sip of her coffee and, I think to build my suspense. "A single firefly was up by the loft window. I remember tossing pine cones at the damn thing till it flew away.

My stomach was instantly twisted in a knot. I wanted to leave for home right then. I couldn't figure out a way to convince your father. Can you imagine the conversation?

'Honey we need to leave because some fireflies want to take your son.' I never told him any of the other stories, not even the dancing with lights. When he saw you dancing he thought you were just a strange child.

Leaving wasn't an option, so I was determined to keep watch on you night and day. I was not going to let those insufferable bugs get you. I brought a blanket to the hammock and told your father I was going to watch the stars till I fell asleep. He thought I was strange sometimes too. See where you get it?

From all of our previous encounters I thought if I could keep them at bay till three in the morning then you were safe for the night. I had a book in hand, a pot of steaming, percolated coffee, and settled in to guard the door.

It was a beautiful night. The heat of the day had given way to a cool, even chilly, night. The sky was clear and I have never seen so many stars in the sky. I want to say it was a quiet night, but crickets sang all night. An owl of some sort kept vigil with me, too. The coffee kept me alert while I read. I looked at my watch at half past one, thinking I hadn't long to go. I was awake enough not to worry about sleep when I saw the lights approaching the house. I reached down to a pile of stones gathered for this contingent. My plan was to pelt them with stones till they left. But as I watched them come, the fight drain right out of me. The patterns the lights made were so mesmerizing and beautiful. My hand relaxed and I heard the stones clatter to the floor. I began to smile, for goodness sake, at nothing. It's like I'd been drinking wine all night. I don't recall when I fell asleep but I do remember the dream. It was filled with love and joy and a contentment as if all was right with the world. I can't explain it any better. I..."

"I know what you mean, Mum. It's exactly how I felt when I was with them."

"Anyway, I woke as the sun was rising. I smiled as I stretched into the new day. It dawned on me, all at once. They came. I jumped up, dropping my book and coffee cup that were still in my hands. I ran to the house and climbed the ladder to the loft, but your sleeping bag was still full. Tears of relief stung my eyes. I was standing between Tony and Willy's cots so I bent down, kissed their foreheads, and tucked them in. Willy scooted deeper in his bag with a smile on his face. I walked up between you and James, kissed James, tucked him in, and then on to you. You were gone. The lump was your pillow stuffed in the bag to look like you. I called your name but there was no response. I kept calling your name as I bound down the ladder and out to the privy. As you know, you weren't there either. Your Dad heard me yelling for you. Actually the rangers in the next state probably heard me, I wasn't being quiet. He came running out in his underwear to see what the commotion was all about.

I was frantic and all I could get out is 'They took him! They took my baby! They took him!' I think I said it about ten times in a row. Your dad wrapped me in his arms and held me. He was trying to calm me down, so I could explain what I was trying to say. He kept asking, 'Who took who?' And I would answer with 'They took him!' Not my finest moment but I was a mother in panic mode.

Your father said, 'Okay Anne, you need to tell me, what are you talking about.' By this time the other three boys were there.

'They took Roger, last night. I tried to stop them but I fell asleep or they put me to sleep, I don't know. All I know is, they took Roger!' I said this accenting the words very slowly and clearly as if I were talking to a slow child.

'Who are they?' your father insisted.

And I told him. 'The fairies, Al. The god damned fairies took him.'

And there it was. He gave the, 'I'm looking at a crazy' person look.

He replied very slowly, as if I were a slow child, 'Okay, let's have a look around. Maybe he went out for a walk. He likes to wander. You know how he is. We'll see if we can find him before we start blaming,' and he paused for a second, 'fairies.' he said with all the sarcasm he could muster.

I wished now I could take back the fairy comment but it was too late, I attempted anyway, 'Maybe I dreamt the fairy part but he's not in his bed, he's not in the house, he is outside of earshot or he would have heard me calling, and his shoes are still by the door where he left them last night.' It was my turn to show contempt.

He sent Tony and Willy to get dressed, as he went back in and put on a flannel shirt, jeans and his boots. He was all action now. In his mind he was mounting a rescue, but somehow I knew it was useless. I didn't say anything as he barked orders out to the boys. They were to check the trails between here and the waterfall, while he headed off in the other direction. My job was to stay put with James, and blow three short blasts the whistle, he handed me, if you came back. I listened to the boys yell your name and it got softer and softer as they walked away. I picked up James. He was a bit traumatized by now. We settled in the hammock. I rocked and reassured him till he relaxed.

I waited about a half an hour before I headed into the kitchen to start cooking breakfast. I figured your father and the boys would be back soon and no one had eaten. I don't remember what I made, but I made a lot.

I was finishing up when I heard your brothers come back. They were disappointed they couldn't find you. They wanted to bring you home and be the hero. They assured me they check several trails and all around the waterfall but didn't see any sign of you. I sat them down and piled food on their plates and they tucked right in.

An hour later your father returned. I could tell he was worried. His temper became quick when he was upset. So he was very worried. He grabbed a couple of pieces of toast and filled them with eggs and bacon. He took a large bite and said, around his mouthful of food, he was headed to the sheriff's station in town to get help. He took off and the station wagon spit dirt back as he raced down the road.

By late afternoon, we had all sorts of folks buzzing around the cabin. The Sheriff's Department and Forestry Service each had dozens of folks out searching. I had to drive back to town for more supplies to feed all the people. I spent the whole afternoon making coffee and sandwiches.

The day wore on and the sun made it's weary way across the sky. A weird feeling come over me. It was about eight at night and the sun was setting when I had this irrepressible urge to grab a flashlight and head out down a trail myself. I told Tony to make, damn sure, none of your brothers left the cabin and I would be back shortly. By the look on his face, I think I scared him a little. He did as he was told without the usual whining about how he should come and protect me.

I can't explain why I picked the path I did. I was drawn to it. I walked for about fifteen minutes, and was completely isolated. With every step, my anger built. I stopped and shouted at the sky, 'God damn you fairies, I want my son back!' Out of the sky, a light that was pink, yellow, and blue all at the same time drifted down. It landed on the trail, right in front of me. The light flared so bright, I had to cover my eyes. When I could see again, this beautiful, young, woman was standing before me.

'Anne, please do not fear. No harm will come to you or your son,' the creature said.

'Do you remember the peaceful feeling I told you about earlier?' Mum continued.

I nodded.

'The peaceful feeling started to descend on me, but I was too heartbroken and angry to feel the contentment.

I turned to her and said, 'Listen bitch, you took my son and I want him back. Where is he?'

'My name is Naomi and I can understand you are upset, but your son is unharmed. He will be returned to you in two days hence.'

'I want him home now. What are you doing to him?'

'He was selected before he was born and is now being prepared.'

'Prepared? Prepared for what?'

'His future.'

'Riddles? You steal my son and answer me in riddles?'

'I came to assure you. He is safe and will be returned

completely unharmed.'

'Yeah, I heard you the first time, two days hence. What are you doing to him?'

'He will be home soon,' Naomi simply repeated and flashed into a dot of light and rose till it blended into the night sky.

'As she predicted the following two days of searching turned up nothing. As the sun set on the second day you came wandering up a trail, happy as can be. I remember your smile spread from ear to ear. When you saw all the cars and people you asked, why they were here.

You actually whispered to me, 'I didn't know we were having a party.' As you looked at me you saw my tears, 'Why are you crying Mum?'

'Honey, you have been gone for three days.'

'No I haven't, I followed those pretty lights, because they said they wanted to play. I followed them down the trail. They disappeared, so I came right home.'

This was the night you took off into the woods and were prepared. Prepared for what I still don't know, but I haven't seen the lights since. I hope to God I never see them again."

Mum took another sip and sat quietly. Her story was told and now she wanted to forget it.

"Roger, I know how these things get under your skin, but please let this fairy nonsense go. They scare me. We have little or no control of ourselves when they are around. That night in the woods, Naomi could have snapped her fingers and killed me. For her, it would have been like slapping a mosquito."

"Mum, I know what you mean, but it's not so easy. They are everywhere. I feel them watching me, wherever I go. I am not looking for information out of curiosity. I am trying to make it stop." I said in frustration. "Thanks for telling me all this. I now have a starting place to begin my research. I need to know, was this preparation for my encounter with Naomi or something else? By the way they keep watch, I don't believe they are finished with me yet. It would be nice to know, what other fun is in store for me."

That night my dreams were filled with images from Mum's stories. Actually, they felt more like memories than dreams. I following the lights out of the house. They took me to the clearing, where we saw all the flowers. I remember either swimming or washing in the pond, but the memory was fuzzy. Images began flooding into and crystallizing in my mind when the alarm buzzed. The buzz dragged me away from my newfound memories, leaving them behind in the land of slumber.

The remainder of my visit with Mum was a normal visit. Mum dismissed all attempts I made at engaging her in talk of the fairies. So we spent the day being mother and son.

Within a couple days I had my bags packed and was headed out the door to return home.

"Well Mum, this certainly was an interesting trip. Thank you for telling me." I could see how the strain of telling her stories had bothered her.

"No thanks needed. I should have told them to you long before this visit. I just..."

"No, Mum, I get it, I really do. Those little bastards know how to mess with your head."

"They do, love, they certainly do. Drive safe." She put her arms around me and we embraced.

"Bye, Mum," I croaked holding back my tears.

As I headed out the door I had no idea where this knowledge would take me.

Until now.

Chapter 35

ME A FLIRT?

The memories of my visit home were still fresh, as I put my turn signal on. I pulled off the road in the town of Independence, Kansas. It was time for food and gas. We stopped at a small gas station called Miller Brother's Fast Gas. Behind the counter was a young guy who wanted to be anywhere but here.

"Hey, can you tell me where I can get a good meal?" I asked the guy as I gave my cash. He couldn't be bothered to remove the ear buds so he acted like he didn't hear.

"You might try Brothers Railroad Inn down the road," offered a lady who was next in line.

I turned, "A good place to eat?"

She replied, "One of my favorites." She was about four-five, brunette, and very good looking. She smiled and it seemed genuine.

I smiled back, "Thanks, shall I tell them you sent me?" I said playfully. Now I need to point out, my family has accused me of being an insufferable flirt, but I disagreed. I'm only being friendly.

"Sure hon," she said smiling. "Tell them Cheryl sent you."

"Will do Cheryl, I'm Roger," and I offered my hand. Her smile brightened, "I take it you're from around here?"

"And you ain't," she said back as she put her money on

the counter.

"No ma'am, I'm not." I do believe she was flirting with me. Oh well, no harm will come of it. I'll be on my way soon and I'll never see this pretty lady again. She was pretty, from her perfectly shaped eyebrows all the way to her toes. I need to go now.

"Well Cheryl, thank you for the recommendation. It was a pleasure meeting such a pretty lady." Dear Lord did those words come out of my mouth? I turned for the door. Kalen was waiting in the truck as I came out. "I found a place to eat."

"Good, I'm hungry," he said flatly.

"Are you okay?" I asked. Kalen seemed off today.

"I'm well enough," he replied.

"All right? What the hell does that mean? What is wrong?" Through our bond I actually felt something was wrong.

"I'm not sure. Ever since the contact with the Warg I haven't felt quite right."

"Were you using magic to track them at the diner?"

"Yes, why do you ask?"

"Do you need more?"

He paused to think about the offer. I knew by the pause, he needed a magic refill, but was too proud to ask. This bond was quite useful. "How does this work? Do you take the magic or do I somehow give you some? I can't have my protector like this."

"It's best if it happens in a fairy realm after sunset," Kalen insisted.

"Can we use the stick glen?"

"Stick glen?" Kalen asked.

"Yeah, you put the stick down, mumble something, light flashes and pops, and we fall into the glen, Stick Glen."

He only smiled at the description. "Yes, the 'Stick Glen' should work."

"Will I be able to work out?"

"We will both be tired from the transfer, but we should be able to get in a light workout."

"Cool, let's go get some grub."

The restaurant was only a mile or so down Main Street. It turned out Cheryl's recommendation was right on. We were greeted at the door. "Cheryl told me name dropping was the thing to do."

"Indeed it is. I'm Mike, and Cheryl is a friend of mine. You get the best table in the house." Actually they were all pretty good.

As we walked to the table, I noticed Kalen seemed to be on high alert. Something here was bothering him. We sat and ordered drinks, "What's up?" I asked.

"Something is close." By this he meant something from the land of Fae was close.

"You sure?" I asked jokingly. He glared at me. "I can't wait till you get your mojo back. You've got no sense of humor. So how close are they?"

"Not very, but it either has departed or has a very weak signature. It could be Phengard, because their magic is usually weak. Let's eat and go."

Now, I was watching everything and everyone too. We both ordered an Italian dish, and though I don't recall what it was, we both enjoyed it.

I saw nothing out of the ordinary. I looked up to thank our waiter and in she walked. Cheryl sat at the table next to ours.

"Hello again," I said in greeting.

"Hi. Fancy meeting you here," and she smiled her crooked smile. It was cute.

Kalen kicked me under the table. "We don't have time for human mating rituals," he said quietly.

I was taken back by the bluntness of his words. "Wow, Kalen, don't mince words on my account. How about you tell me how you really feel?" But Kalen ignored me. I guess I really do flirt.

"So, are you in town for a while?" She asked. I wasn't sure how to answer. We were trying to keep a low profile and I really knew nothing about this lady beyond what I could see.

"No ma'am, we are simply passing through. We are trying to get to," my brain was whirling, trying to think of cities to the south, "Tulsa before we stop today." Thank you 5th grade geography teacher.

"What's in Tulsa?" she kept the conversation going.

"Got my nephew's wedding," damn I was good.

"I do love a good wedding. Does it have a theme?" Now she was just being pushy.

"I have to be there and wear my good suit or else my mother won't forgive me. I'm not a wedding guy. I wouldn't be going except for mom."

I turned back to my plate and began to eat. Kalen was looking intently to my right.

"Is he acting…normal?" he asked. "I mean, for a human.".

I looked and the bus boy was clearing a table but he was moving as slow as I'd seen anyone move. He was close enough to have heard my conversation with Cheryl. He turned and stared back at Kalen and me with a menacing look.

To cover the fact we were looking at him I called, "Hey you, yeah bus boy." and I waved him to our table.

"What are you doing?" Kalen hissed.

"Trust me, and watch." The bus boy came. "Sorry, what's your name?"

"Uh, Bobby," he spoke slowly like he had to think about the question.

"I don't see the waiter around here. Would you ask him to get us some bread?" Before he could turn, "Hey Bobby, that's a nice tat. Did you get it done locally?"

"Yeah, there's a place down the street," he said giving me a closer look and he even smiled.

"It's a beaut. Thanks for getting the bread." He turned and headed for the kitchen. "Did you sense anything from him?"

"Yes, but it was faint, almost nothing. It wasn't quite what I felt earlier. For a moment when we came in I sensed it coming from you."

"Weird. Did you see his arm?"

"You mean the tattoo you inquired about?" Kalen asked.

"I was checking a theory and it paid off. Did you see the bite marks on his arm? He had at least three and they were disguised by the tattoo. I think we found our Steve." I held up a finger to Kalen and turned to Cheryl. "Cheryl, I was wondering if you could help me with something."

"Sure what would you like?"

"Do you know the bus boy, Bobby?"

"Sure," she said without knowing where I was going with this line of questions. I picked up my drink and joined her at her table.

"What can you tell me?" I found myself strangely attracted to her. I need to shake this off.

"He's a strange boy. His parents passed away a few years back. It was horrible. The family was camping up north of here in some preserve. A wild animal attacked them. I heard there wasn't much left of them. Bobby walked away unhurt. Since then he's never been quite right," and she touched her head.

"Poor kid, that's a lot to handle for someone his age," I sympathized.

"Yes it is," she changed the subject with a smile. "Can I convince you to skip the wedding? I will make it worth you while." She reached across the table and rested her hand on the back of mine.

"Shit," I thought. I turned my hand over grasping hers. "If I only could. Maybe on the return trip."

"I hope so," she smiled. Thankfully the waiter came and I asked for my bill.

"It was nice to meet you, Cheryl." I said and found myself meaning it. "Who knows? In another life it could have been fun," I said and smiled at her.

"Me too," she replied and handed me her card. "If you come back this way, call."

"I will," I said knowing full well I wouldn't. My attraction to her was strong and it scared me a little. I paid the bill and Kalen and I headed for the door.

"Do you think he made us? I mean, he heard the bullshit I fed Cheryl."

"If he is with them he heard everything you told her," he said throwing his thumb over his shoulder. "But there is no way to be sure."

"Shit, where to now?"

"We keep going. They may not know our destination and may believe it's to the south."

We climbed in the car and headed south out of town. We needed to go a few miles before we wove our way back to our original route.

Chapter 36

I DON'T SWING THAT WAY

The afternoon's drive put us both in dour moods. We thought we were flying under the radar. It seems I could have made this trip in a tour bus with a neon sign on the side advertising our itinerary. Hopefully, our little jog to the south put the wild Fae off our trail.

After a few dozen miles ticked by I turned to Kalen. "Something about Cheryl struck me as odd."

"Odd? How do you mean?" Kalen answered in earnest.

"My attraction to her was overwhelming."

"She is an attractive woman, for a human. Not quite my taste, but I could see why you were taken by her beauty." Kalen said this with a smile dancing across his lips.

"I'm not kidding, Kalen. This attraction has me a little spooked. There was something about her that made me desire her. It wasn't normal."

"It has been a while since you..."

"Yes, yes," I interrupted him, "but that isn't my point. Normally, I can restrain myself. If she was using some sort of magic, would you have been able to detect it?"

"I did sense something, if you recall," Kalen offered.

"But you targeted Bobby, not Cheryl."

"Bobby was magic touched."

"You also sensed it around me."

"Yes?"

"Did you sense my magic? Or was it something different?"

"I always sense your magic, but what I was talking about was different."

"So was it possible she put a glamour or some sort of whammy on me that made her irresistible?"

"I would have sensed the amount of magic needed for a glamour."

"Did my magic change? I mean could someone make me use my magic without my knowing?"

"You think Cheryl put a glamour, or to quote you a whammy, on you with your own magic? And she left no signature? Roger your hormones are simply getting the best of you."

I shook my head. I really felt that this was more than a simple attraction. If it was magic, Kalen would have sensed more than he did. If so, then who was Cheryl, a fairy queen? Really, a lady I met in a gas station? Kalen was right. I settled in and chased the sun as it raced for the horizon.

The rest of the drive was uneventful, except for the constant feeling of being watched. We didn't make it to Colorado, but we stopped only a little shy. We could have pushed it a little further, but we would have to stop in a National Grassland. I've become afraid of any green area on the map. These fairies are like roaches. They are everywhere, especially in these little green areas.

Kalen said there were only two wild Fae to worry about. How about the non-worry kind? Are they giving us away, and how many are there? This train of thought had me feeling paranoid, but if they really are out to get me, then I am not paranoid, I am prepared. "Kalen, there are more than two kind of Fae out here, aren't there?" I was tired of wondering.

"What is it you want to know?"

"I thought I was clear. Are there more than the Phengard and Warg out here?"

"Yes," was given as a one-word reply.

""Yes, is all you are telling me? Yes, come on Kalen you

owe me more than yes."

"Not now. I will give you more while we practice."

We finished the drive into Hugoton, Kansas. I'd found a B & B called Shady Lane. I hoped this would take us a little off the grid. Also, I wanted something other than a roadside motel and a fast food breakfast.

We pulled into the Shady Lane Bed and Breakfast and grabbed our luggage. We were met at the door.

"May I help you?" asked a kindly gentleman at the door.

"Yes sir, we talked earlier about a room?"

"You Mr. Burr?" he asked and gave Kalen a quizzical look. Kalen was clueless as to why he was receiving this scrutiny, but this was small town America. When small town America sees two guys show up at a B & B and one of them is a gorgeous twenty something. It made them think about a parade in San Francisco.

"Yes sir, I was the one who asked about the two beds?" I stated as a question. It seemed to me, he thought we were a couple and I wished to convince him otherwise. I feel I need to explain my response for not wanting to appear as a couple. As I stated before, this was a very small town in a remote section of a very rural state. A gay couple checking in would be a juicy bit of gossip for the town folk to chew on. I didn't want anyone talking about us. I couldn't care if they thought me gay or alien. Anything gossip worthy needed to be stopped. God only knows who or what was listening.

Our host's name was Neal. "Neal, this is a beautiful house," I said.

"Thank you, Mr. Burr."

"Please, I'm Roger," and extended my hand. "And this is my little brother, well half-brother, Kalen." Kalen reached out his hand.

"So what brings you boys this way?"

"Our sister is marrying a lawyer from Los Angeles and we are required to go his bachelor's party in Vegas." I rolled my eyes to show a my contempt of Vegas.

"This seems a long way to go for a party." I do believe Neal was sensing my bullshit.

"My brother and I have been so busy with our own families that we decided a road trip was in order. And here we are." Neal nodded with acceptance, and if it did make the grapevine, our destination was Vegas.

Neal showed us our room and it was large and comfortable.

"If you boys need anything, give me a holler. I hope you enjoy your stay."

"Thank you, Neal."

"Inn keeper, I bestow my thanks upon you." Yep, this raised an eyebrow.

I chuckled, "He does a lot of civic theater back home and he loves channeling Shakespeare." Thankfully, Neal was appeased. We settled our things and headed out for training.

We drove about ten minutes out of town and found a dirt road. We drove down the road a mile or so and arrived in a pristine meadow. I know this sounds like we wandered randomly but Kalen gave me directions, like a native. I'm guessing, it's a fairy thing.

We got there a bit early and had to wait for the sun to set. We sat on the tailgate drinking the bottled water we snagged from the room.

"Roger, why did you introduce me as your brother?" Kalen asked.

"Neal saw us as a couple," I offered, but this didn't seem to register. "He thought we were lovers," he now displayed the desired look of shock, "and in a small remote town, gay men are news."

"Happy men?" I lost him again. I often forget he is from a different world and time.

"Gay is a term we use for lovers who are the same gender. Anyway, male lovers are big news in a small town and would draw unwanted attention to us. Two brothers headed to Vegas for a bachelor's party is passé."

"Where is Vegas?" He asked and I pointed a little south of due west. "Nicely done," he added.

As the sun closed its eye on us, Kalen knelt down and placed the stick, and we descended into the glen.

Chapter 37

THE FORCE IS STRONG WITH THIS ONE

As I stepped into the wooded circle, I felt like we weren't alone.

"Kalen," I asked, "are we alone?"

"No," he said, "I invited some others to join us."

"Others? What others and when did you..."

Kalen held up his hand and I fell silent. "When you asked about the other Fae, I thought I'd let you meet a few friends."

"When did you invite them?" To this question he raised an eyebrow in reply. "Have they always been around?"

"Every once in a while we'd cross one or another. They keep a low profile. They fear Warg and Phengard. I sent word about a meeting tonight and here they are." He raised his hands to the trees and on cue it was Christmas at the Griswold's. There had to be thousands of pixies. See how I didn't call them fireflies? But they did look like fireflies.

Kalen stepped into the circle and bowed deeply and I followed his lead. In a deep but gentle basso voice I heard, "Greetings General Kalen and Wizard Roger. I would like to welcome you to the wilds."

"Prince Orin, you do me honor beyond my worth."

"Nonsense Kalen, arise and be greeted." As we rose,

there stood a young man, not a bit like I expected from the voice I heard. He was thin and pale, but not sickly. He looked extremely fit and capable. He too, had the same ancient look in his eyes that set Kalen apart from humans, to me at least. He and Kalen greeted like long lost friends. First with the warrior handshake and then they wrapped each other in an embrace complete with a European kiss on the cheeks. I must be too American, because the double cheek kiss always looks strange to me. "And you must be the young wizard, all are talking about."

"Yes, Prince Orin, I must," I said restraining a chuckle. A nineteen year old was referring to me as young. Okay, I know he is probably seventeen billion years old but still they could at least look older. I looked to Kalen for guidance. I was mentally beaming him WTF? But as always he was waiting to see how I handled the situation for myself. "So Prince Orin..."

And he stopped me and reached out his hand, "If we are to be friends you must call me Orin. Out in the wilds, titles like Prince have no true meaning."

I looked around at the Fae in attendance with this non-prince. It meant something. "Okay, Orin, it is a pleasure to make your acquaintance. How do you and Kalen know one another?" I asked, still shaking hands.

"As a lad he was my sword master and my aunt's Master of Arms."

"I still am," Kalen chimed in.

Now I was confused, "Still are what, Kalen?" I asked.

"Both, except I am now your sword master," he said to me.

"You still serve my Aunt Naomi?"

"Aunt Naomi? You are Aelfric's son?" It was a mistake to mention his name. Before the 'n' on the word son was even pronounced, the place went nuts. The fire..., shit. The pixies went berserk. Orin's grip tightened around my hands like a vice squishing a melon. Kalen placed himself between Orin and me, putting a pleading hand on Orin's chest.

"Quiet!" rang Orin's voice. And even the crickets were

afraid to speak.

"My apologies Orin. I meant no offence. I still am new to talking with fairy folk and do not know the forbidden subjects."

"I'd have thought your mentor would have taught you, but if I recall correctly, Kalen always liked to see if you would swim or sink on your own. I do believe he let you sink a bit." This struck Orin as funny and he began to laugh and the chorus of lights joined in.

I was a bit pissed now, but Orin saw this and laughed even harder. He slapped Kalen on the back and I found myself starting to laugh.

You know how you can watch a baby laugh and it cracks you up? It was like that, but only more uncontrollable. I had tears streaking down my face and a stitch in my side from this laugh. Must be a fairy thing.

As the laughter subsided, "Yes, he did father me, but we here are his enemy. I did not agree with how he took his kingdom and how he used his magic against Fae."

"And if I recall, you made sure he knew your thoughts," Kalen added.

"You are right. I was a bit outspoken in my youth. Mayhap for my brethren, I should have held my tongue, but the passion of youth and a great injustice released my restraint. My words brought banishment for these good Fae and me. Our lives now depend on our ability to remain unseen. And one day I will return to my father and make right all he destroyed." As he was speaking I could see his passion stirring and the lights in the trees shifted and moved. They, apparently, were agitated by Orin's righteous indignation. I too, found myself caught up by his words and emotions.

"Sorry my friends, as you see the old wounds still fester. Kalen, it was you who called this meeting. How can I be of service, old friend?"

"We came here tonight to transfer magic through the bond and practice weapon training. I knew you were in the area and thought..."

"My royal blood will make this transfer easier."

"Yes, my Lord. If you wouldn't mind."

"Not at all, as long as I can test my sword against you once again."

"It would be my honor." Kalen raised the eyebrow in question, "Have you been keeping up with your lessons?"

"You will have to wait and see," Orin challenged.

Kalen and I walked to the center of the circle and took seats upon the ground facing one another. Orin motioned to the side and three cups of the delicious fairy brew floated out to us on the backs of a few pixies. We drank deeply and placed the cups back on the tray.

"Roger, please close your eyes," Orin instructed. I saw Kalen's eyes were already shut. I felt Orin place his hand on my head and as he did I heard him take in a sharp breath. I actually felt my magic leave through his hand then heard Kalen take in a breath. Orin removed his hand.

"No blood this time?" I asked wondering when the blood exchange was going to happen.

"Once a bond has been established, blood is no longer required. Though if Prince Orin was not available. I would have needed blood." There was still so much to learn.

"You have much of the old magic, young wizard. It is no wonder why so many are excited by your presence. But more talk later. It's time to train."

Kalen removed his bow and placed his quiver on his back. I followed his lead. We began shooting. I started off with hitting the target seven out of ten times and I was ecstatic. Something was different today. I improved to ten out of ten within four rounds. My concentration was better and I was able to focus on the feel of shooting. It was kind of a Zen thing. I know it's not a good explanation but I was in a zone.

"Kalen, how am I doing this? My improvement is not normal."

"Yes, you might even call it, magic," Kalen added sarcastically.

"Magic? How? Why now? I don't understand."

"Did you feel the magic when Orin passed it to me?"

"Yes."

"Was this the first time you felt it move?"

"Yes."

"I thought, instead of the blood transfer, I could get someone of royal blood to transfer the power through the bond. It would give you the chance to feel your gift. You cannot see it, but you glow with your magic. The barrier has been breached and you now have access."

"I do feel good. I actually feel like I did when we ate the bread last night."

"A main ingredient is magic."

"Why did we need someone of royal blood for the transfer?"

"Well, now that the barrier is breached you can pass it without blood or help, but royal blood is the purest among the Fae. That purity allows them to transfer magic."

I turned back to my target and began grouping my arrows in the center of my target. I didn't get center shots or split arrows, but all arrows hit within a six inches of center... consistently. I liked this magic thing.

"Am I using up my magic?" I asked wondering if I was wasting it like water on the ground.

"No, it simply remains available, but while it is flowing, you must maintain control of your emotions. A flash of anger has the power to kill if it is not controlled."

"Shit," this scared me a little. I didn't want to kill anyone and I felt the magic snuff out.

"Easy, Roger, you must remain in control. Close your eyes and let it flow." It was easy for him to say. I closed my eyes and took a few deep breaths and then I felt it flow.

"Cool," was all I could think to say.

"Put away the bow and try your hands with the sword," Kalen directed.

With the magic flowing, the sword felt like an extension of my arm. Kalen had me try the forms I had stumbled through last night. Today, it seemed like I'd been doing them my whole life.

"Does this magic work like this on all I try and do?"

"Yes it does."

"I don't understand how Charles could have given this up?"

"It was a great sacrifice for a greater good. He was a strong and wise man."

"Should I be messing with this magic? Wasn't magic responsible for the conflict between the wizard and Fae?"

"Not magic, the wizards and Fae were responsible, but it was decided by the fates when the wizards would come again."

"Fates? What do you mean?"

"You were give an enormous amount of magic and your granddaughter is also blessed. This is a signal of your return. It is up to the fairy world to welcome, not exploit you. This is why Naomi took such a great interest."

"If her interest is so great, then why am I forced to go see Ael...sorry this other guy who everyone says is a royal douchebag? And he can't have a good reason for wanting me."

"We do not know what the King wishes of you. He has the right and the power to demand a magic carrier to attend him, if he wishes."

"Wait a minute, you said magic carrier, right?" At this statement Kalen smiled, "I was a carrier, but now that I am using it, I am a magic user. Does this change the playing field?"

"It does indeed. But he won't know whether you are a carrier or user till he sees you use your power. He will notice that power has been released, but he knows of our bond. Actually, a messenger has told him to expect me."

"En guarde!" I said and attacked Kalen with my sword. He easily deflected my blows and proceeded to return the favor. My hand and body moved of its own accord. I was able to flow from one form to another and keep his sword from striking home. We kept this up for a while and I felt sweat pouring from my body. Kalen attacked and we locked swords.

"Break and retreat," Kalen commanded. I followed his

order and stepped back and saluted with my sword.

"Holy crap, that was cool," I exclaimed. "I'm digging this magic stuff."

"Roger, maintain your humility."

I raised my hand, "No, it's okay. I'm cool. The newness of this has got me psyched."

"Well met, young wizard. Kalen, how long have you been his sword master?"

"One day," and a collected gasp echo from the trees.

Orin laughed, "I've never seen you with such a keen wit Kalen. It sounded as if you said one day."

"I did."

"Oh," was all Orin said as he looked at me.

The only thought coming to mind was 'the force is strong with this one' but I kept it to myself because it would be lost on this bunch.

Orin offered us another drink and Kalen and I both drained two glasses of the nectar. Orin turned to Kalen and said, "We need to talk."

"Roger, we are finished with our training. If you wish you can wait at the truck. I believe the beer you brought should be cold by now. I won't be long. I would like to catch up with an old friend."

"I'm not stupid, Kalen, but I will respect your privacy. Orin, it was a pleasure meeting you. I'm not a big one on formalities so," I extended my hand.

"Wizard Roger, the pleasure was mine. Till our path cross again may the fates smile upon your journey," and he shook my hand.

"Later, Kalen," and I left with all of the weapons. I descended back to the meadow and nestled the weapons in the toolbox.

The sky was amazing. Out here the world was flat and the sky touched the horizon. The stars descended and you could dance among them.

I knew that I, or rather my magic was the topic of conversation back in the glen and ten minutes passed before Kalen came out and removed the stick. Which meant, they had several hours of catching up. Bullshit, they were planning something and I think my life got a little more interesting.

Chapter 38

IT'S NOT THAT SIMPLE

The drive back to the B & B started quiet, almost too quiet. I was waiting for Kalen to break the silence but he sat stoically, appearing deep in thought.

"How did the battle planning go?" I asked.

"To what battle are you referring?"

"I felt it was implied in my question." I volleyed back. Through the bond I felt a tension and knew he was attempting to deceive me. I stopped the truck and turned to him with a level look. He sat there looking straight ahead with a relaxed pose. He had the advantage of a couple hundred years of practice.

I continued, "You spent several hours with Orin. You did more than catch up. You are planning something and I'm in the middle of it all. Please don't treat me like a fool. You know than I'm not."

"I never implied you were foolish. I only wish to keep you safe. My Queen charged me with your safety. I am honor bound to do as I am charged."

"Okay then, what did you discuss with Orin for such a long time? Don't try to say life at the court or some such foolishness."

"We did discuss plans, but the rest I am unable to tell you."

"What if I guess correctly? Will you let me know if I am

close?" Kalen nodded.

"First off, he wants my power to use against his father." Kalen nodded.

"He wants you and I to distract the king while he masses his troops." A nod.

"He mentioned they have developed the ability to remain unseen. So, somehow he plans to exploit the skill to sneak through the border and possibly flank their forces." He nodded again and looked impressed.

"How do you know these things? Kalen asked, "You were not there."

"Like I said, I am not a fool. I had over twenty years of military training and I put one and one together. Before I continue this conversation I need to know something. Is Aelfric as bad as they all say? Did he really abuse the magic and kill the Warg, mercilessly?"

"It's not so simple. I watched the boy grow to be a man. I taught him to hold a sword much like I did his son. Many nights we shared stories by the starlight." Kalen stopped and took a deep breath, "He did kill those Warg. I wasn't a witness to it but at the time, wild Fae were something to be pushed out of your way. If humans build a house, they first clear the trees. Humans never worry about the trees and this is how we thought of the wilds. Using the old magic to eradicate them was over the top, way over the top. A treaty was being formed allowing them both use of the land. Orin was pushing for the treaty. And Aelfric held tight to his prejudice against the wilds, especially the Warg. He utterly refused to share his rule with another."

Kalen's face was pale after telling this tale.

"Let me see if I understand. You believe Aelfric's actions were wrong. You believe he should be removed from power but left unharmed, out of respect, loyalty and love. Orin has been plotting revenge for three hundred years and now here I am. He has learned to hate his father and wishes him punished. What does Orin plan to do if he succeeds?"

"I never asked. The truth of the matter is I didn't say much. I did fill him in on life at Naomi's court," Kalen answered wearing a grin.

"Does Orin consider this great injustice to the Warg or to his pride?" Will he remove the Pixies and restore the land to the Warg?"

"I do not know, but suspect the Pixies will not leave, regardless of what Orin decrees."

"Another thought, let's talk numbers. How many warriors do either side have fighting for them?"

"Aelfric's warriors out number Orin's warriors by four to one."

"Orin hopes to use my magic to level Aelfric's advantage, like his father did with the Warg?" I asked getting irritated. "I thought life was precious to the Fae. This is genocide. Can we appeal to a governing council?" I was working myself up when Kalen put his hand on my shoulder to calm me.

"Without your," and he reemphasized, "YOUR, magic it would be a suicide mission." Kalen added.

"So to Orin I am the big ole bag of magic he needs to get back at daddy."

"Yes, you are a vessel," Kalen tried to soften the language.

"Yeah, vessel is a nice way to put it." I put the truck in gear. "What is your plan?"

"Other than seeing you safely to Aelfric, I haven't got one," Kalen said plainly.

"Is there a way to resolve this conflict of interests without a complete genocide?" I asked.

"I would like a peaceful resolution very much but I don't see how it could be done."

The next ten minutes we drove in silence. As we pulled into the drive I asked, "Has Orin formed any sort of relationship with the Warg or Phengard?"

"No, there is little trust between us and the Warg. Even less between anyone and the Phengard."

I parked the truck and wearily headed in the house. We met Neal as we passed by the living area.

"Hi ya, boys," he said cheerfully. "You look hot and

bothered." I had forgotten about the workout and realized we were in need of a shower.

"Yes sir, we got a little exercise."

"Looks like more than a little."

"No, the heat got to me." I couldn't explain that it was a three to four hour workout in fairyland but only a half hour went by. This fairy stuff is screwy. "Can you recommend a good place to eat?" He gave us directions to the best steak joint in town. It was the only steak joint but steak did sound good. We headed for the shower.

As the hot water washed the day's hard earned sweat an idea started to form, but it had a few loose ends, very loose ends.

Chapter 39

IT JUST LOOKED ME IN THE EYE

We were in the truck driving to Gary's Santa Fe Steak House and I realized we hadn't spoken since leaving the truck earlier. It was probably my fault. Regardless, I had an epiphany in the shower. I now needed to flush out the idea.

"Kalen, what I'm about to share with you is only an idea. I haven't fully figured it out and I know it is full of holes, but it could work."

"Pray, do tell."

"We will have to get the Warg and Phengard involved and Orin will have to make a few of unbreakable fairy promises."

Kalen looked a little worried, "Sounds like a long shot already."

"I know, I know, but if we can put those forces together combined with my power, we might be able to depose a king and resolve this dispute," I said.

"We only have a couple of days till you are expected. How do you plan to put this together?"

"Luck, hard work, luck, and lots of time on the other side of the stick." I said as we pulled into Gary's. "I'll tell you more inside. As I climbed out of the truck my eye caught movement in the back seat of the truck. A moth flew from the back seat out my door. It floated and looked me in the eye. It wasn't even flapping its wings and it was stuck in the air at eye level. It only lasted about two seconds but it seemed much longer. "Holy shit, it's blue! Damn it!" I yelled. A Phengard spy was a stowaway. It turned around and moved so quickly my eye had a difficult time following its path. It was gone in a flash. "Shit, did you see that?"

"See what?" Kalen replied.

"The Phengard spy was a stowaway, for God only knows how long."

"Are you sure?"

"Did I give the impression of not being sure? It scared the crap out of me. It was so weird too. It fluttered out of the back like a butterfly should and froze at eye level. It froze in the air. Then it blasted out of here like a bat out of Hell." I stood there shaking my head with disbelief.

"Sounds like you encountered a Phengard," Kalen said nodding.

"How come your Spidey senses didn't pick it up?"

"My what?"

"Oh dear God. On the return trip we are watching a different movie every night. This is getting ridiculous. Why didn't you sense it?" I spoke this last part very slowly.

"It didn't want me to."

"Is it really that simple?"

"If you know what you are doing, yes."

"Let's go eat." We sat and placed orders for rib-eye steaks, loaded baked potatoes, and veggies. We planned on having coffee and dessert when we finished with the steak. With the order placed and our waitress serving others, I proceeded to lay out my idea to Kalen. Kalen stopped me a couple of times, asking for clarification. I felt like I was giving a mission brief back in the Air Force. Somewhere in the middle of the brief, the food came and I continued to talk and eat and even gesture a few times with my knife and fork, usually laden with steak. By the time I finished the brief I looked down and my plate was empty. The whole time Kalen was nodding with approval. The waitress took our orders for coffee and an overindulgent chocolate dessert.

"Roger, you are more of a warrior than I've given you credit. This is a reasonable plan. My only question now is how do we get the Phengard involved?"

I opened my mouth to answer and in walked Cheryl. Walk isn't the correct word for how she moved. Glide, sashay, float are better words, but they too fall short. Whatever the correct word, it was sexy. My eyes were glued to her and mid-gawk Kalen kicked me under the table.

"Use your magic," he hissed through clenched teeth. I did and she was still a damn fine looking woman but the compulsive need to mate, as Kalen would say, was gone. I do believe her smile faulted a bit.

"So nice to run into you again Roger," she said, completely ignoring Kalen. "You seem a little off course. Where were you headed? Tulsa, Oklahoma? Your momma wanted you at a wedding?"

"So," I replied, "are you an emissary of the wild Fae known as Phengard?"

"My, my, my, aren't you clever. You might say I am. I am Danaus, Queen of the Phengard." She stood all regal watching us. I believe she was waiting for us to prostrate ourselves, or something. We sat there.

"What do we call you, Dana or Cheryl?" I asked feeling quite pleased with myself.

"Cheryl is my human persona, but my true name is Danaus," she said slowly. She thought I didn't hear her the first time. I did and this was fun.

I gestured to an empty chair at our table. "Your timing is impeccable. Please, join us for coffee and dessert." This was much better now that her whammy didn't work on me. She sat ever so delicately next to me. Damn, she smelled good too. This lady was the whole package. I am glad the hormones were in check.

"Cheryl, what opinion do you hold of Aelfric?"

"You mean the old world intruder who annexed part of my kingdom?"

"One and the same. Okay, what is your relationship with the Warg?"

"Our lands are divided and the borders are secure."

"What are you doing tomorrow night?

Chapter 40

LADY YOU ARE A PIECE OF WORK

Cheryl raised her eyebrow at my question. It was nothing more than a facial gesture, but it conveyed volumes. Our waitress arrived with our coffee and dessert.

"Thank you," I said, "Danaus, may I order you anything?"

The waitress turned to Cheryl and wore a goofy grin. She must still have the whammy juice flowing.

"Do you have this effect on all mortals or only the ones who can't protect themselves?" It must have worked because the waitress snapped out of his daze with a shake of his head.

"Ma'am, may I bring you anything?" She looked at me with a smug expression.

"I would like a glass of water and one of those," she pointed at our chocolate creations.

"No bother, here have mine. I seem to have lost my appetite," I slid my plate across to her. I leaned in to Kalen. "Kick me again if she turns the whammy back on."

"Are you sure?" Kalen was concerned and he had reason to be, after all she was a Fae Queen.

"What do I have to fear? I have General Kalen to protect me."

"General Kalen, you are the General Kalen, Breena's Kalen?"

"Aye, your Majesty, she first blessed my sword," Kalen replied stiffly.

"How is my cousin these days?"

"From what I have heard in court, she is hale."

"I see, so who 'blesses your sword' these days good warrior?" She purred this almost as if she was offering to 'bless his sword.'

Kalen's expression hardened and he instinctually moved his hand to his sword. What Cheryl said was considered the highest form of insult for both the warrior and his liege lady. I put my hand gently on his forearm.

"Easy, Kalen, you are being baited." I turned to Cheryl, "Queen Naomi is now his Liege Lady," but this was not news to her.

She wore a satisfied smile and took a dainty bite of the proffered sweet. "Oh my, this is delicious. Thank you, Roger," and she wasn't talking about the dessert.

"Lady, you are a piece of work. What is it you want from me?" I was tiring of all the games.

"Isn't it obvious?" She said as she slowly placed a second morsel in her mouth. She slowly pulled the fork from her lips, then held it up in front of her mouth and slowly licked the remaining chocolate from the tines. "I only want a taste, and it would be pleasurable for both of us. Of this, I am certain." I brought my magic up and Cheryl squealed with delight.

"All this is about my magic? I have news for you darling, it's not going to happen. No one gets that much."

"Don't you mean again? No one gets that much, again? Who took your magic when you weren't looking?" She paused. "Wait, was it Naomi?" and she laughed with delight. "I do believe Breena's baby girl had a taste of you. This is good, very good." She genuinely seemed pleased at this news.

"Can we please get passed the kiss and tell portions of the program? Would you please tell me your terms for joining our little foray?" I was tired of the cat and mouse game and wanted to be done with her. Even with my magic protecting me I was almost ready to jump her bones. Thank God Kalen was there.

The Summons

"To help with your, foray is it? You must help me first. I need magic. Aelfric annexed our sacred glen when he murdered the Warg. There is much sickness within my kingdom and precious little magic remains. Without my glen, I cannot pull what I need from mother earth to care for all my people."

"For your participation I will give you magic, but you won't get as much as you were trying to seduce from me. Naomi took what she wanted. That was before I learned about my magic. Now I know, and will never allow anyone unfettered access to my magic again."

"Wizard, you are learning," she said this with an honest smile.

"This seduction magic you are attempting with me… please stop. I would like to lower my magic and talk in earnest?" I released my magic and she stopped. She stopped playing games and I found her even more alluring. But we talked.

"How about we start with your glen. Can you tell me its location?"

She paused. I was asking a lot with this question. The location of a sacred place isn't commonly shared between Fae, and me being human made it worse.

"Look Cheryl or Danaus, wait a second. What do you wish me to call you?"

"My usual reply is Danaus but I like the way you say Cheryl."

"Okay, Cheryl, you want your glen back and I need to know where it is so I don't promise it, accidentally, to someone else? I don't need the exact location; a general area is fine."

"How could you even begin to promise it to anyone? It is held by Aelfric."

"For the matter of this conversation, it isn't important. At the meeting tomorrow night I will explain all. To a few interested parties, I will provide more. I hope you will join. The whole plan will be revealed and you can then decide if you are in or out. In the mean time I need information."

"You are going to invade Aelfric's realm?"

"My idea is a bit more subtle, but again, tomorrow we will discuss my plans. I need to know what piece of earth you will want back."

"My glen is in the northwest corner of the state you call Wyoming."

"Let me see," and I pulled out my phone to check the maps. "Yellowstone? Your glen is in Yellowstone?"

"Those were our lands also, but the glen isn't exactly there. It's to the south, in Grand Teton National Park."

My life has gotten so surreal. I am in the process of promising a National Park to a Fairy Queen. What ever happened to riding a motorcycle across country for my summer vacation? No magic, no fairies, no worries and my family safe and sound at home with no impending doom. The next few days will be busy or possibly my last, if the plan didn't work. In the heat of battle plans are often turned on their ear. So I had better call my kids tonight. They are all pissed off at me, as usual, and I'll probably be leaving voicemail, but I needed to try.

"You would like to regain Yellowstone and south," I stated.

"No, humans have polluted our land. It is no longer useful to us, but Grand Teton and south would replace what was stolen."

"Grand Teton," I repeated as I jotted down a note.

"Roger? Are you promising to give our home back?"

"I am promising you, I will try. Again, tomorrow night there will be a meeting at sunset. You, Orin son of Aelfric, representatives from the Warg, Kalen and I will meet in Kalen's glen." She looked to Kalen. He spoke in a language I would call the old tongue and handed her a small strip of bark. She was satisfied.

"Cheryl, do I have your word of honor as Queen of the Phengard that neither you nor your subjects will take any action to compromise the safe passage of all who attend, or accompany those who attend this meeting be it in this world or the Fairy Realm?"

"Yes, you have my word of honor. Remember this…I will not join your fight without your old magic."

"I know and it will be addressed tomorrow. You and your retinue will also be afforded safe passage, you have my word as Wizard."

"Thank you, sir Wizard," she said formally and bowed her head.

"Just Roger," I added.

As Cheryl rose to leave, we stood out of respect and I even followed Kalen's lead with a bow.

"On the morrow, good Queen," Kalen offered.

"I look forward to seeing you again," I said finding I really meant it. She was growing on me.

She glided from the room and I couldn't take my eyes off her.

"You have to be one of the luckiest beings I have ever met," Kalen said as the door closed behind her.

"How do you mean?"

"Our biggest obstacle was finding the Phengard and having a representative attend the meeting and this one fell in your lap."

"I wish, but I get your meaning."

I watched him ponder my reply for about ten seconds, "I wish?" he asked then he laughed, " Oh yeah, in your lap, this is funny." But it wasn't that funny.

The fact that he got a piece of ill-conceived humor led me to believe I was indeed corrupting a poor unsuspecting fairy. I am not sure if this is a good or bad development. If I have corrupted him this much, I can't wait to see the effect our movie-fest will have, but first things first.

I took out my phone. I located Chepi's number and made the call.

Chapter 41

THERE'S NO PLACE LIKE HOME

The ride home from Gary's was quiet. It's funny how now where I placed my head, becomes home. The concept of home used to be a constant in my life. I'd spent many years flying around the globe, but home never changed. The location changed every several years, but home was always where my family laid their heads at night. It was a place of joy, tears, laughter and love. I wasn't sure where home was anymore. My wife let her cell phone go to voicemail, and I wasn't calling her sister. I'm sure they were together somewhere, but I hope my wife is checking her messages anyway. After her announcement I left the following:

"Hi it's me. Right now I'm in Kansas. I know you don't understand what I'm going through. I barely understand myself. I've never meant for us to end up this way. I hope you believe when I say the tryst with Naomi was beyond my control. Oh God, I wish I could make you understand.

For my twenty years or so years in the Air Force I have been off and on the road. I never knew where I was going to lay my head each night, but I always knew you were my one constant. You were my home. I am about to pick a fight with a bully for folks I don't even know. Yet I fight because it needs to be done. That's not important right now. I feel adrift, lost in the woods. I no longer have a home. The house is fine, but an empty house is but a tune on the wind, undone and unheard. Without you it isn't home.

The Summons

When I dialed I wanted to say I am sorry and I love you. I don't expect these words to change anything but I need to say them and I hope you want to hear them.

Sam will have the details of my journey. She said she would only tell you if you asked. The truth of this trip is beyond belief. Hell, the Grimm brothers told more believable stuff, but I know now, there is a lot of truth in their words...but I digress. Anyway, I have to say, goodbye love."

I hung up.

It was with a heavy heart I said those things, but who knows what was going to happen and she deserved a goodbye.

I began my calls to my kids and one by one they all went to voicemail. This is kind of odd. My kids spend half of their day texting and updating statuses on one social network or another. Their phones are always on and no more than a foot away. They would have them surgically implanted if it were possible. But a call from dear ole Dad goes to voicemail. I need to exempt my oldest. He was busy with his own family. He is finding out for himself why I did what I did. I rejoice that his life is free from the fairy's touch. My messages were a variation of the following:

"Hi, this is Dad. Sorry I couldn't get ahold of you. I wanted to say I am sorry my actions caused you pain, but I didn't do it with the intent of hurting your mom. I'd hoped to be able to explain, but if I can't, I want you to know I love you and hope your life is full of wonder and free of regret. Goodbye love and I hope you find true happiness."

Before I finished and called Sam, I needed a break. I grabbed my flask and headed downstairs in search of a glass. I found the kitchen and located the glass. As I closed the cabinet door, Neal was standing behind the door and scared the piss out of me, figuratively.

"Good evening, Roger, finding everything okay?" he asked without accusation.

"Uh yeah, thanks. I needed a glass," I said holding up the flask. "Care to join me for a bourbon?"

"I've been known to have a taste now, and again. Who are we having?"

"Jim's black," I said receiving a nod of approval.

"Would you care for a nibble? I came down here for a bite to eat."

"Sure, if it isn't too much bother, thanks."

"No bother at all, my lad." Was it me or did he now have an English accent instead of the Kansas drawl I heard earlier?

Neal moved about his kitchen with practiced efficiency. Within minutes we had cheese slices, fresh fruit, and an assortment of crackers sitting on a plate between us.

"Cheers, mate," I offered my raised glass. We clinked and drank. The brown liquid was warm and smoky. It was what I needed. I closed my eyes and let it wash away my regret.

"Want to talk about it?" Neal asked timidly.

"Yes, but I really can't," I replied.

"You're not headed to Vegas," he told me.

"No sir, I am not," and he had my attention.

"And Kalen isn't your brother."

"We aren't lovers, either." I wanted it on record.

"I know. I was surprised he didn't recognize me. It has been a few years though."

"You lost me. Care to explain, Neal?"

"Actually you can call me Uncle Neal. Your mum, Anne, is my niece."

"Seriously, what is this? How do you...? Where did you...?" I stammered, unable to form a proper question. After the day I had, this was about to wig me out.

He put his hand on mine and instantly I knew it was all going to be okay.

"Easy lad, easy. Your Granddad, was my brother. I was the one who took off and I'm guessing they never talked about."

"Granddad wasn't much of a talker, but you were never mentioned, at least to me. I do believe, we need more than I have in my flask." He held up a finger and walked to a cabinet to pull out an unopened bottle.

"Will this do?" He held up a bottle of Woodford Reserve and yes, it would do nicely.

"For a start," I replied. As I watched the kitchen light

play across his features, he did look a bit like my Granddad.

"You favor my brother," Neal said as if reading my thoughts.

"This whole thing is too weird to be coincidence. Got any theories?"

"I was told someday, I'd be called on, but I suppose you need a tale," he uncapped the bottle and filled my glass.

"As a lad I grew up in Eric's shadow. He was a great big brother but was eight years older. I'm sure I was annoying to him, but he was quite tolerant of me. He typically would include me in most of his excursions.

I remember one summer, he had a visitor, your friend Kalen, and he hasn't aged a day. He came to teach Eric. For some reason, Eric needed to learn to use a sword. I didn't learn why till after Kalen left.

Every night, right as the sun was setting, they would go out to a field a short way from the house and they disappeared. To be truthful, I only saw them disappear once. I assumed they did it every time when I couldn't find them. This nightly ritual went on all summer long.

It was bazaar. They were only gone anywhere from a quarter to half of an hour. The bazaar part was their condition upon their return, actually Eric's condition. Kalen was always as fresh as if he'd never gone. Eric was ragged. He was exhausted and drenched in sweat.

Sometimes they would retrieve me and we would all go for a swim in the pond." As he related his story, his eyes shone with the memory. In them, I saw my mother's eyes the previous summer.

"When Kalen left Eric at summer's end, I became his practice partner. He taught me to use a sword, a real honest to goodness sword. For the next few years till he left, he would take me to the field, but we didn't disappear. There he taught me about swordplay, fairies and life in general. He taught me about how our great, great and few more greats Grandfather worked with the Fae. He taught me about the magic.

It's funny what pops in your head. I remember the

author Johnny Tolkien…you know, the guy who wrote about some ring or another. They made a movie about it. He and Eric would trade stories for hours about fairies, Warg, and all kinds of weird stuff. It was right before Eric left home. I think he was twenty or so. And…" Neal paused and wore a far off expression. He wiped his eyes with a napkin, "and it was the last time I saw him. A few years after he left, war broke out in Europe and I signed up. I lost too many friends and neighbors during the bloody war. So after the war I came here to Kansas. It was about as far as I could get from the nightmares and memories. Also, I was drawn here somehow, I can't quite explain. When I got off the bus in town I knew I was home. I haven't had physical contact with my family until you showed up in my drive. I know all about you and your brothers. Eric and I wrote each other often. He was asked not to tell your Mum about me by the Fae for some odd reason, with the assurance that all would be understood in time. What do they know of time when they don't age a day in eighty odd years? But here you are."

"I don't recall you at the funeral," I added. "I can't imagine you missing Grandad's funeral?"

"I went when you all left, to pay my respects and say goodbye. I loved my brother but these Fae, out here, don't know me or my connection to their world. But I know them. Now it's your turn. Tell me your tale. How did you ever end up here?"

"Where do I start?" I pondered as he filled my glass. I began with Mum's story.

By the evening's end we didn't finish the bottle, but we put a serious dent in it. With our tales spun and the moon high, it was time to sleep. I rose from the table and extended my hand. Neal took my hand and pulled me into a hug. Tonight, I found family. I guess I was actually home.

Chapter 42

I GOT SOME S'PLAINING TO DO

I stumbled back to my room. I wasn't sure if I'd be able to sleep. I had an Uncle, and eighty years ago he had hung out with Kalen. The strange part of this whole situation was that it fit within my concept of reality. The truly weird and macabre were my new normal. Right now, my old life seemed a million miles away.

I snuck in the room. Kalen was surely asleep. As the door cracked I heard his voice and saw him in a chair that was turned to the window. He sat there with his stick in his hand. Now, this isn't some euphemism for some perverse behavior. He was literally holding the stick from his grove. Who knew it was a cell phone too?

The reflection in the window showed he had his eyes closed and seemed to be deep in conversation. I grabbed my phone and quickly retreated. He seemed to have the same idea as me.

I was about to make my toughest call. Toughest, because no machine would be acting as a liaison. I dialed.

"You have reached Sam's voicemail. I'll get back to you as soon as I can." I was surprised. I was now six for six, actually seven for seven, counting my wife. I hung up before the beep.

"Shit!" This exasperated me. Oh well, at least my family was consistent. As this negative thought formed, my phone vibrated and there was Sam's pretty face smiling up at me.

"Hi Dad, what the hell is going on?

"Hi Babe, what do you mean?"

"In the past two hours I have heard from every one of my brothers and sisters, also Mom." I laughed because not one thought to call me. You know, the one who left the farewell message. Yep, this is my family.

"Sorry I was going to call about an hour ago, but something came up."

"Please Daddy," her voice changed. The self-assured woman became my little girl with the word Daddy. "I'm scared," she continued, "they all felt you sent a goodbye message. You aren't going to do anything to yourself are you?"

"No love, it's not like that at all. Do you have a little time?"

"Yes, the kids are down. Anyway Rye has kid patrol tonight." Rye was short for Ryan, her husband.

"Go grab yourself one of those fruity drinks you like and swallow it down. You will need it."

"Would a shot of tequila work?" My Baby was growing up.

"Sure, but tequila?"

"I wanted to be ready to…I mean with the calls from my siblings and all."

"I get it, what do you think I was doing before I called? Cheers, love." I heard the shot glass slam on the table.

"Yuck! How can you guys drink this? Okay, I'm ready, talk to me Daddy-O. Sorry it's the tequila talking."

"So soon? Anyway, my calls to the others were a goodbye, but it was more of a just in case goodbye. Before I get into my story, I have some good news. You have a, wait let's see, it would be a great, great uncle."

"So you have a Gunk?" I'd better explain. I am a Gunk because I nicknamed my great niece, Goose. She gave me the name Gunk in return. It is short for great uncle. If you say Great Uncle fast you can hear the gunk in it. Goose is sort of the same. Saying Great Niece produced geese, but she is only one geese, so she would be a Goose. It is silly, but she's my Goose and I'm her Gunk. Her brother got the name Goo from basically the same logic.

"Yep, I have a Gunk. My Mum's dad had a brother and he is the proprietor of the Shady Lane Bed and Breakfast in Hugoton, Kansas. I happened, just happened, to stop here for the night."

"Shit Dad, oh sorry."

"Babe I haven't even started. Are you sitting?"

"I am now."

"Okay, before I get all doom and gloom, I have a few things you have to know. Harmony is special and not the short bus variety. She is Chosen, too. Can you see outside her window?"

"Yes," she offered tentatively.

"What do you see?"

"Well, it's kind of dark, but there are a few fireflies outside her window. Hey, I've seen those there before." I could hear the tension in her voice.

"Easy love, you are about to step through the looking glass, Alice. Can you handle the trip?"

"Do I need another shot? This is about Harmony?"

"Yes, I need you to know."

"So these fireflies are fairies?"

"Yes, and their leader is called Tink. I know, I know, but his name is Tink and it's not short for anything. Please invite them in and allow them to befriend your children. Ryan will have to believe too, but there'll be no clapping. They should have shown up a couple of days ago."

"They did. Why didn't you warn me sooner?" and she was down the rabbit hole.

"I have been quite busy. I asked for them to protect and watch over you guys, especially Harmony. Tink is a good guy. Please trust him. Kalen had nothing but the highest regard for him and I trust Kalen with my life, literally. Please Love, let them safe guard you. There are a lot of ugly things in the night."

"Is there a special way to invite them?"

"Go to the door and gaze in their direction and say this: 'Noble Fae,' when they approach bow your head and continue, 'Sir Tink, please be welcomed to my home. General Kalen sends his regard and wishes for you to continue as you were charged.' Once you say the formal crap, you can talk normally to them. They like chocolate if Kalen is typical, but talk to them about their needs. They will keep your babies safe, especially Harmony. When I am finished with this trip and she gets a little older, I will teach Harmony to use her gift. Until then, there are many beings who will attempt to steal her magic." While I was telling her this I heard her open her door and she spoke the words I gave her.

"Dad, that was cool."

"Oh yeah, they are Pixies and don't like being called fireflies. To them fireflies is the f-word.

You know I'm on a quest of sorts. The incident with the Warg hasn't been the only thing happening. I mean, everyday has been a new challenge." I continued with a recap of the whole trip and explained about the possibility of a battle at the end. I told her how I was now able to access my magic and how I glowed like the kid's toy, when I used it. How I became a Jedi Knight when I flamed-on, she understood. As I relayed the whole of my story, all I heard from Sam was a repeat of a word every now and then in the form of a question, like Magic? Blue butterfly? Another Queen? His son? Jedi? Wolf? As I wrapped up the tale, "and tomorrow is the Council of Elrond and the next day, well we will see." I knew she'd get my Johnny Tolkien reference.

"Don't go Daddy, you don't have to go."

"Actually Babe, I do. I have to go. I have no choice and I need to fix this. I am the only one who can."

"What will I tell Mom?"

"The truth, though she probably won't believe. Don't forget this conversation. Learn all you can from Tink and teach your kids."

"I will. Maybe I'll introduce Mom to Tink."

"Get his permission first."

"I will."

"I love you Babe and need to go."

"I love you too, Daddy." I reluctantly hung up. I bent my head and let the tears fall.

It took the better part of ten minutes for the waterworks to stop flooding my cheeks. Now my resolve was fixed. I was going to live through this and all would be well…I hoped.

Chapter 43

HOLY FLAMING FAIRIES

I dropped my head down on the pillow. I was exhausted, physically, emotionally and mentally. Thoughts about the next couple of days threatened to steal my sleep. It was only an idle threat. The darkness and silence descended on me.

My dreams were of the normal variety, completely forgettable. Somewhere in the night they got hijacked.

"Hello, Naomi," I said as soon as the weirdness happened. The veil of darkness parted and I was back in the glen. A light who was Naomi fell from the branches and flashed. There stood dream Naomi. She was beautiful as always in a flowing, pale yellow gown. The gown seemed to move as if it were underwater and caught in cross currents. It moved here and there at an almost random pace. I found it difficult taking my eyes from it. Although it moved all about, there was no wind. It was a dream and this was normal, even expected.

"Hello Roger, it is so lovely to see you."

"Please good Queen, get to the point. I need my beauty rest," and gestured toward my face.

"My, my Roger, so impatient. It is unbecoming on you."

"Yes, actually I am. What can I do for you? I wanted to sleep."

"I am here to ask what I can do for you?" She fainted innocently.

"How do you mean?" I retorted.

"I understand you've become a General of sorts. You will be trying your hand at taking my brother's throne?"

"And?" I knew Kalen had been reporting.

"And I offer my assistance."

"In return for what? There has to be a big old catch. Don't even try to act as if you are being altruistic. We both know the word has no translation in fairy."

"I am deeply hurt," though she didn't look hurt. She looked amused. I am so glad I am here to entertain her. I didn't take the bait and stood there with my head cocked to one side waiting for a truthful answer. She looked back at me, smiling.

My mind wandered. I was wondering if fairyland had crickets. I couldn't hear any, but maybe it was because this was dream fairyland.

After what seemed to be a lifetime, I turned and headed for the exit. I decided to test my magic and it worked. I heard a slight gasp from Naomi.

"So it is true," was all she said.

"Don't know what you heard, but I can touch and use my own magic now."

"This changes everything. I would like to help so I can create allies in the land across."

"Orin could use a few reinforcements, but beyond his needs we have it under control. When we finish and are successful, Kalen would be an excellent choice for an ambassador."

"I will consider your words." She reached to a table appearing behind her. "You have proven yourself ready to bear this." She was holding a beautiful sword. "It is called Peace. My mother had it forged with both human and fairy magic for Charles. When he gave up his magic, he returned the sword to Mother. He said, 'one day my children will return. This is for them. Make sure they know the name, Peace, is more than a name. It's a pursuit, a hope. A hope it will help maintain the peace wherever it is used.' I must also caution you, it is infused with a magic all its own."

"Infused? What does infused mean?" I asked gently.

"If you are using magic while wielding Peace, it will help you see your foe more clearly. Your ancestor was considered unbeatable with this in hand." She said this as she laid it across her hands and offered it to me.

I will do my best to relay what happened next, but even for a dream it was strange. I took the sword in my hands mimicking the way it was proffered. It was vibrating, or rather pulsing, like a heartbeat. I gave Naomi a questioning look.

"Peace is restless, and you must wield it so you and she may bond." Fairies and their bonding.

The sword was beautiful. The blade shone with an inner light. It was about three feet long and two and a half inches across at the hilt. It tapered slowly toward the tip and had a slight curve. I tested both the front and back edges and they were sharper than any blade I've ever felt. The hilt was an engraved image of a pixie holding a sword and an olive branch. The grip was very simple in design. It was made of wound threads alternating between gold, silver and a green vine looking thread. On the pommel was a rune, as I expected. The rune was two diamonds stacked point to point. There was a line running inside the diamonds from the top to the bottom point. The bottom diamond was missing its bottom left side. I figured this was the symbol for Peace. I carefully wrapped my hand around the grip to test the weight. I raised the sword in salute to Naomi, and then it bit me. Yes, something was biting my hand. I opened my hand to release the grip but I couldn't move my hand. I whipped the sword down and to the right trying to shake the damn thing from my hand. No luck.

"Fear not, young wizard," Naomi laughed with delight.

I brought the sword up to examine and to see if there was anything I could do. I saw movement on the blade. The engraved fairy was glowing red and moving. She was flapping her wings and flew slowly up the blade. She seemed to squeeze through the tip and disappear. I turned the blade over and she emerged from the tip and flew back to the hilt.

She flowed over the hilt on to the back of my hand and where she landed, it burned. She slowly melted into my hand going feet first. As her shoulders disappeared she stopped, looked up, winked and laughed, as she was absorbed. The fairy was the spitting image of this queen standing before me. When she was gone I regained control of my hand. I quickly sheathed the sword in a scabbard at my waist. I never even questioned how the scabbard got there. After all, I was in a dream and dealing with the Fae.

As I released the grip, the burning faded to a memory. I examined my hand. No marks were left on the back of my hand, even though it burned as she passed through. I was a bit surprised it wasn't a third degree burn. On the center of my right palm was a rune, a twin to the one on the pommel.

I held my hand up to Naomi, "Peace?" she nodded. "I see as a young fairy you did a little modeling?"

"You noticed," she seemed pleased I saw the resemblance. "My mother had me pose for this when I was very young."

"Was the bonding a one-time deal, because in a battle that could be distracting?"

"Yes, only this once. You are now bonded with Peace. No one will be able to wield Peace in battle except you, while you live. You can forfeit your bond only if you are willing. Once you release her, she will never be yours again. You are still new to your magic, so have a care when you wield her.

"Have a care, don't get angry, maintain control…I wonder, will I turn green and hulk out?"

"I don't know what you mean by hulk out, but you will have great power at your control."

"And with great power comes great responsibility, right?"

"Well said," replied Naomi. If she only knew. "Come forth, wizard," she commanded. I cautiously approached. I had already been burned once today, quite literally. She laid her hands on my head and gave a slight push. "Sleep," she incanted and I fell back into my pillow and slept a dreamless sleep, carefree for the rest of the night.

Chapter 44

ROGER YOU FOOL

I woke the next morning with a start. The sun rose over the windowsill and a beam of golden sunshine stole past the blinds to make me wince. I usually enjoy this time of day as my brain calibrates. I would slowly transition from a deep slumber to wakefulness. Today was different because last night's encounter with Naomi collided with my beautiful morning.

I blinked my eyes to clear the sleep and tried to focus on the throbbing in my right hand. There it was, right in the center of my palm. I was branded. I gazed about the room and found Peace leaning against the headboard. Already my heart was pounding and I found I was sweating. Visitations in my dreams followed by changes in my physical world tended to freak me out.

"Roger, are you well?" I heard Kalen ask from across the room. He startled me and I jumped nervously.

"Uh, Good morning. I'll be okay in a minute."

"I see you had a visitor," he said nodding to the sword.

"A visitor is one who comes welcomed, not one who…." I stopped because of the confused expression on Kalen's face. "Yeah, I had a lovely chat with Naomi and she gave me my great whatever Granddad's sword…"

"Peace," he said finishing my sentence in a reverent tone. "May I?" again he nodded to the sword.

"Sure," I said as I reached back to grab Peace and then handed it to Kalen.

"Sorry Roger, I cannot take it from you this way."

Of course not, what was I thinking, I thought to myself. "Okay, let's pretend I've never owned a magic fairy sword before. Especially one who bit and branded me as a how do you do." I stopped myself, realizing I was taking all my frustration out on Kalen. "Sorry mate, I guess I'm in a bit of a mood. Please explain what I must do." He actually smiled with understanding. I guess he'd had to deal with Naomi a time or two also.

"Do you remember how Naomi handed Peace to you?"

"Yes," and I shifted the sword to present it two-handed.

"You also must grant me permission to handle your blade."

"Wow, that sounds wrong, but I get what you mean. Any special words or incantations?" He shook his head no. "Kalen, I grant you permission to examine and test Peace." The blade vibrated in response. "Holy crap, is this sword alive?"

Kalen accepted Peace, "Sort of. Whenever fairy and human magic meet, they leave a residual spirit and it imitates life. It is why he put an engraved being on the blade. It acts as a focus, binding the power to the blade."

"You mean Little Naomi is the spirit of the blade? Does she share consciousness with anyone? I mean, can anyone convince her to turn on me?"

"No, only the one who holds the bond is connected."

"I guess you mean me," and I held up my palm.

"Do you truly understand what this means, Roger?"

"Sure, Peace," thinking he was asking about the rune branded on my hand.

"No, you fool. What being bonded to a blade like Peace means?" I'd never seen Kalen this insistent before. Yeah, he'd taunt me on the practice field but never like this. I didn't much care for it either.

"Obviously not," I said with disdain. "Why don't you explain."

"Only three swords like Peace were ever created. Only one fairy, well fairy half-breed to be factual, had the ability to forge them. He held both fairy and human magic. His name was Axton. He was born to a fairy princess and a very powerful wizard. Let me explain this union. Though we lived together and coexisted peacefully, the interbreeding of our people was forbidden. When he was born his parents were exiled, or so the stories say. I know differently. I learned at my father's knee that there are times when serving the Royalty will challenge your beliefs. They were escorted away from the village to a far off place where neither Fae nor human resided. There they were bound and executed. You need to promise me on our bond and on your magic this story will never leave your lips."

"On our bond and on my magic I so promise. So what happened to Axton?"

"He was raised as my brother. The Fae would never harm a child with Fae blood. He grew to be a metal craftsman. His blades are still the best. It is believed his mixed blood caused him to age more quickly than fairy, but slower than humans. He passed from this realm over a hundred and fifty years ago.

He made many fine swords over the years. His hands wrought the blade I carry. Swords like Peace were different. He made only three like this," he said and held up Peace for dramatic effect. "Each time he was commissioned by either a powerful wizard or a fairy Royal. The first was commissioned by one of the most powerful wizards who ever lived. Axton named it Love, but in human legend it was called Excalibur."

"You mean the sword was real? Merlin and all?"

"Yes, Merlin was the wizard who commissioned the sword. Some of his magic was forged into the steel also. The second was Faith. This one was for a fairy king from a land to the northeast, the land you call Norway. Today the whereabouts of Faith is unknown. It seems the king was fighting a battle with some creatures to the north. He lost the battle, his life and Faith. The last created was Peace.

The making of these swords cost my brother dearly. He would drain his magic into the sword as he folded the metal. He would ask fairies and wizards to donate their magic as well, but his was the controlling magic. The folding of the steel and the blending of the magic would take many weeks. When it was finally infused to his standard he would take as much time again honing the edge and polishing the blade. Finally, he would wrap the grip and engrave the marks. The final step involved a journey to the highlands up north where he would quicken the blade. This action breathed life into the sword. He always made these journeys alone and would share none of the details of the quickening, other than what I explained. Upon his return he always appeared half-dead and it would take a month before he returned to full health. He never recovered after Peace. One year after Peace's quickening, Axton died and I lost my brother."

Now, I felt like crap, "I am sorry Kalen. I meant no disrespect. I will cherish Peace and your brother's memory. I will pass this story on with Peace when it is time for us to part. I will bear this brand as a badge of honor."

Steel rang as Kalen set it free and began running it through its paces. Our room wasn't huge, but he waltzed through the room with the blade singing through the air. He was more graceful than any dancer on a stage. His face glowed with the memory of his brother and the joy of the movement.

I sat on my bed mesmerized by the performance. I wondered why I had been given this blade of legends and not Kalen. Surely it belonged in his hand.

He concluded his form and flowed to one knee with the sword sheathed. He presented it with outstretched hands. It was so smooth I thought it was part of the form. I was waiting for the next movement.

"I thank you sir, and return Peace to it's bonded mate."

"Oh," I said in surprise, "thank you, Kalen."

"No, it is I who must thank you. It was nice to dance with my brother again. He taught me the form you saw and many I have taught you. I forgot to mention he was my master of swords."

I was at a loss for words, "Let's go get some breakfast, but first I need a shower." But weirdly Kalen didn't. I worked up a sweat watching him, but the fairy was calm, cool, and sweat free.

"Fairies," I muttered as I trudged to the bathroom.

Chapter 45

BACON, SAUSAGE AND EGGS OH MY

Breakfast was an affair to remember.

The best word to describe the small dining room was cozy. It was like having breakfast at an eccentric aunt's house. None of the china matched, none of the silverware matched, no two chairs were alike and everything was perfectly different. All were the highest quality but nothing matched. When I mention china it was good quality bone china. It seemed to have been collected one piece at a time. It was truly a bizarre phenomenon. The colors were so different they matched. Uncle Neal went eclectic and it worked.

"Good morning," I said in greeting to a young couple sitting at one of the tables.

"Good morning," was their muted reply as they turned back to their coffee. It looks like I won't be making new friends today.

The air was thick with the smells of coffee, crisp bacon, sausage and something sweet. All the goodness emanated from the kitchen and made my mouth water. On a sideboard were several kinds of juice and milk, but in the corner I found what I sought, coffee. I grabbed my cup from the table and headed to the sideboard.

"Kalen, coffee?" I offered to be polite. I knew he preferred any type of fruit juice.

The door to the kitchen swung open and out came Neal with a tray laden with food. Eggs, bacon, sausage, homemade bread toasted, fresh fruit and French toast. All for the couple I greeted earlier.

The plates of grub filled the small round tables.

"Morning, Unc," I said as he finished piling the food on the table.

"Morning Roger, hungry I hope?"

"Starved," and I was famished, even more so now that I saw the food.

"Good morning, Kalen," he said more like a question.

"Morning, Neal, it is quite good to see you again," and Kalen embraced the old man. "I am sorry I didn't greet you properly yesterday, but it wasn't my place." He nodded toward me.

"I understand, old friend," Neal replied. Kalen had recognized him but wanted Neal to tell me we were related and how.

Neal began, " How fare you good f…" he looked to the other table, "Uh, good sir. It has been a long time.'

"Indeed it has. I suppose you are aware of the events occurring in your realm?" Kalen asked.

"Roger and I had a long chat last night and I believe I am familiar with the current events. I would like to be at this meeting."

"Will you share our travels or will you simply care to join us in the glen?"

"I would care to join you in the glen. I have a sanctuary in the garden." When he bought the house years ago he had created an English garden. An assortment of flowers and rose bushes lined the paths as they wound through the garden leading to the center. Instead of an ornamental fountain or birdbath, there was nothing but a ten-foot round patch of grass. It was perfectly manicured, but was only grass. He was preparing for today. "Kalen, I will need a token to your land." He needed a piece of the stick to get to fairyland.

"Do you know the words?

"How could I forget? You drilled them into Eric's brain and he did the same for me. Did you visit Eric over the years?"

Kalen nodded and Neal continued. "Was he as happy as he said in his letters?"

"Yes, though he missed his brother. He understood the need but didn't much like it." Kalen said, "He was never afraid to tell the Queen, or me, how he felt about this forced separation."

"I do remember his quick wit tended to get him in trouble. Also, I ended up on the receiving end of his tongue a time or two," added Neal. This brought a smile to both of them.

"So Kalen," Neal asked, "the usual?"

Kalen lifted an eyebrow and in reply, "Please."

"You lad, will get the house special."

"Sounds good," I said. Kalen and I settled into our chairs. I doctored my coffee with sugar and real cream. We sat in a comfortable silence. Kalen appeared to be caught in a pleasant memory and I was right at home.

In the kitchen came sounds of cooking, pots clanking, knives chopping and Neal whistling softly as he worked. The other guests were eating their fare with much gusto. I heard sounds of silverware scraping on china and a few of those yummy sounds people unconsciously make. They also spoke in hushed tones about how much they enjoyed the food.

I sipped my coffee and enjoyed the cacophony of silence. When Kalen roused from his memory he took a sip of his purplish juice.

"Kalen, I'd like to get a practice session in this morning. We haven't far to drive and now everyone and their brother knows where we are going so we haven't anyone to fear, do we?"

"No, a treaty is in place till we meet this evening."

"So we can drive on the interstates and get there faster." Kalen sat there examining my face for what seemed a long time.

His face split into a smile, "You want to try Peace," he

accused me.

"Well of course I do, and I would like to work on the bow as well. I may need to rely on my abilities tomorrow night."

"Fair enough, we can use his sanctuary."

"You've seen it?"

"I took a walk last night and found the gardens, peaceful."

"How about an hour or so after we eat?"

"Sounds fine," Kalen replied. Our schedules were set and out came the food. My side of the table was overflowing with the same fare I'd coveted earlier, much to my delight. In front of Kalen he put a large plate, no that's not quite right, it was more like a platter of food. The platter was covered with all kinds of fresh fruit. Balanced on top of the heap was a generous hunk of homemade bread. Kalen's eye sparkled with delight.

"Neal, is this your Mum's sweet bread?"

"Yes it is, I remembered how you liked it." Said Neal beaming with a smile from ear to ear.

"You remembered, but how?"

"Who do you think had to help Mum in the kitchen when you two would traipse off? I don't make this bread too often. My guests tend to like the overly sweet cinnamon rolls. I remember how you had to have it every morning and Mum loved to watch you eat it." I asked for a taste and it was quite pleasant.

"Do you think I could get the recipe. I am family," I asked.

"Sure, I'll give you my Mum's original. I don't need it anymore." And he tapped his head. "I have it here. I have a pile of dishes calling my name. Enjoy boys." he directed at Kalen and me. He paused mid-step for a fraction of a second after he realized what he said. It was nice to see the fairy weirdness had the same effect on someone else.

We dug into our plate like we'd been starved for weeks and it was good.

Chapter 46

OKAY, IMPORTANT SAFETY TIP

Most of the breakfast dishes were cleared and I was sipping on a cool cup of coffee. Neal, Kalen and I were alone in the house. The other couple had finished breakfast and checked out.

"Neal, when can I expect you back east? I know my brothers and my Mum would love to meet you."

"Maybe when the dust settles in your wake, lad."

"Okay, keep Christmas open," I turned to Kalen. "I'm going to head up to change. Will you be ready in twenty minutes?"

"Sounds good," Kalen agreed as I departed.

"Ready for what?" Neal inquired.

"Roger and I are going to have one last practice session. Naomi visited him last night and gave him a present he's anxious to test."

"Don't tell me, he got Peace?"

Kalen was surprised by his directness and by the fact that he knew Peace. "How do you know Peace?"

"Do you think you are the only one to visit Eric and me? You may have been the first, but certainly not the last. You've tasted my sweet bread. The bread alone, in and of itself, would attract Fae. But Peace, she was my ancestor's sword. Some of the Fae thought we would like to know our history. This means…"

"Yes, Roger has learned to use his magic," Kalen interrupted. "Peace was destined for magic users within your family line. If Naomi had decided to withhold her, Peace still would have found her way to Roger. Naomi is a fairy with great honor, so she did as honor would dictate."

"Is it as wonderful as they say?"

Kalen smiled from ear to ear remembering his dance a short while ago, "Yes."

"May I join your session? It has been quite a while since I tested my blade against another."

"Have you kept up with your forms?"

"Every day." Kalen nodded approval. Neal rose and cleared the remaining dishes. He went through the door and piled them in the sink.

At the prescribed time we met at the sanctuary. Oddly enough, we all arrived at the exact same time from three different paths in the garden. There before us was the grassy circle.

"Neal, I'm a bit curious. Why a circle and why this size?"

"A circle because it is the center of an English garden and it reminds me of the glen where Eric and Kalen trained. It is also at the heart of my garden and provides much privacy. I can practice my forms without interference. A ten foot circle is plenty of space for most of the forms. Only a couple need extra space, and paths suffice for these."

We approached Kalen from either side. I had Peace sheathed on my belt and my quiver strapped to my back. I carried my practice sword and my unstrung bow. Neal had a katana which appeared well used, but in excellent condition. Kalen placed the stick, but rose again before he spoke the words.

"Neal?" and he invited him toward the stick.

"Thank you, Kalen; it would be an honor." Neal knelt and opened the passage to the glen.

"Roger, on our return trip I will teach you the words of passage."

"Thanks," I said as I mentally prepared for training. We descended into the glen. I placed my practice sword, bow and quiver aside and strode to the center. I embraced my magic and reached for Peace.

Kalen stayed my hand before I could reach the grip. "You do not need to hold your magic with Peace."

"I thought I needed the magic to reach my highest potential."

"Peace has her own magic. Please, try without."

"Okay," and I released the magic and set Peace free. She became part of me and strength flowed in my veins. I began to move through the forms. I was surprised by how effortlessly I moved.

The sword took me and guided me through my forms. I flowed from one to another, moving always faster and faster. The trees around me were a blur as I spun with Peace slicing through the air, whistling as it parted before her. I finished my forms with a two-handed slice and a jumping turn followed by a two-handed overhead strike taking me to one knee. Peace was out to my right while my left hand moved symmetrically in the opposite direction. My head was bowed reverently and my breathing was deep but controlled. I slowly came back into focus and found Neal clapping with delight. Kalen smiled and nodded.

"Holy crap," I blurted as I sheathed Peace. "That felt great. How'd it look?"

"Your forms were perfect, even the two Peace taught you."

"What are you talking about?"

"The last two forms you performed I never showed you. It seems Peace wanted you to know them."

"As I flowed from one to another they all seemed so familiar."

"The magic of the blade."

"What if I use my magic as I use the blade?"

"Then you must be extremely careful," he said a bit louder. I expect to emphasize the point.

"It sounds sort of like crossing streams of proton packs."

"It kind of is," added Neal. "It would be bad." I smiled, finally someone who has seen a movie and I couldn't resist.

"I'm fuzzy on the whole good / bad thing. What do you mean "bad"?"

Neal smiled back, "Try to imagine all life as you know it stopping instantaneously and every molecule in your body exploding at the speed of light. Total protonic reversal."

Now I was chuckling. Uncle Neal was a movie guy. It must be in the bloodline. So, I finished the line from Ghostbusters, "Right that's bad. Okay. All right, important safety tip. Thanks Egon." I raised my sword tip to Uncle Neal in salute. He tapped it with his. Kalen stood there shaking his head, muttering, not too quietly, "Humans."

"Joking aside, what are the risks of holding power and using the sword."

"If your control slips for a moment and you lash out with your power it could eliminate all life around you."

"How far would this circle of death reach? Are we talking feet or yards?"

"No, more like miles or dozens of miles."

Neal whistled, "He has that much juice?" Kalen nodded.

"Shit, okay, important safety tip." I turned to Kalen with Peace in hand, "Let's dance." I was ready to spar.

"Put Peace away. I will not cross swords against Peace."

"Really? We are only going to spar."

"No. She knows only how to fight, not practice."

"Mind if I take her for a spin while you two cross your swords?" Neal asked.

"Not at all," and I presented Peace, granting permission. I embraced my power and saluted Kalen with my other sword. Peace's lessons remained within me and I found I was able to best Kalen, at least half the time. We danced for a while and when we stopped Neal returned Peace. I sheathed Peace and the three of us took turns fighting each other. Neal was good, very good. He didn't have the fairy's speed, but was able to anticipate and deflect Kalen's attack.

When we fought I didn't use my magic and found we were evenly matched. During my break, I practiced with my bow and filled the target with arrows. I was feeling ready. I was confident in my abilities with both weapons, but had no idea how I would fare in battle.

"I stood and watched as Neal and Kalen finished."

"Hey Neal, not bad for an old guy."

"You ain't too bad for a young pup, either." He was definitely family.

"Kalen, do you think we will come to blows with Aelfric?"

Kalen took a moment to ponder and said, "Yes. He has too much pride and confidence. There is only one way to avoid conflict. Give him all he wants." He said it like a challenge.

"So, a fight it will be."

Chapter 47

FAIRIES IN THE KITCHEN, NOW WHAT

As we left the glen Kalen turned and retrieved the stick. He took his blade and carved a small curl of bark and handed it to Neal.

"We will meet at sunset. All who travel have been afforded safe passage to and from the meeting."

"Thank you, Kalen," replied Neal formally. "I will see you tonight."

"I have to hit the shower and change before we get on the road." I said out of habit. I'd had a hard workout and it usually meant I would need a shower. I found I hadn't even broken a sweat. I worked harder today than any previous session but I wasn't sweaty.

"Magic - the perfect antiperspirant for today's warrior. One spray before a battle and it will last you through a lovely dinner in the conquered city, worry free." I thought to myself. Wow I was losing it. Instead of a shower I changed my cloths and dragged my luggage to the truck.

I walked back in the house after stowing my gear. I headed to the kitchen to find Neal. I swung the door open and saw blurs of light zipping out the window. A plate clattered on the counter and a pot clanged on the floor near an open cabinet. Other than the plate and pot, the kitchen was spotless. Looks like Neal has a few kitchen helpers. On the counter was a large paper sack with 'Roger and Kalen' written across the side.

"Oh, there you are," Neal said as he entered. He walked to the plate and pot, casually put them away.

"I was looking for you and I saw...."

"Good, you found me," he interrupted shaking his head as if to say 'stop talking.' He plated half of a dozen cookies and placed them on the counter.

He grabbed the sack and my arm and took us both out of the kitchen. He whispered, "I have a few helpers and they are very shy. They don't like me talking about them either."

I'd read about these fairies called brownies. They would help with cleaning and such around the house.

"They like cookies I gather?"

"Pretty much any baked sweet. It's not a requirement, but anyone who helps me, deserves some sort of thank you."

"I'd love to sign them up at my place. Did they make the sack lunch?"

"Yes, they did. The word is out among the Fae about how you two plan to make things right."

"Thank them for me."

"I did. This is what the cookies are for." He had walked me toward the truck. "I will see you tonight. Tomorrow, my blade is yours."

"Thank you I accept. It will be good having family watch my back. I trust Kalen implicitly and know he will protect me, but I think he, or rather Naomi, has her own plan."

"Even the good ones, and Kalen is the best of those, have to answer to someone."

"True enough, but I do have the bond and the oath."

"You two are bonded?"

"Well yeah. I assumed it was a typical deal for them."

"Have you asked Kalen how many times he'd been bonded? And how many times with a human?"

"What's the big deal?"

"Bonding lad. It is a huge deal in their world. I would bet you are his second bond. The first will be his wife."

"Bonding is a marriage thing?"

"Yes and no. They do bond when they marry. You can

see the advantage of a marriage bond, right?"

"It does make sense."

"But a warrior bond, while similar in the exchange, isn't quite as intimate."

"They do like to gloss over the details. I didn't know any of this."

"It is an honor of the highest form. To be offered is a big deal all by itself, but to have a warrior, one of Kalen's stature? Yes lad, this is a huge deal, really huge."

Neal was beside himself over this bond. I'll have to find out more about this bonding stuff.

Sometime during the conversation we had arrived at the truck. It was loaded and Kalen sat swinging his legs on the tailgate, waiting patiently. I gave Neal a hug. "See you tonight, Uncle."

"Drive safe and get me a room when you get there. I'll need a place to lay my head this evening."

"I will."

Neal and Kalen exchanged what I called a warrior's handshake. It's when they grasp each other's forearm instead of hands. They also touched foreheads. I guess Neal has been around the Fae a bit more than I have.

We climbed into the truck and hit the road. It was nice to drive without watching out for the wild Fae. They won't be popping around corners or jumping from shadows on this leg of the journey.

Our route was along the interstates today, but we still had a healthy drive ahead of us. We settled in for the ride. Tonight we would be staying at another bed and breakfast in Casper, Wyoming. I wonder if I have anymore fairy adjacent relatives waiting for me.

And the miles ticked by.

Chapter 48

OMG

The drive to Wyoming was boring. Kalen and I spent hours discussing that night's itinerary and our plan when we met Aelfric. Without the threat of imminent death hiding around the next bend it was a simple road trip. Actually, before I started this journey, I expected the trip cross country to be exactly like this.

We were staying at another bed and breakfast tonight. This one was recommended by Uncle Neal and was called the Sunburst Lodge. It advertised lots of acreage and hiking trails. To me that meant wilderness and good places to set the stick.

While we drove, the sun rose and stretched across the sky. The sun was half way to the horizon when we stopped for dinner. Tonight the menu was simple - drive thru burgers. Burgers were on the menu a lot lately. It's a good thing I like burgers. Now that dinner was complete we only need to concentrate on the meeting.

We saw the lodge from down the road and it looked like a log castle on a hill. Uncle Neal knows how to pick a place to stay. When we pulled up, Paige and Johnson greeted us. These were the friendliest puppies I'd ever met. Mary was a step or two behind her pups and greeted us as if we were long lost relatives. She gave us a quick tour and showed us our room. Our room was the Dreadnaught room. It had five beds, granted four of the beds were in the form of bunk beds, but it would do. I explained to Mary that my Uncle would join us later.

We settled in the room and I strapped Peace on my back. I was getting good at concealing it beneath my jacket. Our bags were settled and we were off to hike a trail and look for a spot to enter the glen.

The hike was pleasant. It felt good to stretch the legs after sitting in the truck all day. The vistas were majestic. They made me think of every cowboy riding into the sunset scene I'd ever watched, but this was better because I was seeing it for myself. We quickly found a spot close to the lodge, but hidden from view.

We keep hiking to pass the time while we waited for sunset.

"So Kalen, what does Naomi have planned for tomorrow?" I asked bluntly after we'd hiked for a half hour.

I do believe I caught him off guard, "What do you mean?" was all he could get out. I saw he was flustered by the question.

"I'm thinking somehow we are doing her bidding with our plan. Maybe we aren't doing it the way she wishes, but the end result is what she is hoping to see accomplished."

"What makes you say this, Roger?"

"Lots of little things have been rattling around up here," I touched my head. "Her wanting to meet me on the first leg of my journey. Aelfric summoned me, not Naomi. She provided me with a warrior to guide and protect me. Don't misunderstand. I appreciate all you have done with and for me. I truly value your friendship. But you are Naomi's to the core." He nodded at this. "While I'm rolling, how many bonds have you held?"

"Your bond was my second," Kalen replied without hesitation. Uncle Neal was right.

"I'm guessing you are married and your wife holds the other?"

"Yes," he said nodding again.

"Is it your wife who you talk to through the stick?" I

wanted to see if I could get him to talk about his life in fairyland.

"You noticed?" It was my turn to nod. "Yes it is."

"I assume she is back at Naomi's realm?"

"You could say she was." He was being a bit evasive about her identity.

It hit me like a brick, "No, it couldn't be," I couldn't believe what I suspected. "Please tell me I'm wrong, but you are married to Naomi?"

Normally Kalen was able to react to anything I said or did with a look of, well, indifference best describes his reaction. Kalen, the Hun's have invaded your village..."Okay." No reaction. A grand piano is falling from the heavens to crush you..."Alright." Disbelief. Nothing seemed to ruffle his feathers except this. "How do you know this?" He actually yelled. "Who told you?" and his hand went to the hilt of his sword. Mine went to Peace in reaction. He was scaring the hell out of me.

"I figured it out...I guessed!" I yelled back. "And it seems I guessed correctly." I should have kept my big mouth shut.

Like a switch being thrown, he calmed himself. Bipolar doesn't even begin to cover it. One second he was a bull pawing at the earth ready to charge, and the next a lamb grazing in the field.

"Damn, Kalen, what the hell happened? How do you switch gears so quickly?"

"I am sorry, Roger. I didn't mean to lose my temper. Naomi and I are married, but marriage among Fae is a very private matter. We don't have elaborate weddings like humans. We bond alone with the stars as our witnesses.

Now I felt awkward. The memory of last year when I had my little dalliance with Naomi in the glen, came to mind. He hadn't once even mentioned it. Could this be why he didn't react at the diner? Was he waiting for the right moment to end me? "I have to ask, last year when Naomi and I were in the glen..."

"Let me stop you right there. Don't judge our marriage

by human morals. What Naomi did with you in the glen was not a violation of our bond." He was saying the words with his mouth but his eyes were far away. "She is a queen and needed your magic. And besides, she was in her human form."

"So human form indiscretions don't count?"

"The way fairies exchange love is through the bond. I could demonstrate?"

"Hey dude, I don't swing that way, but no judgment."

He laughed, "No it's not what you think. Love is exchanged through the spiritual not through the physical. You saw Neal and I do so earlier today."

"The warrior handshake and head bump thingy."

Again he laughed at the stupid human, "Yes, but because you and I are bonded, you will experience something closer to the exchange I was describing. It won't be as intense but will give you an idea."

"Okay," I said reluctantly, "but be gentle. I'm a bond-sex virgin." Yep, it went right over his head. Why do I even bother? I have to admit I was a bit nervous.

"Relax, Roger. We are completing a normal greeting or parting gesture among the Fae. It is to us what a handshake is to you."

I found his words reassuring. I offered him my hand. We clasped forearms. At this connection a tingle moved up my arm. He pulled me toward him and our heads touched. In the words of a teenage girl, OMG!

When I was a kid, we'd go swimming in the lake as soon as the calendar marked June. It didn't matter that the water was freezing. To us it was summer, and summer meant swimming in the lake. As to how you entered the frigid water, there was only one sane choice. You jumped in without hesitation. Any other method would allow you to talk yourself out of swimming. It sounds like a horrible experience, but only the first shock of cold water surrounding your body is excruciatingly painful, and only for about a second. Once you give your underwater primal scream your mind and body simply accept the feeling as pleasurable, or rather refreshing.

The first moment of the bond was like the shock of cold water which was quickly followed by a warm embrace. The embrace was euphoric and flushed all of the toxins that life's stresses left behind. My mind cleared. All the worries I'd been harboring, my wife, my kids, bills, work, the impending battle, everything was gone. I knew only the presence of Kalen and felt loved. All too soon the feeling evaporated and the world returned with all of its baggage. I was standing in front of Kalen slack jawed. I was speechless.

"How long were we doing the bond thing?" I stammered.

"Less than a minute. Naomi and I stay together until the stars fade so the marriage bond is much more intense."

"You are kidding. How could it be more intense?" It was hard to conceive.

"Yes," he said nodding with a sly grin across his face.

"Thank you for showing me this. I'm sure there are other things I should know about your customs. For instance, is this always an appropriate greeting?"

"If you feel a handshake is appropriate then this is what a Fae would do."

"Will I get all bug-eyed with others, or was this an element of our bond?"

"With your magic, you will feel a stronger connection than most humans, but it won't be as strong as you and me."

"Cool, I need to make more Fae friends. How about when I meet King Aelfric or even Queen Cheryl…is this a good greeting for royalty?"

"Yes, especially when you greet royalty, but expect more intensity from them. Aelfric knows you've been travelling with me and will expect you to know our ways."

"This is the first thing you've showed me."

"I know, and now I am telling you more. I know you are a quick study."

I found a place to sit and he continued class. The sun slowly sank toward the horizon. He stopped the lesson as the sun reached the hilltop. We stood and watched. It was magnificent. The sky danced with color as the sun was pulled lower and lower till a green flash shot across the sky.

"Are you ready?" Kalen asked.

"Yes," I reached out my hands grasping either side of his head. I reached out with my bond and filled Kalen with my magic. "Now we both are."

Kalen placed the stick and opened the way.

"Let's do this, Kalen." With grim determination we stepped into the glen.

Chapter 49

YOU ARE ONE EVIL TEMPTRESS

Kalen and I were first to arrive. Our crossing put us in one of the many entrances of the glen. I'd never really paid too much attention to the other pathways, but today they would not escape my notice.

I felt a hand on my shoulder, "Easy, Roger," Kalen sensed my nervous tension. He had on his typical blank expression. I was grateful for it at this moment. I found it calming. Kalen waved his hand and a comfortable chair formed from the root of the tree.

"Roger, sit here and practice a form."

"How can I practice a form while I sit?"

He tapped my head, "Close your eyes and practice here."

I did as he suggested and found it to be very soothing. I felt my magic rise and my emotions stabilize. I was a lean mean fighting machine. Peace's magic touched me and everything grew sharper. The glen came more into focus. Details I'd not noticed before came into view. I saw a bright glow surrounding Kalen. It was his magic's glow. I don't know how I knew what it was, I simply knew.

"Kalen, thanks, I needed that. Were you able to form the chair because of the magic refill?"

"Oh yeah," he said a bit enthused.

"How much did I actually give you? I was shooting for the level when we first bonded."

"You missed. You will want to back off the amount by a lot when you give the Royals power."

"Giving them less isn't an insult?"

He chuckled, "No, not in the least. You really don't know how much magic you have, do you? I now have enough to challenge Naomi for her realm. You gave me twice the amount she took."

"I gave you that much?"

"Yes, and as tempting as it is, I believe you need to take some back."

"Wait a second, won't this help us in the fight with Aelfric?"

""The temptation is too great. I don't want to abuse the magic, like he did. With this much power it would be too easy to use it. How did you visualize giving me magic?"

"I know it's silly, but I poured my power into a glass. I simply filled the glass."

"To the brim, I'm betting." I nodded. "You definitely need to take some back. You filled me to the maximum amount I could contain. Fill my glass to no more than an eighth full. And do the same for any transfer to any fairy, never more than an eighth."

"Okay, are you sure?"

"At an eighth it is as powerful as any king or queen. I was almost as powerful as a god."

I took him by his head and saw the glass dump all but an eighth back into me. Then I gave back a splash or two.

"Thank you," he sighed with relief. "You left more than I asked."

"Yep, live with it. I want you to be above all I deal with today. Don't take this personally but I don't trust the Fae. I trust you."

"He took my head and touched his forehead to mine. I had a flash of the warm embrace. "You are wise, Roger, thank you," he said quietly.

"Now can you teach me the chair making thing?" I asked brightly.

He chuckled, " You never stop."

"Nope, " I smiled back. Then came a sound. It was like someone walking through dried leaves, and out popped Uncle Neal.

"There you are," he said to us and greeted Kalen. He came to me and put out his hand. I clasped his forearm and touched foreheads. No warm embrace. I really didn't expect one, but you never knew.

"Someone has been learning fairy customs."

"Yep, Kalen has been teaching me my Emily Post," I said pretending to raise a teacup with my pinky properly extended.

"Am I the first?" and no sooner were the words out of his mouth than three wolves padded into the glen silent as death.

The leading wolf was what I would call an average size for a wolf. She was pure white, the white of freshly fallen snow. Her eyes were an iridescent blue. On her flanks were two of the biggest beasts I'd ever seen. Those two males made her look like a puppy, by comparison. The one to her right was black. The black offered a complete contrast to her white, but he had the same eyes. The beast to her left had a beautiful grey to white coloring bringing to mind a Husky, if a Husky was two hundred plus pounds of teeth and claws. The eyes on this one glowed a bright daffodil yellow.

Their transformation was astounding. It wasn't at all like what you see in the movies. They simply stood up and by the time they were upright they were human. There stood Chepi Luna. Oh, did I forget to mention they were fully clothed? Beside her stood two large, heavily muscled gentlemen. I was glad they were on Team Roger.

I greeted Chepi first. I clasped her forearm and said, "Thank you for showing yourself. Be welcomed." We then touched heads. Kalen never warned me about the difference that greeting a female would make. Chepi was a royal in her clan so it bumped the octane, but the sweet feminine pull damn near curled my toes. I almost, now I said almost, lifted my foot to the back. There was no shock of cold here, only a tidal pull into erotic pleasure. I backed off quickly to see her smile at me. She knew, and was somehow controlling it. I'd have to talk to Kalen later.

Chepi stepped back and said, "Allow me to introduce Dubhan, Alpha of the Moon Runners, Descendant of the Silent Death, and Conor, Alpha of the Shadow Killers." I greeted Dubhan first, following the order of introduction. "Dubhan may my hunting grounds fill your belly," and we touched heads. Next I said, "Conor, may your pack prosper."

All seemed pleased by this formal greeting. "Allow me to introduce General Kalen of the Realm to the East and my Uncle Neal White," and greetings were exchanged. I noted that no one else seemed to have a hard time with Chepi's greeting. I also noted a flash of recognition when Neal and Dubhan greeted, but it seemed amicable.

"Neal, please show our distinguished guests to the offered refreshments." The corner where they entered was to be their area. Kalen had fashion four areas with tables and chairs, and each table was laden with food and drink. This setup at the corner where they entered enabled me to only have to watch two more corners.

I pulled Kalen aside, "What's the deal with greeting females?"

He smiled guiltily, "Oh, I should have warned you. Women can twist the exchange and make you an offer with it. You did fine with Chepi. Always remember to embrace your power before touching your head."

"She was making me an offer?"

"Probably not, but she judged your reaction. She sized you up."

"How did I do?"

"Great actually. I've watched dignitaries get lost in the embrace but the women claim innocence. It can be a social embarrassment. You did well, actually very well. Remember to use your power and it will provide you with a bit of an advantage. Cheryl won't expect it and maybe it will lessen her effect."

"I am a little worried about Cheryl or rather Danaus. Sorry, I'll get it right when I need to. I have the name Cheryl stuck in my head."

The next to enter was Orin and two of his retainers. When I first met Orin I thought he was a good guy albeit a bit disgruntled. Today he stomped in muttering angrily.

His voice was raised for all to hear, "Why are my people barred from entering?" This next comment was directed toward Kalen, "Are your own kind, no longer welcome?"

Kalen leaned as if he was going to deal with this jerk, but I placed my hand on Kalen's arm, "This is mine," I said quietly.

I approached Orin with a pleasant smile on my face. It was killing me to placate such a pompous ass. I extended my hand in welcome, "Prince Orin, I bid you welcome." He slapped it aside.

"How dare you refuse entrance to my people."

"Are these two not of your people?"

"Don't play games with me, human," he turned from me. "Kalen, attend me," he commanded so loudly his voice echoed in the glen.

"Kalen, stand fast," it was my turn to command.

Orin's hand went to the blade on his hip.

I continued, "Dare you threaten your host, or do you wish to practice the sword with me?" By now Peace was sitting comfortably in my hand. I heard a collective gasp from around the glen. I was attempting to maintain a pleasant smile but was told later I'd failed miserable. I instead looked rather insane with the smile I wore.

"Are you threatening me?" Orin asked. He had lost a bit of the commanding tone.

"No, I thought you wanted to practice before we begin the meeting I invited you to this evening. I am simply trying to oblige my guest." The whole time my eyes were on his hand. It moved away from his sword. "No?" I asked innocently and smoothly put Peace away. "Then allow me," I wasn't really asking and my tone reflected this, "to greet you in the spirit of Peace." Yeah the double entendre wasn't lost on Orin. I saw him blanch slightly. I extended my hand again. He took my hand in a human greeting, again with the insults. I slid my hand to the fairy greeting and embraced my power. I pulled him toward me to touch foreheads. It was more like a quick head-butt but it sufficed.

He then introduced me to the two warriors at his side. The first was a young lady named Raise, which in human tongue would be Rose. She had a slight athletic build and was stunning. I am still waiting to meet an ugly fairy maiden…but I digress. As I met her eyes, I saw a grim determination. She was leery of me after the little pissing match I had won.

I extended my hand, "The roses of my land pale with jealousy at the mention of your name," and we touched heads. The embrace was warm and quick.

"Well met, wizard," was her reply.

Kalen had prepared me for these exchanges. He'd guessed correctly as to who would attend the prince. The other attendant was a large man who looked to be of an age with me. He wasn't as big as an alpha, he was close, but his face was used to laughing. His eyes shone with joy as a grin split his face. He had nothing to prove to anyone. He was called Foster, guardian of the forest.

I took his hand, "The trees I meet on my travels sing of your deeds. Be welcome." His hand fit all the way around my forearm and overlapped on itself. When our heads touched, a warmth, missing from the previous two greetings, washed over me in waves. It infused me with the joy I saw on his face.

"Thank you, wizard."

"Please call me Roger," I'd offered my name only to him.

"Orin, did you not agree to the conditions of this meeting?"

"I did agree, but I am a Prince," as if being a Prince carried weight with me.

"So you agreed to the conditions, good." I said ignoring his complaint. "Please, we have provided refreshments for you to wash away your travels. Enjoy while we await the arrival of our other guests." He wasn't happy but he turned and headed to his corner.

I turned and headed back toward Neal and Kalen, hoping my shaking knees didn't give me away. I found all eyes watched me, and the Warg were reevaluating their first impression.

"So how'd I do?" I whispered to Kalen.

"Holy cow, Roger, that was bloody awesome," interjected Neal as he clapped me on the shoulder.

"He is right," added Kalen. "Orin hoped to take control of the meeting with his ploy. He figured he needed to act like a King here so he could claim his father's throne after we depose him. You shut him down. I thought he was going to draw on you but you pulled Peace so fast. I never saw you reach for her and there she was in your hand. Peace was truly meant for you. He will try again when the meeting starts, but if you maintain your authority no one will pay him heed."

"Will he accept the position we have in mind for him when this is finished?"

"It will be either him or someone else. So his choices are the position offered, or the old country with the father he helped oust. He'll accept."

Our conversation was interrupted by menacing, throaty growls. I looked to Chepi, Dubhan, and Conor. They were now wolves growling at the empty corner.

I turned and watched. Around a tree came harmless looking but deadly butterflies. There were three blue Phengard flitting, as butterflies will do. The largest one landed and with a flash of light became Cheryl. She was wrapped in a Grecian tunic that seemed to defy gravity as it hung on her. It covered enough to call it clothing, but left absolutely nothing to the imagination. It shifted and moved when she walked, always threatening to fall to the ground. The other two butterflies alighted on her shoulders.

"Wish me luck, boys," I muttered as I stepped toward her.

"I bid you fond greetings, my fair Queen Danaus." I took a deep breath to steel my nerve and extended my hand. Her hand was soft as she gently laid it on my arm, but her grip was firm. As our heads closed on each other she said, "I would prefer if you called me Cheryl. I told you, I love the way you say my name." The next part all happened within a one second time period. I was about to embrace my power to soften the effects of the greeting but felt I needed to answer. As I drew breath to form a reply I inhaled her essence. And we all know what her essence does to me, so I answered dreamily, "Okay, Cheryl," and then our heads connected. What washed over me was warm, passionate, and ever so inviting. What Kalen sent through me was love. This was pure high-octane unfiltered lust and oh, it felt good. My heart was hammering in my chest and my breath quickened to match my heart's pace.

Do you remember the first time you fell in love? When I see it as an adult I call it puppy love, but as a kid it was the kind of love about which epic poems were written, where daughters defy parents and run to their lover's arms, and every song on the radio was sung to exclaim your feelings. For me it happened in middle school and she was all I could think about. My first thought in the morning and my last thought at night. My daily quest was to get a glimpse of her beauty or hear a gentle word. This exchange was ten times worse. As I floated along this river of love, a vision of Kalen flashed in my head across our bond saying 'come back.' My eyes popped open. I drew a gasp of air and yanked myself back. I stumbled back a few steps. Cheryl laughed with such joy I heard it pass contagiously around the glen. Hell, Orin even joined the chorus. After a moment or two I joined in.

"Cheryl, you are one evil temptress," I said with a smile playing across my lips.

"Thank you, but I wished to more than tempt. I was hoping for a taste," she said smiling coyly back.

I regained what dignity I could muster. "Please introduce me to you attendants."

"I haven't the magic to spare," she said humbly. "Please, if you would allow them to touch a single drop of your magic they would be able to join us." I held out my palm and willed a single drop of magic to pool in my palm. The two butterflies flew, landing on my hand. Through my bond I felt Kalen tense. Two tiny balls of light flew from my hand and formed a pair of breathtakingly beautiful maidens. They were as scantly dressed as Cheryl and were kneeling before me with their heads bowed.

The one named Lily had pure white hair. The other was Heather and had hair the color of pale lavender. They smelled like a field of flowers and I embraced my magic as I remembered what Cheryl's scent did to me.

I greeted each in turn and they didn't mess with me the way their Queen did. I walked them to their refreshments. Cheryl took my arm and floated along beside me.

"I need you to turn off the pheromones during the meeting. I don't want to have to hold my magic and we do not need the distraction."

"I will behave," she purred and kissed my cheek as she let go of my arm.

As I walked back to Kalen and Neal I could see they were resisting the urge to laugh.

"Go ahead, I deserve it," and they did a bit louder and longer than I'd hoped for. "She distracted me right before we touched heads and I forgot all about the magic. Thanks for the help Kalen."

"You are welcome. She is a good one to have as an ally." Kalen added.

Neal asked, "Are they really as deadly as the stories say?"

"Looking at them in human form it is hard to believe, but yes, Neal, they are among the most fierce and deadly Fae."

I took a cup of cool, clear liquid from our table. I whispered, "Here we go." Then I raised my voice for all to hear, " I would like to raise my glass to once again to welcome you to this conference. May our talks become the actions which will return your land and free your spirit. To success," and I drank deeply.

All raised their drinks and joined me in my toast, "Success!" resounded thru the glen.

Now the work begins.

Chapter 50

YOU'D ONLY ANGER HIM ANYWAY

"Kalen, if you would," I asked gesturing to the center of the glen.

He closed his eyes and a slight rumble shook the glen. In the middle rose a large round table with stools tucked neatly around.

"Arthurian enough for you?" he grinned.

"Wow, now you start with the jokes?" I said back. "It's perfect. How did you make the table again?"

"I asked the trees politely."

"Tell them, thank you." The table was beautiful. It was polished to a brilliant shine and had the rune for peace embossed in the center.

"Please, if you all would join me at the table, we may begin." I planned for two sessions with a break. In the first session, I would lay out the plan to retake the land, and in the second, I would introduce the plan to govern the land we took. Everyone settled in a spot closest to his or her corner of the glen.

"First I wish to thank you for coming. My hope for our action tomorrow is to return your lands to each of you. Granted, some concessions will need to be considered, but I will address these later. I would first like to discuss our plan of attack." They all nodded approval. "I say attack, but I hope we can avoid spilling blood unnecessarily. I am not naive enough to believe that no blood will be spilled, but I hope we…" And Orin started.

"Wizard?" he interrupted. "May I speak?"

"If you could wait…" I hadn't even answered the question before he started.

"I propose we walk in and demand he give us our land back."

"What has stopped you from doing this already?" I asked.

"Power, more specifically, magic."

"So you have access to this magic now? Then why am I wasting your time?" I stood to exit. I got a step from the table when Raise and Foster appeared in front of me.

Orin continued, and I believe, he thought he'd won. "Yes, we have magic, your magic." He stood there with a confident smile.

I wheeled around on my heel wearing a cold smile on my face. "My magic? You said we walk in and now it's my magic you want. How do you plan to take this magic? Is this a threat?" I asked gesturing to his warriors. When I raised my hand vines shot from the earth below Raise and Foster's feet. It wrapped them up like a spindle of yarn, from their toes to their shoulders.

Our other guests sat silently, waiting to see how this little exchange played out. "Orin, I'd have thought you would have learned this earlier. But let me make this very simple. I do not take kindly to threats." Magic was amplifying my voice. "Now if you are through with all this foolishness I will offer you two choices; one, you may gather your warriors and leave, or two, have a seat and play the part I will assign you. Know this, if you leave I will declare you to be a traitor along with those who follow you. This will make you an enemy to Warg, Phengard, and me. I believe I could convince Naomi to agree and follow suit in the East. What say you?"

Orin was livid. I could see he was weighing his options but finally he sat. "I accept your terms," he spat like the words had a foul taste.

I turned back to Raise and Foster to release them. "My apologies for any discomfort, good warriors. I pray you remain unharmed?" I bowed my head in respect. I really was sorry they had to be punished for the actions of Orin, the horse's ass.

"Good. Now are there any other bits of business we must attend?" I looked from person to person around the table. I made eye contact with all. I then began my briefing. I laid the plan Kalen and I had been forming the past few days. The group interacted with the plan, asking questions, clarifying strategies, and making suggestions. For this to work I needed the three groups to buy in to the plan and play nice with each other. The Pixies with Orin had to be able to work with the Warg. It would be their job to conceal the wolves and bring them close to where I was meeting Aelfric, all while remaining undetected. I was hoping for a show of force to deter battle, but if it came to blows then we would have to coordinate an attack.

Orin really had me worried. If he was this arrogant, how arrogant was the one who sired him ? As butt heads go, I'm betting Aelfric is a bigger one.

When I was confident all knew their part of the plan, I called for a break. The refreshments were restocked and all adjourned to their corner.

"Kalen, do you have any of the energy bread you brought from home? If you do, may I have a small piece? I would love a bite or two."

"Yes, I do. Here," and he produced a small piece and gave it to me.

"Thank you, brother. I need a boost before we start up again."

"How did you wrap up those warriors?" Neal asked.

"It was as Kalen said earlier. I asked the vines to wrap them."

Kalen smile like a proud parent and nodded.

"You asked them?" Neal protested.

"I even said please."

Kalen changed the subject back to our real concern. "You will have to watch Orin closely. I do not believe you will be able to trust him."

"You are right. Has he always been so unstable?"

"No, but the past few centuries have been hard for him. I know he doesn't show it but he wants this for his subjects more than he does for himself."

I added, "He has some serious trust issues."

"That is a good way to explain his actions. He does not trust anyone except those he's tested."

"Is this a trait he shares with Raise and Foster?"

"No, they are only following orders. Why? What are you thinking?" Kalen asked.

"You are a Battle General, right? Can we insert you into his chain of command?"

"And what would we do with him?"

"Give me a minute," I held up my finger while I let my wheels spin. "It could work. Okay, we bring Orin with us. I'm betting Foster has more battle experience?" Kalen nodded. "Then you put Foster in control of the Pixies in Orin's stead. He will want one of his bodyguards and I will suggest Raise. We take Orin with us to see his Daddy. We'll bring home the prodigal child, effectively controlling the chaos surrounding Mr. Crazy."

"Sounds good," offered Neal.

"Yes, but who is going to convince Orin?" Neal and I stood shoulder-to-shoulder looking at Kalen. "Okay then, allow me the privilege to suggest this change. You'd only anger him anyway."

"You may wish to tell him this was your idea," suggested Neal. I nodded agreement. Kalen turn and headed to Orin.

I took this time to make my rounds. I wanted to see if there were any concerns not brought to the table. "Dubhan, Conor and Chepi," I greeted each by name as I approached. "I am checking to see if there is any last concerns you might have?"

Chepi started, "Those Pixies aren't expecting to ride us into battle like pack mules, are they?"

"No, they will fly, but you need to keep up with them if we attack. It is imperative you hit the flank simultaneously. But only if I give the order."

"Good. After the battle, what then?" asked Conor.

"This is the purpose of our next round of talks. Any other battle related concerns?"

"No, the plan is sound," offered Dubhan.

I headed to Cheryl. I greeted them exactly like I did the Warg. "Cheryl, Lily, Heather, I am checking to see if there any last concerns you might have?"

"I am concerned that our part is so minor. We would like to be more actively involved in the main battle."

"Indeed, the Phengard are truly a force of reckoning. All Fae know and fear the Phengard and I am counting on that fear. It will do more damage than any sword. I need this fear to cloud their minds. Cheryl, you know the importance of clouding people's judgment?"

"I do see your point. When this is finished may we continue what we started in Kansas?" She asked as she caressed my shoulder giving me a pouty look. "I promise it will be all pleasure and no real harm will come to you."

"Tell you what, how about we discuss this after tomorrow?" I gently put my hand on her cheek. "I don't wish to be distracted. It could jeopardize all of us."

Now it was time for round two.

Chapter 51

L'CHAIM

"Friends, let us finish our talks," my magic enhanced voice boomed. I was using the word friends rather liberally, but what the heck.

When all had settled back at the table I continued, "We must now discuss what we all wish to gain from this endeavor." I stretched my open hand palm up toward the Warg contingent, allowing them to express their wants first and said, "It was you who were first harmed by Aelfric's action, so please tell us what you wish to gain."

Dubhan looked right to Conor who nodded. He then looked left at Chepi and she rose silently.

"Thank you, wizard." Then she addressed the rest of the table. "You all know the atrocity visited to my kin. Hundreds of my brothers and sisters, aunts and uncles fell when Aelfric abused his gift, claiming what he had no right to claim. Our hunting grounds, nay our home was stolen. We became outlaws and renegades. We were hunted and killed within our own homelands. We were forced to flee. We did not have the power to fight the magic bringing us death. All but a few of our pack, Silent Death, perished. Our families to the east, the Moon Runners and the Shadow Killers, accepted our refugees into their packs. They allowed us to run as their own. They will always have our undying loyalty. Wizard, you ask what do we wish? First you have laid out a plan allowing us to face our sworn enemy." As she said this she looked to Orin. "And we will face them with some of their own, as our allies. Many pixies witnessed the action wrought against us. They gave their freedom and their families attempting to right this wrong. Thank you." She bowed her head to Orin. He returned the gesture. "What do we wish? We wish to go home. We wish to hunt, raise pups, and reclaim all we lost. Before the holocaust, we were willing to live in peace and share the land. We would be willing to create a similar arrangement again." She nodded toward me and sat without ceremony.

"Thank you, Chepi Luna, daughter of Dubhan of the Moon Runners, descendant of the Silent Death. Many of you are not aware but Silent Death was not the only Fae to lose their homes by the hand of Aelfric." I turned to Cheryl. "Queen Danaus of the Phengard, Cheryl, would you please tell us your wishes."

She looked me in the eyes and winked coyly before she rose to say, "Thank you, Wizard Roger. A human poet once wrote 'Good fences make good neighbors.' The memory of a Silent Death and Phengard relationship lies with the Phengard alone. We shared a fence, if you will, and became good neighbors. We existed in peace. There were those who would cross the fence, venturing into each other's land. An agreement was established to separate our hunting grounds, not separate our kind from one another. So many would journey to meet their neighbors. One such Warg wandered to our lands. He was little more than a pup and full of life and joy. We did not know it, but his path within his pack was all but destined. He stayed among us for a summer while he grew into the man/wolf you once knew. He and one of our maidens found happiness together. They were seldom found apart. They would often be found hunting together in the deep woods along the border of our lands. They were in love. For our kind too," she paused looking for the right word, "mingle, we must use human form for a wolf and a butterfly have no chance to 'mingle successfully'. But they were quite familiar with this form because of our human neighbors, and they maintained this form within our villages. As the summer gave way to the cool winds of autumn, we were visited by the Alpha of the Silent Death and his mate. They came to encourage their son to return to the pack. Ulfang didn't wish to go for he had fallen in love with Princess Morphini."

At the mention of Ulfang's name the Warg contingent gasped. He was the Alpha when Aelfric committed genocide. Also, he was Dubhan and Chepi's ancestor. "Ulfang knew his duty was to his pack, as he knew Morphini would have the same responsibilities to her rabble. He was told to return before the next moon for his pack was to run under the harvest moon." The Warg nodded understanding.

"To this point in my story their love was youthful and innocent, but all the stories are filled with the impetuous nature of star-crossed lovers. They, too, consummated their love under the stars. His seed grew within her and because it was conceived of two different Fae, she was force to bear the child as a human." A gasp came from the Fae around the table. I found out later, bearing a child as fairy is a joyous event for all, including the mother. It isn't the pain filled hours of labor and childbirth that human mothers experience. Also, when the child is of a mixed mating, all breathlessly await the gender. The gender determines the kind of fairy the child will become. Females follow mother and males follow father.

"My mother was born of their bond." She looked to Chepi and Dubhan, "We are kin. Granted, both Ulfang and Morphini accepted mates within their own kind, but their love never stopped. My mother would tell childhood stories of meeting her father at the border and running with him and my grandmother. So while they fulfilled their obligations to their rabble or pack, they still met in secret. This alone is reason enough to bring me to this table, but my tale does not end here. Aelfric was not interested in lands south of Ulfang's. So he didn't bring the fight to our lands. When word of Aelfric's horrific acts reached my grandmother, however, her heart was torn asunder. She called her forces to arms and invaded the land."

She turned to Orin. "This was after your exile. Aelfric used his magic a second time. He brought his forces south to steal our glen and drive us from our lands as well. What do we wish? First, we wish Aelfric gone. Be it dead or exiled from this continent, gone. Second, our people have suffered greatly being separated from our glen. You Pixies have several glens around the continent where magic to live and heal is able to be freely drawn. Warg had other packs to accept them. We had but one glen and had to rely on magic we could take from our food. It is enough magic to live, but my people grow weaker and weaker as each day passes. Like you, I tried to tempt the wizard here." And she smiled at me, but she was not the overconfident vixen. She was vulnerable and exposed. As much as she drove me crazy, right then, my heart went out to her. "I now see he was wiser than I, and I am certain that this plan could restore balance in this realm. So, I wish to have the lands surrounding our glen and south. This puts us well south of our traditional border, but most of our land has now been polluted by humans." She really didn't like what we did to Yellowstone. "This is my wish." She sat.

"Thank you, Cheryl, Queen of the Phengard, descendant of the Silent Death." Chepi raised her hand like a schoolgirl in class. "Chepi?"

"May we take a short break?"

"Sure, let's take five minutes." She rose and walked directly to Cheryl with a pained expression on her face. I wasn't sure what was going to happen. I looked to Dubhan and with my eyes I asked, "What the hell?" He shook me off, silently telling me to let it happen and watch. So I waited breathlessly, wondering if this was all going to fall apart.

Chepi stood directly in front of Cheryl. What happened next was a variation of the greeting. Instead of one hand they used both and touched heads. But before the contact Chepi said, "I see you, Sister." And Cheryl returned, "Share my flower, Sister." When they touched heads I averted my eyes. I don't know why. It only seemed right. I found I wasn't alone in this sentiment. All present gave them the moment alone. When Chepi finished with Cheryl she greeted Lily and Heather the same in turn. Dubhan came over and greeted Cheryl in the traditional fashion. When I later asked Kalen about what I had witnessed he gave a long-winded explanation, but honestly all I remember is that it's a girl thing. I was relieved the plan would continue without a new glitch.

When all returned to their seats I turned finally to Orin. I thought 'here we go' and found I was holding my breath. "Prince Orin, son of King Aelfric, would you please tell us your wishes?"

Orin actually looked humble as he stood, "Thank you, Roger."

Forgetting to use wizard in front of my name was supposed to be an affront to me, but I wasn't used to being called Wizard yet so I missed the insult. I found all eyes around the table waiting for me to do something, but I hadn't a clue till Kalen explained it to me later. But no reaction turned out to work in my favor, for Orin paused to await my comment. I only sat waiting for him to continue, pondering the attention and the pregnant pause.

Orin stumbled through the next few lines of his speech. He was prepared for another confrontation with me and didn't get it. Oh well. He continued, "While I lived in my father's realm I was able to establish many friendships with the Silent Death. I would often run with members of the pack. I would sit and talk for hours upon end with Ulfang while we were trying to establish a treaty. His desire was to be able to run and hunt freely. He would allow us to establish several villages provided they didn't impact their hunting grounds. In return, Aelfric would infuse their cave with magic from the old country. Their cave, as many of you know, acts as our glens. Its magic wasn't low, but he thought the old magic would make his people stronger. He wasn't looking for a huge amount of power. As it turned out, my father used more power exterminating them than was requested for the cave. Aelfric wanted to share with no one.

What do I wish? I wish to reign in my father's stead. I would humbly submit myself to be your king and provide peace and stability for all my father's lands. Queen Danaus, you would have unfettered access to your glen and the surrounding lands. Dubhan, you would be permitted to hunt our lands freely after each harvest moon till the vernal equinox, provided none of my subject's livestock become your prey." The Fae around the table began to stir restlessly. "So you see, I have your interests at heart. As king, I will be available to help resolve all disputes and maintain peace and prosperity throughout the realm." He smiled brightly, looking more like a presidential candidate than the spoiled princeling he was. And he sat feeling confident.

By now the stirring gave way to muttering. "Let us take another short break while I consider your requests." I was able to say this because nothing was going to happen without my power and they knew this, so my word was to be final. No sooner had I returned to my table for a drink, than Cheryl and Dubhan flanked me. They weren't happy about the prospect of a king permitting them access to their lands. I anticipated this, and I wasn't going to let it happen either. This break was to give the appearance of considering each request and weighing the options. Actually, I already knew what they wanted, but I hadn't known all I heard about Cheryl and the cave. So it was good that I let them talk. I tried to appease Dubhan and Cheryl by saying I understood their plight but that they had agreed to the outcome of the meeting. I also asked them to keep the faith in me. I actually felt like breaking into song with 'Have a Little Faith,' but they wouldn't get it. Duly appeased, they returned to their corners.

Neal asked, "You good?" I nodded, "Know what you are going to say, lad?"

"I do, Uncle. I knew before we started but I needed them to tell their tales to each other. Look what it did for the Phengard and Warg relationship." I turned, "Kalen, how will Orin react?"

" I believe he will react stoically, but will attempt to get what he wants through deception. He has tried you twice today and found you can't be beaten by a frontal assault. Tomorrow he will come at you from the side, after you depose Aelfric. Don't underestimate him. Yes, he is a bit unstable, but he is strong and smart."

"Thanks. Here we go. If we could gather back to the table." I began, "First, I would like to thank you all for your contribution. I have thought long and hard about how this realm will be divided and governed. I must remind you of your oath to abide by my final decision. Here is what I have decided.

No one will be king of this realm. Peace reigned for many centuries before the advent of a king. Instead, I propose a council of governors, one from each of you. I will leave it up to you to elect or choose your own representatives. There will also be a representative from Queen Naomi making it a council of four. For any disputes, either a representative of my choosing, or I myself, will be available to resolve the issue. This power of resolution will be handed down my bloodline.

Cheryl, the lands you requested will be granted. Dubhan and Orin, your requests, I feel, were similar. The division of land and hunting rights must be equitable. I will make this the first task of the board of governors upon our success tomorrow. Until then, you will cohabitate peaceably within the villages and yes, among the humans. The cave will be the sole property of the Warg, and off limits to any others without express permission from the Warg governor. Are there any questions?"

I could see by his posture, Orin was not agreeable, but Kalen was right he knew he couldn't win this fight here. Tomorrow will be very interesting.

"I have been summoned to appear at sunset. I need to be there at sunset. You know where you are supposed to be and what you are supposed to do. Without your complete cooperation none of us will succeed. We will meet here tomorrow at one hour before the sunset. I will give you my magic then."

"But you said we'd get it tonight." Orin insisted.

"No! I never agreed to tonight and there is no need till tomorrow. Do you need more than an hour to distribute it among your warriors?"

He backed down, "No, but it was promised."

"The promise has not been broken. The promise was for power to be given before the battle and it will be," I thought to myself, and no promise was made as to how much. "Till tomorrow, sleep well and good night." All exited in muted conversation.

I sat in the chair in our corner enjoying one more cup of the delicious elixir. "Tomorrow this gets resolved, one way or another. Tonight I raise my glass to family and friend. Without you two, I probably would have ended up fairy food by now. Thank you."

"To success," Kalen added.

"L'Chaim," added Neal. Kalen and I looked at him. "What, you're the only one who can quote a movie?"

I laughed and drank with Neal. Kalen shook his head at the both of us and drank. I made a mental note adding 'Fiddler on the Roof' to the movie playlist.

Chapter 52

AN STN...STICK TELEPORTATION NETWORK

When we departed the glen, night had fallen and the near full moon was high in the sky. The sky was so full of stars it was hard to see where the sky ended and the world began. My mind and body were exhausted. Thankfully, there would be no driving tomorrow. Orin's camp was close to where we had to enter Aelfric's domain. When we met in the glen we would simply exit through Orin's portal.

"Kalen, what's to stop us from establishing a stick teleportation network?" I asked as I thought about tomorrow.

Neal grinned. Kalen said, "A what?"

"Sorry, you know how we plan to use the stick to travel the last three hundred miles tomorrow? Well, how difficult would it be to set up a transportation system to travel back and forth? An STN...Stick Teleportation Network."

"The trouble lies with glens like mine. Mine is temporary. My Queen provided it for me and said it would remain viable until four days after the moon."

"Isn't four days after the moon arbitrary?"

"You had your audience on the day of the moon. She figured our business would be completed by the end of one evening, and that it would take four days to travel back to her realm. So it's not arbitrary at all."

"No, you are right. You said the trouble lies with glens like yours. What other kinds of glens are there?"

"Ones like Naomi's or Cheryl's. Also the cave's of the Warg fall into the other type."

"What difference do they make?"

"In Naomi's case, Steve has a permanent portal set up in the park. He has a talisman he uses to travel to and from the glen."

"Like the shavings you gave the others for your glen?"

"Yes, it is similar indeed. Steve's is more permanent in nature. Naomi would only give them to trusted servants."

"So let's see if I got this straight. We could have a network set up among these permanent glens. All you need is a talisman granted by the boss of the glen."

"Yes," replied Kalen.

"So if, say I wanted to travel around the country without the hours of driving. I could bop here and there provided I have a token from each as well as permission. Does Aelfric have a glen?"

"Yes, I believe he established one when he became king."

"Could I have one?"

"I suppose you could. They are constructed from a bond with nature and magic."

"You know how it's done?"

"Yes."

"Here is the million-dollar question. Is there a way to bind the permanent glens together? If I build my own and I gain the required permissions, could I enter my own glen and step out into someone else's glen? Or could I establish glens of my own around the country, or world, to create a way to travel."

"I don't know."

"Who would?"

"Possibly a Queen."

"When we are through tomorrow I'll have to talk with Cheryl. The STN would be a good way for me to visit out here occasionally." As I finished this statement, Paige and

Johnson greeted us back at the Lodge.

I introduced Neal and Mary and headed up to our room. Only an hour had past here but I'd spent too many hours awake today already. It was time to sleep. I grabbed a shower and hit the rack. Kalen had his stick in hand and was looking for a quiet place to commune. Neal took a fancy to his fellow innkeeper and they were deep in conversation down in the living room.

As I settled in the sheets, I realized I had nothing on my agenda tomorrow till almost seven at night. Good. I had some errands to run and now I'd have the opportunity to accomplish them.

I announced to the ceiling, "Leave me alone tonight and no hijacking the dreams, please." I knew no one was listening, but I had to try.

I was asleep before I could count five sheep. And the dreams came.

I found myself walking in a deep forest. It was familiar and foreign all at the same time. I had my sword in my hand and my magic was ready to use, which was weird for I didn't know how to do much with my magic anyway. But it was a dream and I was ready and confident. The light of a full moon lit the forest, but there were neither moon nor stars overhead. Something drew me forward.

Ahead, I saw a small fire burning. It looked like a campfire. I approached cautiously and remained outside its circle of light. I didn't know if this was a trap or what the hell it was. I knew I was dreaming but the smells and the textures were very real. You can never be too careful when you deal with fairies.

"Roger, join my fire and warm yourself," said a voice I knew I could trust. I knew because it was my Granddad's voice, my dead Granddad. Like I said, weird things happen in dreams.

"Do I have a guarantee of safe passage? Swear on your word and on your magic." They laughed for now there were two voices.

"Yes lad, you have mine and Charles' word. Now come

in out of the dark."

It really was my Granddad. God, I missed him. I went to him and he wrapped me in his arms. "Hello Granddad, how can this be?"

"Magic lad, magic can do many things. This is why you are here with us. Allow me to introduce you to my, how many greats? Well, anyway, Charles. I believe you've recently heard about him?"

"Charles the Keeper?"

He gave a hearty laugh, "I haven't heard that name in quite a few centuries, but yes, I am he." He offered me his hand and I greeted him in the fairy fashion. When our heads touched I was rewarded with a feeling of warmth and love. "I see you've been learning the ways of the Fae."

"You could say, I've been taking a crash course." This got a raised eyebrow. "Uh yes, I've had to learn quickly this past week. Kalen has been teaching me their ways."

"General Kalen?" Charles asked at the same time Granddad asked, "Kalen?"

"Yes, to both of you. Neal told me of the summer he spent with you guys. Why am I here?" I asked pointedly.

Granddad rose to leave, "Lad, you can trust Charles. Hear what he has to offer you and learn your magic. Please tell Kalen I said hello. Oh, and give my brother a hug from me. Tell him he was my last thought in your world."

"Do you have to go so soon?"

"I'm afraid so. I was allowed to come so I could introduce you to Charles. I did and now I have to leave."

I hugged him again, "Goodbye, Granddad."

"Tell your Mum I still love her bunches. Use bunches, she'll know what it means."

"I will," and he faded from sight.

"Now down to business." Charles started. "I know I am Great, Great, etcetera Grand whatever but please call me Charles. I am here to prepare you for the pompous ass you will meet tomorrow."

"Wow, like father like son."

"So you have meet Orin. Be leery of him. When you

meet Aelfric he will be your best friend. When he puts his arm around your shoulder and if you are not prepared, you will be his best friend. You will need some sort of cloak to wear, or a jacket. We can put protections on the jacket but it needs to be done ahead of time. You can bind your magic with the threads in the material creating a protective garment. It will repel magic thrown toward you. It won't be much good against blades and the like but that won't be a problem for you and Peace. It is true, I never lost a duel with her.

You were warned about using magic and the blade simultaneously?" I nodded. "It can be done, but ground the tip of Peace before you release the magic. Peace's magic tends to be deadly. By grounding her magic before using yours you soften the blow to the bystanders."

"To be clear Charles, if I release magic while holding Peace I place her tip in the ground. Do I release her grip?"

"I wouldn't. It could distort what you are doing with the magic. Remember you will be using her magic as well. Grounding her lets her know you have a specific target in mind, not a general 'I am being attacked from all sides' spell."

"I have so much to learn."

"And you will, in time. But come here. My time grows short." He took me by the head in the same manner I gave magic to Kalen. When our eyes met I heard his thoughts in my head. There was so much and it was coming so fast.

I shot up in bed, gasping for breath. My head felt full. But I knew stuff too. I knew how to make a ball of fire. I looked at my hand and exclaimed, "Holy shit!" Okay Roger, calm down. And it extinguished because I asked it to with my mind. I looked around the room and saw Neal and Kalen sleeping soundly. Even with my little outburst.

I guess I have a few more things to do tomorrow.

Chapter 53

MAGIC IS FUN

When the sun's light came to wake me the next morning, I jumped out of bed excited and recharged. In the past week my twenty-four hour days have been lasting thirty to forty hours because of our little trips into the land of Fae. Today promised to be the longest of all, but I didn't care. Last night's visitation filled my head with ways to use my magic. I needed to try some of this stuff. I also had to go to town to run a few errands. I bound out of bed excited to start the day. I hit the shower dressed and headed to breakfast.

I came around the corner in the dining room to see Neal and Mary chatting quietly over a cup of coffee.

"Morning folks," I greeted them.

"Morning," answered Mary.

"Morning lad. You're early," Neal said.

"I am? What time is it?" I asked in earnest.

"Put it this way," and in answer he waved his hand around the room showing me that we were the only ones there.

"I'm sorry," I said to Mary, "is the dining room open?"

She laughed at my distress. "Breakfast won't be ready for another ten minutes but there is coffee, tea and juice. Please join us. Your Uncle has been telling me you've had quite a journey cross country."

I looked to Neal who seemed unfazed by her statement. "Yes Ma'am, it has been a string of long days." I was silently begging Neal to help me out. I know he didn't regale her with stories of the Fae, but it would help if he could tell me what he did tell her. No, there he sat with a grin on his face, enjoying my pain. "We have been driving mostly the back roads, so it's taking a bit more time."

"Where are you headed?"

"To depose a fairy King," I thought but said, "Spokane."

"What's in Spokane?"

"None of your business, lady. Isn't there something in the kitchen for you to cook?" Again this was my internal voice, "An old Air Force buddy, I'm planning to visit. His daughter is getting married and well, I've known her since she was a tadpole."

"How sweet."

"Would you excuse me?" I headed over to the coffee to pour a cup and to get the hell away from the questions. I was standing there shaking the sugar packets when Neal joined me.

"What the hell, Neal." He was still wearing a stupid grin.

"Nicely done lad, nicely done."

"Why did you set me up? What have you been telling her?"

"Nothing as elaborate as your story."

"I had to come up with something," I said.

"How are you going to explain staying the extra night?" Neal asked.

"Why do I have to explain anything?"

"Because this isn't a motel. And she's a real sweet lady."

"How about I say my Uncle wanted to hang out for another day." It was my turn to screw with him.

He smiled like he enjoyed the idea, "It could work," he said.

"I take it you don't get a lot of single female visitors at the Shady Lane?"

"No, but there are a few ladies in town. When you get to be my age, if you have a pulse and an income you become catnip to their..."

"Okay, okay, enough already." A shiver went down my

spine. Hell, I wanted to stick my fingers in my ears and sing, "La la la la I'm not listening." But it was too late and this will never be unheard.

Uncle Neal stood there grinning like a fool. "You are enjoying this," I accused.

"Yes, I am, very much." Mary had retreated into the kitchen and a few more people came into the dining room for breakfast.

I raised my coffee in a salute, "Morning folks."

"Good morning," Neal added.

"Hello," was the response I received. Neal and I sat at his table.

"So, you and Mary?"

"Not yet, she's a sweetie and is quite a pleasant conversationalist, but I've got a few other things to occupy my evenings while we are here," he said pointedly.

"I'm headed to town. I need to hit the Wal-Mart, and I have to pick up a few trinkets for the grandkids. You need anything?"

"How about a lift? I wouldn't mind looking around. I've never been here before."

"Let's meet a couple hours after we finish breakfast. Have you seen Kalen?"

"He went for a walk saying something about seeing the sunrise, and a ritual he performs the morning before an impending battle." Neal looked up, "Talk of the devil."

I finished, "and he's presently at your elbow." Neal nodded agreeing.

"Nice to see your Mum taught you a few thing from back home." He turned, "Morning Kalen."

"Neal, Roger." His tone was somber. It looked like he was getting his game-face on a little early.

"What is your plan for the day?" I directed at Kalen.

"I will be heading up the trail to meditate on the upcoming events."

Kalen's timing was perfect. Mary entered with plates of food. Today was French toast day and each plate was filled with the toast, several types of breakfast meat, and fruit. The food was arranged on the plates to look like a work of art. My food was pretty. This presented a moral dilemma. Do I sit and enjoy the aesthetic beauty or give in to the rumbling behind my belt buckle? I took out my phone, took a picture, and then tore into the delectable treats. Dilemma resolved, and it was heavenly.

"Neal," I muttered behind a mouthful, "you got her beat in quantity, but her food is much prettier. You ought to marry this one and combine your efforts."

He laughed and kept eating. I notice Kalen's plate was devoid of French toast and meat. It was piled high with fruits and bread. "I see someone has been talking to the chef."

Kalen looked up with a blank expression. Neal interjected, "I might have made a suggestion or two. Kalen, did you taste the bread?" He picked it up and took a bite. This put a smile on his face. "We were waiting for the sweet bread to come out of the oven when you came down, Roger."

"Nice," the rest of the time was dedicated to enjoying this delicious meal.

Breakfast was finished and I cleared our table, ignoring the protestations of our gracious host. After such a wonderful meal, I felt compelled to help with the cleaning. A rule in our house is that the cook shouldn't have to clean. It's a rule that I try to follow and it's the right thing to do. I headed to the kitchen laden with the dirty dishes.

"Roger, stack them in the sink. I'm not allowed to have guests back here. It's an insurance thing, but thank you." Mary said as I began to enter the kitchen.

I placed the dishes and headed out to the main room.

"So Unc, I'll see you out front in a couple hours. Kalen, which trail are you going to hike?"

"The one we were on last night, why?"

"I need to do a little reflecting myself and I don't want to disturb your meditation. I know how important it is to you.

I headed away from the house to test out my newfound skills. This was going to be fun. I found I was anxious and smiling like a kid headed to Disney World for the first time. Magic is fun.

Chapter 54

A SMILE WOULD STEAL THE CORNERS OF THEIR MOUTH

I jogged north for about a half an hour. Mary told me to be careful, because I was headed off into the wilderness. In other words, devoid of human and hopefully fairy contact. I brought several bottles of water and had my quiver and bow. Of course, Peace was securely fastened to my back.

I found the pond Mary told me about. There was an abandoned shack at the north end and an access road surrounded it. This would give me room to work.

My first task was to practice holding and releasing magic. I'd already acquired a certain level of proficiency, but my new memories told me my level was equivalent to a small child. So I found a place to sit quietly. There I held and released my magic. I did this for a half of an hour and by the end I was able to embrace magic at the speed of a thought.

My next task was to do the same thing except while engaged in an activity requiring my concentration. I strung my bow and explored my surroundings for a viable target. In the shack I found an old stained mattress and propped it up against the wall. I paced off what looked to be a distance we shot from in the glen and loosed a few arrows to test whether this would work as a target. On the upper third of the mattress was an old brown oval stain and I focused my aim on that. Without my magic I was hitting the stain, not the center, but hitting the stain was good.

The drill was to engage the magic as I released the arrow, just soon enough to let the arrow fly magic enhanced but no sooner. Before I started I'd wondered how I would be able to gauge my success but my new thoughts said it would be obvious.

On the first attempt, I was too late. The arrow struck the mattress at the bottom, an inch lower and it would have obviously been in the dirt. I'd lost my concentration and the arrow proved it. The next shot was perfect but I'd engaged too early. This went on for about five minutes, early, late, late, early, and then I nailed one exactly right. When the bowstring left my finger it sounded like a string on a guitar playing a clear note, resounding perfectly in tune. The note resonated through my body. Wow, the voice in my head was right, it was obvious. The arrow struck dead center and buried itself up to the fletching. I put my bow down and walked up to retrieve my arrows for another round. The perfectly shot arrow had penetrated the wood on the house and was a pain to remove. I went in the house and dragged out a box spring to put behind the mattress. Hopefully it would make the arrows easier to retrieve.

Back at the shooting line I simply tried to repeat what I had done on the fateful shot. I was able to duplicate it after three more shots, then it was every other, and finally I had it. I now knew how to shoot creating a beautiful song.

The box spring kept the arrows from the wall but between the springs and the material, retrieving the arrows was a bit of a pain at first. I recalled the roots in the glen and how I asked them to wrap around Raise and Foster, so I asked the arrows to extract themselves. To my surprise they did. They backed out of the target and floated to, then nestled themselves in the quiver.

My next task was to mess with the fireballs I produced last night. I moved the mattress and propped it on a fallen log adjacent to the pond. If I lost the focus and missed I had water to back me up. Thank God, I had the water. Making the fire was easy. Hitting the target was the tough part. My first few attempts created several columns of steam rising from the pond. I didn't even come close to the mattress. On one of them I was lucky to hit the pond. I was getting frustrated. I tried tossing them like baseballs, overhand, underhand, and side-armed. The sidearm one was almost a disaster but luckily fell short into the pond. I even tried a Frisbee throw, singing my shirt and lastly I tried spiking it like volleyball. It bounced along the dirt until it fell in the pond.

The more frustrated I got, the worse my aim. I sat down in the sand. I thought through all the training sessions I'd had the past couple of days. I took a few deep breaths to clear my mind and relax. I put my hands at my side, still with my eyes closed, and asked the fire to hit the target. The balls leaped from my hands and blasted through the mattress one after another landing in the middle of the pond. I found that all I had to do was ask my magic and anything could be accomplished. I threw the balls and asked them to stop halfway to the target. I could change targets or extinguish the flame. The shape of the fire was whatever I desired. I even sent a pair of fire ducks and let them consume the mattress for I was finished with my session. The ducks perched on the mattress, pecking at it. The mattress was quickly consumed by fire. The earth below the mattress was untouched by flames, but the mattress was reduced to ash.

I checked my watch and found that I needed to get back to the Lodge quickly. I engaged my magic and ran. Trees blurred past and I stepped into the field behind the lodge two minutes after I last checked my watch. My breathing was normal and I wasn't sweating at all. It had taken me a half of an hour to forty-five minutes to hike there, but only two minutes to get back. Now, I was the Flash and I was hungry, starved actually. I guess magic burned calories as well. I was going to like this magic stuff.

I was late before I even thought to run back. When I came to the front yard, Neal was leaning against the truck waiting for me.

"Hey, Neal. Been waiting long?"

"Two minutes at most."

"I need to drop this bag up in my room and I'll be right down. Here," I said as I tossed him the keys. "Start it up and get the AC going." I ran to the room and dropped my bag on the bed. I debated whether I should leave Peace, but decided against it and left it strapped to my back. I hustled back down to the truck. Neal was perched in the passenger's seat and the truck was running. I jumped in behind the wheel and said "Where to?"

Neal directed me turn by turn. It seems Mary gave him directions to the sights. I stopped in front of a marker for some historic event, letting Neal out. "Where'd you want me to pick you up, here?"

"No, I'll find my way back," he said, but his smile was a bit too broad.

I took a stab, "So where are you taking her to lunch?"

"I don't know what you are talking about," he denied.

"If I come back here and grab a bite in say two hours, I…"

"Okay smartass, eat on the other side of town and Mary will bring me back."

"I know. Have fun."

"I plan on doing so."

I was happy for Neal. Who knows what was going to happen tonight?

My truck turned toward the drive-thru. I was starving and ordered two large double cheeseburgers and fries, a large soda and a milkshake. I told you I was starving. I drove to the address I found in the phonebook and parked in their lot. The lot was filled with pickup trucks with gun racks. I was in the right place. I sat on my tailgate and scarfed down the greasy treats. Wiping the mess from my mouth and hands, I headed in to make my purchase.

"Looks like all the paperwork is in order, sir." He stapled the receipt to the bag and I headed for Wal-Mart.

I was looking for my protective cloak. The only criterion was that it had to be made from non-synthetic materials. Leather or cotton was what I was expecting to use. Actually, in Wal-Mart I wasn't expecting leather. I hadn't taken into account this was cowboy country. They had a few racks of the leather blazers and dusters. Right next to those were the denim jackets. I could wear a jean jacket.

With my purchases in the cart I headed to checkout. I stopped and looked around for a moment or two. I was in a normal non-fairy environment for the first time in what felt like a long time. The strange part was that I felt like I stood out here. I didn't belong. Wal-Mart was for normal folks and I was no longer normal. I could make fireballs with my mind. I was walking around with a sword strapped to my back. This was my new normal. I decided then and there to keep the weird away from Harmony for as long as I could as she grew into her magic.

I paid for my purchases and headed back to the Lodge. Once there, I went up to my room and brought my spell ingredients with me. I put the new ceramic bowl on the desk and added the following in order while reciting the incantation Charles taught me last night. Bay leaf, lavender, ginger, and eucalyptus were all mixed in apple juice. He had said to use blood, but apple juice would suffice for the bulk of the liquid. Ten drops of my blood was the minimum needed to activate the spell. To add power to the protection spell he suggested I add Echinacea. At this point, I did. I would add the blood right before applying the potion to the jacket. I first had to cleanse the object by reciting another incantation and spraying the coat with lemon juice.

Next I used the tip of Peace to prick my finger and counted out my ten drops of blood. A curious thing happened when drop number ten hit the herbal stew I'd created. It started to bubble like it was boiling, but there was no heat source. I decided to add more blood to be on the safe side. Besides, I'd cut my finger pretty good and it was still bleeding. I carefully poured this new mixture into a spray bottle and soaked the whole jacket. I sprayed every drop covering each spot both inside and out, twice. One can never be too careful.

When I finished I spoke the last incantation over the

dripping jacket. When I spoke the last word there was a flash of light and the jacket was dry.

"I'll take the flash as a good sign," I said aloud to the empty room. The clock read five and I heard a car approaching the drive. I peeked out the curtain and saw that Mary and Neal were only now getting back. They sat in the car talking. Neal leaned in and kissed Mary, passionately. I said aloud to my audience of me, "Good for you, Neal." They got out of the car and acted like nothing was going on between them. I could see the strained body language. They would brush their hands together as they walked and a smile would steal the corners of their mouths when they made contact. This was too cute, but I would keep this to myself, for now.

I laid out my clothes for later and cleaned and prepped my weapons. I set my alarm for an hour and put my head on my pillow for a quick rest.

My mind replayed Neal's kiss, putting a smile on my face as sleep took me away.

Chapter 55

IT WAS FAIRY MADE

I woke from a dreamless sleep minutes before my alarm and silenced it. I felt refreshed. No one had tried to hijack my dreams. I guess I needed to sleep more in the daytime. I quickly dressed and gathered my weapons. I felt a little panicked as I tried to find Peace. She wasn't anywhere in the room and I couldn't remember taking her off and putting her away.

"There is no way she's..." I said aloud. I reached back and there was her grip. I'd fallen asleep with a sword across my back and didn't even notice. She was becoming part of me. I pulled her free of the scabbard and let her sing through the air.

She was alive in my hand and seemed to quiver with excitement when my thoughts turned to my audience with Aelfric. It was a little disconcerting for I was hoping to get through tonight without her tasting flesh.

"You need to help me with this. After all, Peace is your name. I imagine it's hard to ignore your nature. If we dance, please let me lead."

"You talking to someone?" asked Neal as he entered.

I put Peace back in her scabbard, "Yeah, I was talking to Peace."

"You know she's a sword."

"You know it was fairy made," I replied.

"Touché," Neal conceded. "You almost ready? Mary made us some sandwiches to eat before our evening hike."

"Nice, I am a bit peckish. I'll be ready in about half an hour."

Neal left and I picked up my phone. I needed to at least try one more time. I called my wife, Sue. As I expected, I got her voicemail.

"Hey it's me again. I'm about to do something ..." and my phone rang. There was her face smiling up at me so I pressed Answer.

"Hi," was all I could say.

"Hi, you called me?" Sue accused me with her voice tight with anger.

"Sorry...I didn't mean to disturb you. I wanted to talk."

"Then talk." She wasn't making this easy for me. I found my other hand was resting on Peace's grip.

"Okay, here it is," I said as I put a little bass in my voice. "I am sorry you feel betrayed, but I no longer feel guilty about my perceived indiscretion. What happened to me was beyond my ability to control. Had I been a female and Naomi had been a male most would believe I was raped. I did not choose this. It was destined. I know you don't believe in the Fae, but your belief does not change the fact, I said fact, that they exist and I am entangled with their world. When I get home, I will be able to provide proof. I am about to go on a mission tonight to try to oust a King. I don't know if we will ever talk again. So here it is, I am sorry this mess caused you pain. It wasn't my plan to be forced into having sexual relations with a fairy queen. Screw this, I wanted to say goodbye, so goodbye."

"Goodbye? You're hanging up on me already?"

"It's obvious you don't want to talk to me. You don't believe me and think I am creating this whole elaborate scheme. If tonight goes badly, and it very well could, you won't have to worry about divorce. So yeah, goodbye. I hope you find happiness in your new life." I was pulling the phone away from my ear to press End when I heard.

"Wait, Roger, please," her voice had a worried sound to it.

"Okay, what now?" I was tired of being on the defense. This was an extension of a conversation we'd been having for a little over a year. I will only feel guilty for so long. Enough was enough.

"Say, I believe."

"All right you believe." I couldn't help being a smart-ass. It was in my genes.

"I met one at Sam's. She had me over for wine and well, I met some of the ones hanging around Harmony. How could you sleep with something so little?"

"With magic they morph into human size beings."

"Sam said you might be in danger?"

"Did she show you the wolf clip?"

"Yes."

"Those guys are my allies now. I am headed to see a King, Naomi's brother. He wants me, now I am only guessing, to be his bitch, a magical bitch but one all the same. I have something different in mind. Sue, I have changed in ways you'd have to see to believe and will continue to be involved with the Fae for the rest of my life. So will Harmony."

"My grand-baby?"

"She's my granddaughter as well and she too has been chosen. If I get through this, I will explain all of it to you when I get home, only if you would like?"

"When will you be home?"

"How about I call you tomorrow?"

"How about when you are through tonight?"

"No promises, but I will try."

"Roger, I don't want a divorce."

"Me neither."

"Please be safe."

"Can't promise anything but I will be smart."

"Bye," now Sue sounded meek and a little sad.

"Bye, love." END.

I went into the bathroom and splashed water on my face

and took a few deep breaths. I was ready. I went downstairs to the dining room and found Kalen, Neal and Mary sitting, eating sandwiches and chatting quietly.

"Are you well?" ask Kalen.

"Yeah. I made a call home to Sue. It was a bit stressful." I looked to Mary, "Sue is my wife. We are separated and well, we had a few issues to discuss. These sandwiches look great."

"They are as good as they look. Have one lad." Neal had picked up my 'Let's change the subject' hint and ran with it. I nodded thanks.

The sandwich was good. I ate three. I guess I really worked up an appetite sleeping.

"You guys ready?" I had noticed they were actually waiting for me.

"So where are you going?" Mary asked.

Neal put an arm around her shoulder. "I told you earlier there's nothing to fret about. Three guys on a wilderness hike. I expect we will return sometime tomorrow."

Mary looked longingly up into Neal's eyes and I think she wanted to kiss him goodbye.

"Kalen, there is something in the truck I need to ask you about." I said drawing Kalen away.

Kalen followed, "What do you need to know?"

"Nothing. We just needed to get out of there quickly."

Kalen was confused, "Why?"

"To give Neal and Mary a little privacy."

"Are they going to mate again?"

"Again?"

"I returned while you slept and went looking for Neal. I heard his voice coming from her private quarters. He was very short of breath and repeating the phrase 'Oh lord.' He didn't sound distressed so I figured it was a human mating ritual."

"Uncle Neal, you old dog. No, they aren't mating again. Only saying goodbye, human style."

Neal came jogging up to us. I hadn't noticed it before but Neal looked and moved like a man a lot younger than eighty.

The Summons

I'd have to ask him about his youthful secret later.
"Ready?" Neal asked.
"Here we go again." I said.

Chapter 56

ONE WAY OR ANOTHER THIS ALL WILL BE A MEMORY SOON

We waved goodbye to Mary as we entered the brush. Paige and Johnson turned and trotted back to the lodge. We walked in silence as the sun stretched across the sky. None of us really knew what fate had in store for us tonight. We were headed into a conflict, with a team loaded with more untrusted members than I cared to count. Even those I trusted had split loyalties. If Naomi gave Kalen an order putting my life in jeopardy, could I trust him to stand by me? Probably not, since Naomi was his wife and Queen. Fairy hold loyalties dear. I believe the only one I could trust was my blood. Uncle Neal would have my back and I would have his. I only hoped Naomi would allow my bond brother to do as he was originally charged.

While my mind pondered these questions, my feet carried me to the field with the stick. Kalen knelt and whispered. The familiar pop accompanied by the light flash let us know it was time to travel. Before I stepped over the stick I noted, I had a little over an hour and a half till I met Aelfric.

I shook off the portal travel and adjusted myself to these strange but familiar surroundings. A realization dawned on me.

"Kalen do your realize we have been traveling together

less than a week?"

"You humans view time in such bizarre ways." He said with a smile. He was amused but took no affront.

"I'll bite," I quipped, "how so?"

He walked toward me and his expression changed from humor to one a bit more somber. He placed one hand above my heart and the other above his own. "How can time measure the bond we shared and built? How can it be trusted to know our loyalty and friendship? How can it know of the learning and teaching? It can't. So the measure of time we've spent with each other is irrelevant to what we've shared and received from each other. You are my brother and brotherhood begins as time begins. It will never end. Eric is brother to Neal and I. Think on your brothers. All of them, especially James, are your brothers, as are Neal and I. Yes, I know you give him the honorific Uncle, but he is your brother with a sword at your side. So if we are your brother then our journey began as you began."

I wasn't worried about his loyalty any more. I grasped his forearm and touched my head to his, "Thank you brother. I needed to hear that." I embraced the warmth as it spread over me.

Noises in the corners broke our embrace. "Looks like our guests have arrived. Right on time." Neal and I made bets on how long it would take Orin to demand his magic. Neal had a higher opinion of the little S.O.B. than I did. He guessed it would be five to ten minutes. I guessed as soon as he could get my attention upon entering. The actual guess was less than five minutes. I had to hedge my bet a little. After all, I only make a schoolteacher's salary. As it turned out, I should have bet more. He didn't even wait to get my attention.

"Wizard, I wish to receive the magic promised."

"Hold your horses. I will honor my promises in my own time. Do not for a minute think you have a right to what is mine."

"I only wish to be ready for our venture into enemy territory," he retorted.

"You mean your trip to see your father, the Fae who gave you life and breath? The one who taught you at his knee? Is this the enemy about which you speak?"

"Yes, but do not forget it was this loving father who exiled me and my brethren because we disagreed with his slaughtering of hundreds of innocents."

"You need to know that this foray is not about revenge. I will destroy you if you attempt to exact revenge. It is about resolution, a peaceful resolution if it can be accomplished. I believe you gave me your word of honor to follow and obey me during this excursion?"

"You know I did," he spat back.

"Then obey this; lose the attitude of revenge. It will get more innocents killed and I believe you said something about disagreeing with the 'slaughter of innocents.' Or was I mistaken? Order two; wait your turn and be quiet about it."

I turned on my heel and headed for my uncle. He had the sawbuck in his hand, waiting to pay his lost wage. "Thanks Unc."

"How did you know?"

"Sadly, I've had to deal with my share of jerks in the military and they were all this predictable. Ah, here is Cheryl."

I headed over to her and extended my hand in greeting. Right before she took my hand I said, "Be nice." This got a laugh from her and she did greet me pleasantly. I didn't embrace my power as a sign of trust. She put a little whammy on me. It was quite nice. I felt loved and desired, but none of the primal raw passion was present as it had been earlier. She released me before I had to pull back.

She smiled at me and it was ever so sensuous. "I can't deny my nature can I?"

"No, I expect you can't. Do you have any final questions about tonight?"

"No, I only need your gift and we will be on our way."

I put my hands on the side of her head and gave her the magic I had planned. It pleased me to see her shiver as the magic flowed through my hands and into her.

When I removed my hands, it was her turn to take a step back. Again I derived pleasure from this. She grasped both of my hands. I thought she was trying to steady herself and I embraced my magic. She put her head to mine. Though not a word was spoken I heard her voice loud and clear. "Thank you, Roger. Even if tonight's events do not go the way you have planned, know you have saved my people. The gift you have given me will heal my sick and help my people prosper for a hundred of your years. May your God protect you from harm tonight, and know you and your kin will always be welcomed in Phengard lands."

This time she followed the head touch with an embrace and a kiss on each cheek and the whole thing was whammy free. She turned and left the way she came.

I turned from Cheryl and saw that the Warg were present. I headed to them. As I walked I use my peripheral vision to watch Orin stew at being the last to receive the magic. I'd already given Kalen magic to give to Foster for him and his troops. I saw over a hundred Warg in wolf form trot through the glen and out Orin's threshold. Kalen was to follow the Warg with Foster, transfer the magic, and send them on their way. I saw Dubhan and Chepi waiting patiently for me. Conor was leading the rest of the Warg out.

I greeted them, "I see you Dubhan. I see you Chepi." Kalen told me it was their traditional greeting. We then grasped arms. They were all business. They were every bit the wolves on the hunt even though they were in human form.

"Dubhan, do you have any questions about tonight?"

"No."

"I trust you will remain true to the plan." He growled at me for this. He thought I was questioning his honor and wasn't pleased by this.

"I gave you my honor," he barked.

"I know you are honorable. It is not your honor I call to question." I glanced toward Orin. I went to one knee and turned my head to one side. "I am sorry. I was confounded by another and meant no disrespect." The one knee and head thing was what I picked up from Chepi at the diner.

"Rise, wizard, we now hunt as one again."

I quickly passed magic to him and sent the Warg on their way. They turned from me and morphed into wolves so smoothly it was like magic. Okay, I know it was magic, but give a guy literary license now and again.

Last but not least, in his own eyes, was Orin. Everyone was clear of the glen and the only ones left were Neal, Orin, Raise, and I. I approached Orin. "Are you ready to receive the gift I offer?"

He shuttered slightly, "Yes, thank you, Wizard." Wow I got a thank you and a Wizard. Before he was gimme gimme and now I got a thank you.

The amount Kalen and I decided to give him was about half the amount I gave the others, although he had no way of knowing what I gave the others. It would also be significantly less than I gave Kalen.

I placed my hands on his head and envisioned about a half a shot glass to pour into Orin. He shuttered as it flowed into him. When I broke contact, he was smiling.

"So this is what the old magic feels like. No wonder my father wants you." I raised my hand, about to remind him of his oath. "I remember my promise and I am nothing without honor. Thank you, Wizard Roger."

"You are welcome, Prince Orin. Shall we go?" I raised my hand to his threshold and we left.

We fell out on a wooded area and Kalen stood alone awaiting our arrival.

"All is as you wished, Roger."

"Thank you, Kalen. Orin, please lead the way." Our party of five walked through the woods. The sun stretched to the horizon and shadows grew around us. One way or another, this all will be a memory soon.

Chapter 57

YOUR REPUTATION PRECEDES YOU, WIZARD

We had a two-mile hike to a white house on the Bond Creek Trail. My directions were to drive toward Swan River National Wildlife Refuge. On the south end of Swan Lake, on MT – 83, there was a brown sign with Bond Cr Trail. I was to turn right and drive about half of a mile to a white house and park. I would be met there at sunset.

My STN network had potential. I was able to travel about seven hundred miles in little over five minutes plus the two-mile hike. I knew that what lay ahead could be impending doom, but my mind was buzzing with the possibilities of a worldwide STN. So I hiked along, muttering to myself lists of thing I needed to accomplish to establish an STN. Orin and Raise gave me sideways glances and moved to put Neal and Kalen between us. They thought I'd lost it and the only thing more dangerous than a pissed off wizard was a crazy pissed off wizard.

I heard Neal say to Kalen, "He's on the STN business again."

Kalen shook his head and nodded to Orin and Raise's discomfort, "Let's hope he can keep it together. We don't want him using the STN on them." Upon hearing STN, I saw Orin blanch and Raise tighten her grip on her sword.

"Kalen, you evil fairy," I thought to myself, but I did enjoy the effect of his words.

Neal furrowed his brow with confusion. Seeing Orin and Raise's reaction, he nodded and smiled. Neither of us knew Kalen had such an evil streak, but we liked it.

We arrived at our destination moments shy of actual sunset. I only knew this by the time on my phone. We'd been walking in the dark for the last fifteen minutes. Here in the mountains, actual sunset is rarely seen in the valleys. One needs to be on a tall mountain to view the horizon and enjoy the beauty. As we approached the house, the tree adjacent and the roofline of the house lit up like Christmas.

"Holy shit," I blurted. "There has to be thousands of them."

"Your reputation precedes you, Wizard," Orin said.

A bright blue light came zipping to the ground. Instead of hitting the ground it exploded with light. From the light stepped a warrior clad in armor and ready for a fight. He held himself with a rigid posture but looked ready to use any of the weapons he carried.

"Greetings, Warren," offered Orin.

Warren ignored the greeting and turned to me, "Why did you bring this," he spat sourly, "Princeling and his consort with you. And who is this human?"

"First of all, Warren is it?" I embraced my magic and let it flow through my vocal cords. "My companion extended you a greeting. I have been offered the hospitality of your king and he sent a watchdog armed for war to greet me in what was to be a peaceful conclave. His dog then has the audacity to insult my companion and my kin. It would be within my right to reduce you to ash where you stand." My words stirred up all the Christmas lights for they began shifting, but Warren stood fast. He was only betrayed by a slight widening of the eyes. Warren took a deep breath and went to one knee bowing his head.

"Good Wizard, please accept my forgiveness. I was not expecting you. I was sent to meet a human and possibly a Pixie warrior, no more. Here stands a party of five containing our exiled Prince and his companion. I was not told the wizards have returned."

"Rise, good warrior, all is well between us. Accept my greeting, Warren." I extended my hand. He stood and accepted it freely. Then he turned to Kalen.

"General Kalen, it has been a long time." Warren extended his hand to Kalen.

"Warren, oh I see it is General Warren, you are right my friend. It has been too long." They greeted each other.

"Warren, allow me to introduce my Uncle Neal." He greeted Neal.

I wasn't sure how to handle Orin. I started, "On my journey to your realm, Orin's and my paths crossed. He shared with me his story of exile so long ago and wished to attempt reconciliation with his father. I assumed your King only wished to request my magic and that takes so little time. I thought it would be wonderful to witness a reconnection of the King and his son. I asked Orin to accompany me, so he is here at my request. I have been told if Fae hospitality was extended to me, then it is extended to my party. Is this an incorrect statement?"

"No, Wizard, it is not."

"Greetings, Prince Orin." They clasped arms and greeted. "Greetings, Raise." They also greeted.

"My next question. If I am here under rules of hospitality, why was I greeted by an army?" I gestured with my hands to indicate the Pixies lighting the area.

Warren looked confused by this question. Kalen nudged my arm and spoke quietly to me, "They are mostly children, Roger. There are only six armed escorts; the rest are curious children."

Warren found his voice, "Our young heard a Chosen was coming and a few heard about your altercation with a Warg. Nicely done by the way. The king thought it would be a nice way to greet you with a large audience."

I looked up, "Hello, young Pixies. Thank you for such a lovely greeting. Please, would you light the way and accompany me as I enter your realm?" The air exploded with movement and giggles. The youngsters flew to line the path. It was such a joy to watch and I noticed my companions were smiling as wide as I was. I leaned to Kalen, "Will the kids be present during the whole audience? Or will they be safely ensconced in their beds?"

"If Aelfric stays true to protocol we will have a greeting ceremony with all present, and we will then retire to private chambers to talk. They may not be in bed but they won't be clustered together as a crowd."

"No one is to harm a child or they will deal with me and Peace. If you have a way to get my message to the troops, please do so."

"Do you have your phone?"

"Yes, why?"

"Call Chepi."

I reached in my pocket and pulled out my phone. "Excuse me a moment." Instead of calling Chepi, I texted her. She replied with 'K.'

It took us ten minutes to walk straight up Bond Creek Trail. At the end we took a right turn into the woods. We hiked another five minutes and arrived at a clearing. As the pixies sat in the trees, the clearing became another glen. It looked quite similar to Naomi's back east.

We were escorted toward the center of the glen. By this point I was suffering from major déjà vu. A bright light came swooping from the trees. It landed gently in the center of the glen. Instead of a violent explosion of light, this one grew large enough to encompass a man and out stepped Aelfric. He was a male version of Naomi. This is the best description I can give you. She represented all the goodness a woman has to offer. He was the male equivalent. He stood about six feet tall. He had a medium build and was well muscled. He moved gracefully as he walked toward me. His face was beautiful. He was a walking, talking underwear model for Calvin Klein. As he approached he gestured to the side and as he arrived in front of us, so did the servants with trays laden with food and drink.

"Greetings, Wizard Roger," he said with a slight

hesitation to the wizard part.

"Greetings, King Aelfric," and I extended my hand. By his reactions I believe he was expecting a bumbling human, not me. He recovered gracefully, because gracefully is how the Fae do everything. I was getting a bit irritated by this always-graceful crap. I wanted to see one trip over their own damn feet, just once.

Before we touched heads I embraced the power and noted that there was nothing special about the greeting. No warm fuzzy, no temptation, nothing, I might as well have been greeting a human.

"I trust your travels have been uneventful? I heard you had to dispatch one of those nasty Warg, but besides your confrontation, free from trouble?"

He was fishing for information, but I didn't take the bait. "I did bump into Orin, but it was mostly a long boring drive." To this point he had been completely ignoring Orin. He acted as if he was just one of my retainers.

"Yes indeed, Orin. We will deal with him in a little while." The whole time he spoke he smiled but there was no joy in it. Actually, it felt like he was spewing malice. He spoke again for all present to hear.

"Again, I wish to welcome Wizard Roger and his party to our realm." The trees ignited with applause and bouncing lights.

I raised my hand and said, "Thank you for the wonderful greeting, especially to the youth of your kingdom for such a fine escort." This was received with a renewed round of applause.

Aelfric turned and walked back to the center to sit. This was a signal and streams of multicolored lights headed out the entrance. Branches lowered from the trees holding lanterns. A table sprang up in front of him with chairs around.

"Please sit, we will now talk." Aelfric ordered. We approached the table.

Chapter 58

BURNING AT THE STAKE WAS TOO GENTLE OF A PUNISHMENT

I approached the table cautiously. The way it sprang up from the ground gave me pause. I saw Orin and Raise hadn't yet moved toward the table. We both were thinking of what I did to her and Foster last night as Orin attempted to intimidate me.

"Your majesty, I have heard such glorious things about the beauty of your realm, especially in the moonlight. May we talk as we stroll through the woods?"

Aelfric paused before answering but his expression gave nothing away. "I hoped to provide food and drink in comfort. Surely you must be exhausted from your travels?"

"Actually no. Your youth's energy infected us as we walked here. I feel rested, actually I feel restless. I'd like to move." When I heard myself say this a song from a video my grandkids watched leaped to mind and I almost broke into song. 'I like to move it, move it. She likes to move it, move it, You like to...' I knew the reference would be lost on all present.

"Then let us walk," he moved an open palm down and the table and chairs slammed into the ground. I do think the king has a little temper.

We left the glen and headed into the woods. A group of

pixies encircled us, casting light on the path we took. While I had heard mention of the beauty I would witness, words did this wonderland no justice. The tall cottonwood trees stood as sentinels along the path. I'd noticed on the way in several species of trees blending to populate the forest. Two of my favorites things were the distinct scent of the ponderosa pines filling the air with its vanilla and the numerous stands of aspen. The aspen always reminded me of the white birch back home.

The moonlight splayed through the trees and mixed with the multicolored hue of the pixie escort. The light cast on the terrain created a surreal quality. We were definitely skipping along with Dorothy over the rainbow.

I walked lost in these thoughts for about five minutes when our host broke the silence.

"You are probably wondering why I summoned you to my kingdom?" Aelfric started.

"No, you want something from me." I replied casually.

"I do? And pray tell, what is it you think I want?" He said smugly. Now this made me a little nervous. It was obvious he wanted my magic, but it was obvious to all, so why is he so smug?

"Magic," was the one word reply I gave him.

"I only want your magic, is that what you think?"

"Yes," why mince words.

"Dear Wizard, I wish to offer you a place at my side. A job, if you will. I've heard of your wit and intelligence from my sister. With one so astute at my side I could find ways to interact with the humans within and around my realm."

"You want to extend your realm to include some of the human provinces and think I'm the man to help?" I said as if the idea excited me.

"In a manner of speaking, yes. Side by side we could rule this area completely, restoring the balance of nature. I've been reading your newspapers and I see that humans wish to fix all they've destroyed in nature."

"You envision, you and I will be a force for nature, kind of green, recycling caped crusaders?" Of course this reference was lost. "We will make the humans renounce their technology and machines and return to nature?"

"Yes...they will not be able to resist the magic we will wield." And there it was. He wanted magic to take over the humans now. From what I understood this was trouble on many level. The Fae leadership will not like this at all. But it also confirmed, he was bat-shit crazy.

"I thought the Fae frowned on this type of aggression. Especially one affecting your relations with the humans."

"What can they do? When you give me a fill of old magic and you, a wizard of old, stand by my side, what can they do?"

"When did you come up with this plan?" He paused. The truth was I'd only been a wizard for a few days. I probably became part of the plan in the past few minutes. He'd planned on tapping my magic and doing this by himself all along.

"I thought I'd have to teach you to learn your magic when you arrived. It is why I invited you here. Naomi told me of the magic you possessed and I felt it was a waste if you couldn't learn to use it." He then put his arm around me. "Here in my realm I could mentor you. I would show you how to wield your gift and sharpen your skills with magic. You would be educated in the ways of Fae and we could bring the old ways back. Fae and wizards would no longer have to hide from humans." I felt his magic sliding right off my jacket. I thought I'd play along for just a moment. But first I looked back at the wide eyes of my Uncle Neal. He and our whole party were a bit freaked out by the Kings words. I'd found out later, this was Fae blasphemy of the highest order.

Neal told me later, "It would be like a woman during the Salem witch trails standing in the town center shouting 'I'm a witch and I damn you all to hell.' Burning at the stake was too gentle of a punishment. Aelfric words were worse by far in the realm of Fae."

Still I pretended his whammy was working, "What can I do to help?"

"Fill me with magic right now." His tone was a command. Yep, he thought I was under his influence. I am glad the jacket worked.

I turned to face him. I saw the group trailing, watching me closely. Orin's face was pale with fear. He didn't know about the jacket and thought I was under the influence of the King. I found Neal's eyes and winked at him. He physically relaxed and even smiled. I gave Kalen a slight nod and he too prepared.

"Yes, your majesty, as you wish. Please kneel." And he knelt before me. I placed my hands on his head. "I'm sorry your highness, I am finding it difficult to concentrate with all these distracting lights."

"Royal guard, you are dismissed." One flew down and stopped midair in front of my nose. It was Warren, a tiny, glowing, winged Warren. He glowered at me. I maintained a blank expression with a goofy grin. I wanted the full on whammy look.

He hovered there for about a minute until, "Warren, you are dismissed," Aelfric repeated. Warren turned and glared at his King. He was not over joyed about leaving his king alone with this rabble, but he was a good soldier and followed orders.

We were now alone with the King and if we were going to pull this off, it was time to act.

Chapter 59

BUGGER! BUGGER! BUGGER!

I began feeling a gentle pull on my magic. He was trying to take my magic. "Aelfric, stop pulling on my magic immediately." The pressure increased. I released my hold on his head, moving my hands about one foot away from his ears.

"Aelfric, King of this realm, heed my words. Do not move or your life will be forfeited." Fire blossomed in my hands. He lifted his chin and locked his eyes on mine.

Through clenched teeth, "What has my idiot son convinced you fools to do?"

"Orin was but one of three different tribes of Fae to tell me of the atrocities you have accomplished."

"So the puppies' whines have reached your ear? Who is this third?"

"You have violated everything decent and good. I do not know why the Old World Council has overlooked your digressions."

"Digressions?" he shouted. "Exterminating vermin from my lands is considered a digression?"

"Murdering fellow Fae regardless of how you feel about them is a violation of our laws," added Orin who was at my side with his sword in hand. When Aelfric raised his voice my party drew weapons and encircled me with their bodies facing out.

"You will now have the opportunity to make your argument before the council."

Aelfric began chuckling. There was actual mirth in his laugh and he began to rise. Kalen turned and placed a hand on his shoulder pushing him back to the ground.

"Stay down old friend. You know me. Our threats are not idle."

"You too, Kalen? You let my whelp's words poison your logic? Join me. Together we can defeat the wizards once more. His magic is ripe for our picking. Think of the glory. Do you forget? The wizards ruined everything. How many centuries have we enjoyed freedom from their power hungry tyranny? Now you bring this one here to my kingdom and listen to him try to gain power to himself?"

I'd listened to enough, "Quiet yourself now, Aelfric. Your words have condemned you already. You will renounce your claim as King of this realm and name me as your replacement. Then you will have an opportunity to plead your case to the Council."

He laughed again. "You do have magic, dear wizard, and you have moxie. But you forget where you are. By now, my army surrounds you. While we chatted Warren was putting them in position." He turned his head, "Oh Warren!" he called.

Our world lit up like a Griswold Family Christmas.

"Warren, many will die this night and it will be all on you. Stop this senselessness. You know your King has violated Fae law on many occasions. We are simply here to see that justice is served."

Aelfric laughed again, "He can't hear you, none of them can." And his smile turned to a menacing sneer. "They only hear me. Now, Warren, see that these intruders release me and do try not to kill them. Well, the old man and Orin's concubine are expendable, but the other three I want alive. I do have such plans for them."

As the lights closed in, I threw fireballs into the air. Actually it was more like twenty to thirty fireballs. It was the fourth of July. They exploded high above our heads. This gave the Pixie warriors pause. All stood watching the fireworks. I would have sworn I heard oohs and awes from the crowd. As the last fireball's explosion died, the night filled with the mournful howls of the Warg as they hurtled toward us.

The smile washed from Aelfric's face as the Warg's song bounded closer. He shoved me back and drew his sword as fast as I'd ever seen Kalen draw. Peace leaped to my hand and the battle ensued.

About a dozen warriors hit the ground and flashed to human form. The others flew around our heads like pesky, biting, dare I say it…fireflies.

Aelfric came at me and our swords crossed, throwing sparks in the air between us. I released my magic and let Peace guide my movements. I did not wish to kill Aelfric and found I had to restrain Peace a few times. I blocked his attacks and Peace forced openings in his defense. I then had to stop Peace from killing Aelfric. The results were several small cuts under his ribs on each side and over his left breast. Each touch could have been a killing blow. But nothing I did would slow his attack. I believe he figured out I wasn't going to kill him and grew bolder. We danced around the trees, our swords moving faster than humanly possible.

The Warg arrived with Orin's forces. I saw lights flying into each other. There would be a flash and then one would blink out. I couldn't tell who was who up there. I could only hope our side was winning. The Warg joined the fray and more of Aelfric force flashed into humans to confront the new foe. I'd occasionally catch a glimpse of my original party. Kalen had engaged Warren and he too danced in and out of the trees. I'd seen him pulling his blows too. Orin plowed through several warriors with Raise at his side. Neal was holding his own, but I could see he was getting tired. I saw Chepi was at Neal's back. She had transformed and was dancing with her sword as naked as the day she was born.

I needed to do something. Too many lives had been lost already.

"Peace, help me end this, but please don't kill him." I

know it sounds crazy talking to a sword but she vibrated slightly in my hand as if to say, "Okay."

I renewed my attack. I'd been fighting a defensive battle till now. I was afraid to attack for I feared I wouldn't be able to restrain Peace. Now it was time for Aelfric to feel my wrath. It only took three strikes. The first two made him step back and to his right. It put him up against a tree. The third strike came from behind my head and hit his sword right above the hilt. It broke the blade completely away from his sword. And Peace stopped below his chin with a drop of blood pooling around her tip.

"I do not wish to kill you, but my blade does." He looked at my blade for the first time and saw his sister's image smiling back. His eyes grew wide for he now knew her nature. "I don't know how long I can restrain her."

"What do you want?" he spat.

"Release them."

"They will not stop even if I do release them. Let me go and I can make them stop."

This time I said it through clenched teeth. "Release them! Now! I will not say it again." He closed his eyes and I felt the magic pass by me.

He was right, it didn't stop the battle, but a few of the older warriors did stop. Warren held his sword mid strike and blinked his eyes as if waking from a dream. Several others did the same, but not all. I looked around and saw Neal's opponent stop his attack but a Fairy came from behind and slashed him on his right shoulder close to his neck. I balled up my fist and embraced my magic. I hit Aelfric right in the nose and he crumpled to the ground. I pulled handcuffs from my jacket and cuffed his hands behind his back. With the magic in me I was able to do this in about two seconds.

Neal had fallen to the ground and the fairy was now raising the sword above his heart about to plunge it through Neal's chest. I reached inside my jacket and pulled out the .357 Magnum I had purchased yesterday. The shot rang through the forest and put a neat little hole in the forehead of the fairy trying to dispatch my Uncle. I found out later, I'd pulled my gun and shot on a dead run.

By the time I stopped at Neal's side, Chepi had crawled to him. The attacker I shot had given her a nice cut on the back of her leg.

"Are you okay?" I asked as I knelt by his side. Neal gave me a weak smile.

"Did we win?" he asked and coughed up blood.

"Not yet, but we will as soon as these butt-heads put their swords down. Aelfric is hog-tied over there."

"Boy, know this, I'm glad I met you. Your Granddad would be so proud of what you became," he paused to cough again and closed his eyes.

"Neal?" I shook him gently. "Uncle Neal? You can't die on me. NO! NO! NO, God damn it…you will not die!" I was still holding my power and my voice echoed through the trees. I placed my hands on his chest and willed my magic into him, but he didn't stir. Tears were coursing down my face. I was this powerful wizard with old magic to spare and I felt weak, frail and helpless as I watched Neal's life slip away.

I put my lips close to his right ear, "Unc, you can't die on me. Mum will never forgive me for finding and losing you. You need to meet your great's and your great great's, all of them, even Harmony. Please don't go." My tears were now flowing down his cheek and neck. They fell into his gaping wound and a curious thing began to happen. The wound began to bind itself and close. Neal's eyes shot open and he screamed.

"Bugger! Bugger! Bugger!" He was in pain, intense healing pain and all I could do was laugh. He was alive! Neal will live and consequently so will I, because now Mum won't kill me.

"What the hell just happened? One second I was having a conversation with my brother and the next someone stabbed me in the neck."

"How does it feel now?" He moved his arm to test the area.

"Fine. It's a little stiff and I'll need a new shirt." What remained was a nasty scar, but it seemed all the damage was healed.

Chepi sat next to us smiling at Neal's good fortune. "What's up with your leg?"

"The bastard hamstrung me from behind," and she grinned at her words.

"What's so funny?"

"Not funny so much as ironic. A wolf getting hamstrung?" I too smiled.

"Let me try something. This may sting a little." I wiped my hands on my face. I placed my tear stained hands on the cut naked flesh. She morphed beneath my hand to wolf and howled at the sky. She returned to human and the cut was healed.

When she howled all the wolves joined in and the sound stole the remaining fighter's resolve. They turned and fled into the night. I smiled for I knew what awaited them in the dark. I would concern myself with them later.

I helped Neal stand and took off my jacket, handing it to Chepi. "When you morphed earlier, you were clothed. What happened to your clothes?"

She rolled her eyes, "When we left the glen, we readied ourselves for battle." Seeing my confused expression, "Clothes are cumbersome regardless of the form we take. We shed them when we head into battle." And she rolled her eyes like my teenaged daughter.

"Please, we are close to the village and there are children there. Besides it's distracting. Just put on the damned jacket." She smiled, enjoying my discomfort with her gorgeous naked body. She was in human form and human form had little to no effect on the fairy folk, only us humans.

I helped Neal up and picked Peace off the ground. I sliced her through the air, flicking the few drops of blood from her, and put her away. Warren and Kalen picked up Aelfric under his arms and carried his unconscious body to me. They placed him on the ground before me as a crowd of warriors from both sides gathered around. With the living around me I saw the fallen scattered around the area. There was too much death.

"Look around at your brothers and sisters. Their lives were forfeited for what? Him?" I pointed to Aelfric. "The one who exterminated wild Fae because they weren't Pixie? The one who wanted to start a war with the humans? It ends now. It ends here." I placed my hands on his head and removed all of his remaining magic. It felt like I drank spoiled milk. I turned my head and vomited on the ground. A black viscous substance poured from me. It hit the ground and burnt wherever it touched. I am told they walled in the area I spat out the evil after I left, and it is off-limits to all Fae.

I turned to Warren. "Gather all to the glen, I wish to address your people." He pounded his fist to his chest and bowed his head before he departed to the north toward the village.

From the south came Pixies flying and warriors running. These were the same ones who were trying to get away. My little surprise caught up with them. They broke into our clearing and skidded to a halt.

An impromptu leader spoke, "We must flee. They are coming and they will destroy us."

"Who is coming lad?" I asked.

In flew the Phengard. Cheryl alighted on the ground in front of her force of a few hundred butterflies. In answer to my question, "We are, Wizard."

The local Fae gasped as I stepped toward Cheryl. The others simply smiled.

I embraced my magic and greeted her. "Glad to see you fared well, Roger. Would you like us to clear the dead?"

My face curled up in disgust. "No thanks. We will let them all care for their own dead according to their customs."

"Our way is quicker and…"

"Stop. Please stop. It has been decided." I never thought about that side of her nature.

"So we are finished here?"

"Yes, and your lands are returned. If you see any Pixies

of this realm please send them back," and I paused, "unharmed."

"Farewell, Wizard Roger. Till we meet again." She bowed her head and a light flashed as the Phengard zipped off to the south.

Orin's warriors gathered around the warriors returned by the Phengard and took their weapons.

I looked for Orin and found him off to the side. His expression was grim. I walked up to him, "Orin, please take charge of these warriors and escort them to the glen." About then I noticed that Raise was missing. "Oh God, Raise?"

"She fell toward the end. My wife fought valiantly but was outnumbered three to one protecting my back. We will sing her into the ages."

"You have my sorrow and she my gratitude, Orin." As I said this Foster came up beside us. Orin turned to Foster, and relayed the news of Raise, and passed my request to him. He nodded and took charge of the forces.

They also carried Aelfric with them. When all departed, Kalen, Neal and I were left to ourselves.

"It is done," I said, glad to have the fighting finished.

Kalen only grinned, "It has only begun, Roger."

"What are you talking about?"

Neal smiled at Kalen a knowing smile. "He is still new to this, Kalen. Allow this moment of respite."

"What the hell are you guys talking about?"

"Another day," Neal said as he patted my shoulder. His magic washed the anxiety from me and I took a deep breath.

"Okay, but we are still having a movie fest on the way home."

"Sure," agreed Kalen as we turned and headed toward the glen.

Chapter 60

60 GOLDIE AND SMOKIE

The treetops in the glen were alive with excitement. I'd noticed before that their colors tended to be pastel in nature, usually a soft glow of lights twinkling softly. Tonight the colors were bold and flashed bright like a light bulb about to expire. As I stepped in the glen I could physically feel the noise.

"You ready, lad?" asked Neal as he looked around the treetops.

I took a deep breath. I was beginning to feel the exhaustion I'd been holding at bay with adrenaline and fairy bread. "Doesn't matter if I am, Unc. It's game time."

Kalen squared off in front of me with his hand extended. He had no words for me just a gesture of friendship which I gladly accepted. We clasped arms and touched heads. I felt his love and acceptance and I willed mine toward him. As we broke contact I asked, "Was it good for you, too?" I only got a weak smile in reply. Tonight Kalen was all business.

"Here we go." I approached the center where Aelfric was bound to a chair. "Thank you all for coming." The buzzing sound stopped. It didn't taper off. It stopped. "I am sorry we couldn't resolve our issues without violence. Regardless, the reign of King Aelfric has come to an end." The buzzing noise rose again and I heard Orin's name. "Aelfric will be taken before the council to answer for the atrocities he has committed. You will not be left without a leader, but the time for a monarchy has passed." Warren and another large fairy lifted Aelfric from the chair and escorted him to an alternate exit. Kalen had called Naomi when the fighting was through and Aelfric was our prisoner. She contacted the counsel and arranged for a Stick Network from here to England somewhere. I'd need a map to figure out where. It didn't matter. Aelfric was on his way to justice and my stick network idea had greater possibilities.

A bright light flew toward me out of the trees. It flashed brightly and he stepped forward. He was an older, I want to say gentleman, but who is to say how old he really was. When it came to the Fae, I had no frame of reference. He did look to be of an age with Neal. He extended his hand in greeting. I took it and was treated to a warm, friendly greeting.

"My name is Walter and I am pleased to meet you, Wizard. I wish to bid you greetings." He looked sincere when he said this. "Please b,e patient with us. We have been answering to our beloved king for many centuries. I followed the young Fae and his sister from the old world with dreams of prosperity and joy for my family." He swept his hand around the glen, quite dramatically. "When we found this place we were greeted by Osawaw and Oshota, Ulfang's father and mother. They welcomed us as family and we were cousins of a sort. For a short while, we coexisted in peace. We all answered to the Alpha's authority as was customary for our hosts. Aelfric began to use his magic to influence us to answer to him. I do not believe his magic worked on the Warg. We became restless, wishing to establish our own kingdom. By this time most of the Pixie were affected by Aelfric's glamour and would do anything he wished. His son, Prince Orin fought with his father saying that we should establish a treaty and share the land. Aelfric wanted to conquer and eliminate them. His heart became black with a greed for power. He approached Osawaw and told him he was royalty and thanked him for the welcome he and his people received. I remember the night clearly.

Walter began his story.

Aelfric approached Osawaw, "Greetings, Alpha Osawaw, I am here to discuss business of state."

"Aelfric, how may we help you with your concern?" Osawaw said, but was a bit perplexed as to the visit. He thought his visitors were happy in their new home.

"I am glad you asked. I was born of Breeana, Queen of all the Fae, and it is my birthright to establish my own kingdom. I have chosen here."

"Osawaw actually laughed," Walter said. "He was a good natured fellow, quick to smile and laugh. He thought this was some elaborate ruse meant to entertain. And Aelfric did not like his laughter one bit. No one laughed at Aefric."

"I am glad you are able to find humor when none exists." Aelfric made a slight gesture with his hand and twenty-five of his warriors flew down and grew into human form within the blink of an eye. His magic was quite powerful.

"I remember Osawaw's eyes," Walter continued. "They glowed a bright gold. So bright they cast a golden hue to everything in front of him. Oshota was at his side and instantly became a wolf with teeth bared and rage in her eyes. Sadly, I must admit I was at Aelfric's side, armed and ready for a fight. I do not know why I felt the way I did, other than because Aelfric compelled me with his magic."

"Osawaw are you threatening me?" Aelfric taunted. "You do realize I am a prince of the old magic, heir to the throne." His taunting stopped and menace entered his voice. "Do not try your wolfy intimidation tricks on me. And you'd better heel your bitch before I do." This is when it all started.

"Oshota went for Aelfric's throat." Walter said with downcast eyes. "Aelfric flicked his forefinger and she vanished into smoke. Nothing remained. Osawaw leaped from his chair transforming midair and was sliced in two by Aelfric's sword. I never saw him reach for his blade. Though the Warg were stunned, they restrained young Ulfang. He, too, wished to try for Aelfric's throat. Now, he was the Alpha, leader of his clan. Aelfric addressed him.

"You are their pup?" Ulfang gave a deep throaty growl. "I thought so, so I am your new best friend. No need to thank me, I enjoy helping."

Ulfang snapped, "Thank you? I was thinking I'd like to see you with your throat torn out."

"Is that a doggy thing? A way to say I appreciate the promotion?"

"Pixie, what are you babbling about? You give me nothing but grief."

"Oh contraire, I promoted you to Alpha. So heed me now, puppy. You and your canine brethren will leave these lands before the next moon or else you will make me unhappy. You saw what I do when I am not pleased; unhappy is a whole lot worse."

"You have heard the tale from this point," Walter said. "Until tonight I remembered it all as a happy time. With the glamour removed, I am ashamed and deeply saddened that I supported the genocide." He turned to Chepi, "I see you are a descendant of Oshota. Your face is the image I have carried all these years. I wish to extend my deepest apology and request your forgiveness." He took a knee and bared his neck in the Warg fashion. Then all the lights in the tree zipped down, flashed, and were on one knee with necks bared. Chepi, Dubhan, and all the Warg raised their heads and howled. It was a sad, mournful sound. I found I had tears streaming down my face and as I looked around there wasn't a dry eye in the place.

"Rise, Walter," Chepi said and offered her hands. "All is forgiven now that Aelfric is gone." She and Walter touched foreheads in a warm greeting.

Walter and the Pixies returned to the trees and all eyes turned back to me.

"Thank you, Walter. I am glad to see the healing begin." I proceeded to explain about the board of governors who will lead in the absence of a king. The idea of self-government was well received. Many present were born and raised here on what I grew up believing was U.S. soil. Most were both citizens of the U.S. and Fae, so this type of government was familiar and acceptable. When I finished speaking there were a few questions about details of the new government and I put most of them off with the promise of a town hall meeting within the week with their interim governors. All would be answered and explained in detail then.

When their questions were answered I asked them to return to their homes. Many invited the Warg and Pixie warriors, in my group to their homes. Walter offered Kalen, Neal and I his hospitality, which we gratefully accepted. He gave us directions to his house and departed to prepare for us.

Once again we found ourselves alone in a glen. This was getting to be a habit.

"Looks like our work here is finished," I offered.

"Only the armed battle," said Kalen. "The fighting will go on for some time now. The only difference is that there will be no bloodshed and the governors will have to deal with them."

Neal was testing his shoulder again, "I still can't believe you could fix this wound."

"I have no idea how I did it either, other than it took my tears. Let's not try to test my healing skill anytime soon, okay?" I asked.

We turned to leave and out of the trees a small pixie flew down and landed on my shoulder. She appeared to be about ten years old. She leaned into my ear and yelled, "Thank you." It came across as a whisper. Then she flew to my cheek and kissed me. It sent warmth through my body and brightened the darkest regions of my soul. I still find the memory, of that little Pixie, brings me joy no matter what else is happening in my life.

With an ear-to-ear smile I followed the boys to Walter's house.

Chapter 61

NO ONE MESSES WITH MY FAMILY

Walter's house was a regular house. I was expecting a fairy house made from tree branches reaching down, intertwining with flowers sprouting. Nope, he had a split-level ranch with aluminum siding and a two car garage. The Fae here have integrated with the humans. The humans had no clue. He had three bedrooms and a finished basement. I took the couch in the basement and left Neal and Kalen to figure out who had which bed.

I took a long hot shower and after today it felt wonderful. I shaved a few days' growth from my face and longed to put my head to a pillow. In the mirror I noticed nicks and cuts on my sides where apparently Aelfric's blade made contact with my skin. Most disturbing were the raccoon circles around my eyes. I needed sleep, undisturbed, no awaiting apocalypses, and no summons to answer, sleep. I brushed my teeth and hair and headed for bed.

A couch covered in a sheet never felt so good. It was soft. My head sank into the pillow just right and before I could even register another thought, sleep took me away.

I dreamed I was flying high above the clouds. It was a wonderful feeling. I looked next to me and holding my right hand was Harmony, giving me her goofy smile reserved for when she ran to me calling "Granddad."

She was smiling at me, enjoying the flight. The dream had a surreal feeling to it. I know it was a dream but it felt like so much more.

I called over the wind, "Hi, sweetheart."

She replied in kind, "Hi, Granddad." Her smile was captivating.

I guess I was a little homesick. I was used to seeing my grandbabies at least a couple times a week. This trip, though it was only about a week of human time, was stretched into almost two with all the stick time.

"When are you coming home, Granddad?" Harmony asked.

"Soon love, soon."

"Good, I want you to make that mean old frog stop bothering me."

"I will honey, in a few days." My dream was getting weird now. Harmony is only a little older than two and our conversation was a bit above the skills of a two year old.

"He says he wants to take me home to play with his kids."

"Do you know his name?"

"I don't know if it is his name but someone called him Ucky."

"Do you mean Uke?"

"Yes," she said giggling, for to her it sounded as if I only repeated what she said.

I sat straight up in bed screaming, "No, you son-of-a-toad. No!" I was wide awake by now and I heard footsteps from upstairs headed my way. I fumbled for my phone. Before I could dial Kalen was at my side.

"What is it, Roger?"

"I don't know. I was talking to Harmony in a dream."

"Your granddaughter?"

"Yes, and she said Uke was saying he was going to take her to live with him."

Now I know this conversation sounds a little nuts, but I noticed that Kalen was also worried. Having an adult like conversation with a two year old in a dream was not typically cause for concern. Her talk about a sworn enemy threatening to take her away sounded my alarms. This is all part of my new life.

I found my phone and dialed my daughter's number. It was five in the morning and I had only slept for 4 hours.

A heard in a sleepy voice on the other end said, "Hi, Daddy. Do you know what time it is?"

"Yes, love, I do and this is important."

"Daddy, you are okay?"

"Yes Sam, I am. Please listen to me. I need you to go and check on Harmony."

"Why? Where are you?"

"I'm in Montana. Please Love, do as I ask."

"Okay," she said more to placate me. "So everything worked out with the King?"

"Yeah, you could say. Is she there in her bed?"

"Looks like she's all tucked and bundled."

"Please wake her."

"Daddy, you know what a bear she is when we have to wake her."

"Yes love, please trust me. This is very important."

"Okay," I heard her over the phone. "Harmony honey, I need you to wake up."

Sam told me later she sat right up and saw the phone and said, "Granddad."

"Yes it is. Would you like to talk with him?"

I heard, "Hi, Granddad," in Harmony's sweet breathy voice.

"Hi sweetheart."

"Can we fly again? It was fun." That was all I needed to hear.

"Sure Harmony, but can you do me a favor?"

"Okay."

"Stay with the good fairies and don't talk to the froggy anymore."

"He is ugly Granddad, but he is nice."

"I know, but I don't want you to go away with him."

"He was only being silly."

"Tell you what. Wait till I get home. We can talk to him together."

"Okay, but you have to come soon."

"I will baby, I will. Can I talk with Mommy now? I love you, sweetie."

"Love you, Granddad. Here Mommy, Granddad wants to talk to you."

"What were you two talking about?"

"She was in my dream tonight. We were flying in the dream and she told me about a frog fairy."

"Wait a second. This is about a dream?"

"Honey, she had the same one. I don't exactly know how all this magic stuff works but we shared a dream from over twenty-six hundred miles away. She was telling me about a frog fairy she met. He's bad news and we need to protect her."

"Because of a dream," Sam said again but with disdain.

"Yes, damn it. You need to accept this, Sam. Your baby is at risk."

"Daddy, she's safe now, back to sleep curled up in her bed." I heard her get up and close Harmony's door. "Come home, Dad. You sound tired. I will watch out for her. I haven't seen any," and she paused slightly, "frogs around the house, but we'll look out for them." I couldn't tell if she was saying this to humor me. It wasn't like Sam.

"Okay Sam it will take me about a week to get there, four days if I push it."

"Be safe Dad. Enjoy the ride."

"See you soon."

"Bye Daddy." The line went dead.

By the time the line went dead, Neal had joined Kalen and me in the basement.

"What's going on?" Neal asked.

"Roger had a dream about Uke, a fairy King, who was visiting his granddaughter."

"What's the story on this Uke?"

I responded, "Naomi spanked him recently with my magic. I would guess he's in full revenge mode. Kalen, what can you tell me about him? Can he glamour folks like Aelfric?"

"Why do you ask?"

"Sam wasn't quite herself. She basically placated me. She knew the crap storm we had to face last night and about our adventures getting here. But she wasn't the least bit concerned about what happened to me or the possible threat to Harmony. I'm thinking whammy."

"Let's get going," said Neal.

"Right, Kalen, how quick can you get us back to my truck?"

"How would you like to get closer to home?"

"How close can you get me?"

"Do you remember Steve?"

"Sure I do. You can get me to Chattanooga?"

"Yes."

"When can we go?"

"How quick can you get back to the glen?"

Neal added, "Get me back to the lodge and I'll drive your truck to you."

"Cool." We dressed and were ready to travel in about five minutes. At the glen Kalen went to one corner and spoke some words in the old tongue.

"Neal, this will take you back to the lodge."

"Neal, wait a minute." I fished the keys out of my pocket and tossed them to him. "Thanks, Neal. If you can talk Mary into a road trip, she's more than welcome at my house, too."

Neal grinned, "Good idea, lad. Good idea." He turned and disappeared through the portal.

"Course it's a good idea." I mumbled to no one in particular.

Kalen prepared our way to Chattanooga, or rather Naomi's glen. As we descended through, I was thinking about the STN again. I couldn't help it. This was too cool.

As we stepped into the glen, Naomi and a cast of thousands in the trees met us. They erupted with cheers. Naomi greeted us with refreshments. They had the wonderful elixir and slices of the energy bread. Somehow in the five minutes it took for Kalen to pack, he had called Naomi and arranged this reception.

I extended my hand to Naomi. She took it and I greeted her in the formal Fae greeting. I didn't even embrace my magic.

"My, my, someone has been learning," she said playfully.

"Naomi, you don't know the half of it." I took a sidelong glance at Kalen and added, "But then again, you may."

She smiled warmly, "I am glad to see you returned to me in good health and happy spirits."

"I'll give you the good health part."

"What troubles you?" This surprised me for I thought Kalen would have relayed my plight to her.

I told her of the dream and my need for haste. When I mentioned Uke's name I saw her expression change.

"Do you have any information to aid me?" I asked.

"I hadn't heard about the foul toad travelling south. I will contact Harmony's escort and let them know to be on the lookout for him."

She took a few steps away, sat in a chair, and closed her eyes. Almost on cue my phone rang.

"Daddy?"

"Yes Sam, what happened?" Her voice was an octave higher than normal and I heard panic rising in her tone.

"She's gone, Daddy. We checked on her only an hour ago and now she's gone."

"Shit. I'll find her Sam. I know where the bastard lives and I will get her back. Call your mother and let her know."

"I will Daddy. How soon can you get here?"

"I'm almost in Chattanooga, but I need to make a slight detour."

"How did you get from Montana to Tennessee so quickly?"

"STN babe, but that's another story. I've got to go. Get your Mom there and tell her everything."

"I will, Daddy."

"Bye love."

Shit, just when I thought it was safe to relax.

"Good folks of Fae, know this," I had embraced my magic and my voice boomed across the glen. "Let it be known far and near, nobody, and I mean nobody, messes with my family, least of all my Grandbaby. Uke had the balls to take Harmony and he will pay for his folly with his life and any who aid him in this venture will suffer his fate."

The glen erupted again with cheers of support. Naomi had opened her eyes and her face was ashen. It was as I had thought. Her troops had been sacrificed to protect Harmony.

"Naomi, they will be avenged. Is his stronghold where we met?"

"Yes."

"Can you get me to Chattanooga now?"

"I can," she pointed to my exit. I found Kalen had fallen in beside me.

"Thank you friend, but you are home now and this is my fight."

"You are wrong, brother. Someone messed with my family and it is our fight."

"Let's go kick some toad butt."

"Let's," Kalen repeated and we stepped into our next adventure.

The End.

ABOUT THE AUTHOR

Rob Burgess was born in Whitinsville and grew up in the small town of East Douglas, Massachusetts. He attended Douglas Elementary School and Blackstone Valley Tech High School. He left home after high school and received his Bachelors Degree in Mathematic from the University of Florida and a Masters Degree from Troy State University. He spent 23 years flying around and experiencing the world courtesy of the United States Air Force. Upon retiring from the USAF he settled in Belleview, Florida and began a second career as a math teacher at Vanguard High School in Ocala, Florida. While teaching, he met fellow author G. Kent who encouraged him to write.

Rob was backpacking with Gary and Todd through the wilds of Georgia and Tennessee when this story was born by a campfire.

Rob has been married to his college sweetheart for over thirty years. He has six children and three grandchildren with more on the way.

Rob can be contacted at Firefliesfromhell@aol.com.

Check out other books by Rob, his family and friends.